JAMAL MAHJOUB was born in London in 1960. His family moved to Liverpool in 1961, and then to Khartoum. Mahjoub returned to England in 1981 to study Geology at Sheffield University. In 1989 his first novel, *Navigation of a Rainmaker*, was published by Heinemann. In 1993 he won *The Guardian*/Heinemann African short story competition. His second novel, *Wings of Dust*, was published by Heinemann in 1994. He is married and has two children.

JAMAL MAHJOUB

IN THE HOUR OF SIGNS

Heinemann

3600 2128

Heinemann Educational Publishers
Halley Court, Jordan Hill, Oxford OX2 8EJ
a division of Reed Educational & Professional Publishing Ltd

Heinemann: A Division of Reed Publishing (USA) Ltd
361 Hanover Street, Portsmouth, NH 03801–3912, USA

Heinemann Educational Books (Nigeria) Ltd
PMB 5205, Ibadan

Heinemann Educational Botswana (Publishers) (Pty) Ltd
PO Box 10103, Village Post Office, Gaborone, Botswana

FLORENCE PRAGUE MADRID ATHENS
MELBOURNE AUCKLAND TOKYO SINGAPORE
MEXICO CHICAGO SÃO PAULO
JOHANNESBURG KAMPALA NAIROBI

© Jamal Mahjoub 1996

First published by Heinemann Educational Publishers in 1996

Series Consultant: Abdulrazak Gurnah

British Library Cataloguing in Publication Data
A catalogue record for this book is available from the British Library.

ISBN 0 435 909223

Cover design by Touchpaper
Cover illustration by Hussein Shariffe
Author photograph by Paul Freestone

Phototypeset by CentraCet Ltd, Cambridge
Printed and bound in Great Britain
by Cox & Wyman Ltd, Reading, Berkshire

96 97 98 99 10 9 8 7 6 5 4 3 2 1

PART 1

The Signs

Prologue

On the many occasions in later years when the Khalifa Abdullahi al Ta'aishi was asked to describe the circumstances under which, in the very regions where he himself would eventually be hunted down and killed, he had first encountered the man known as the Mahdi, he always told the same story. It happened like this:

Dust ripped across the bone-dry plain, like a sheet of paper curling from the hide of the world. A man came walking, alone. In the towns and villages that wound behind him in a trail which stretched back to the western reaches where he was born, they remembered him as an outsider. He was greeted with a suspicion normally reserved for lepers, carriers of the plague and men capable of murdering small children. They shunned him, called him names, cursed his people. They threw stones and whatever else they could find; anything indeed that would push him along, help the wind to take him – blow him off towards the dusty horizon.

The roads which had led him here, the voices which told him that he would one day find the answer he sought, still turned in his head. The further he went the more convinced he became that this was not a simple journey, but a *hijra* of the most noble kind. He was in pursuit of that bright shining vein which burned within him like a curse. One day it would come to light, cleansing him of everything he despised in himself. One day he would be saved.

As he drew nearer to the collection of slumped flat-roofed dwellings he felt his fatigue begin to lift; he sensed that he was nearing his destination. One day they would regret their throwing of stones, their curses, which fell like a brutal rain to wash him from their midst. God revealed himself only to the chosen few. It was not their fault, but no man should be treated as he had been.

His mule was dead. He had no possessions to speak of. His family had turned against him. He would not return until he found what he was looking for. They would raise him high, bow down in reverence and wonder, all of them – even his father. He found no consolation in words, for since the work of reading and writing had never come easily to him, he had abandoned it; just as, in its own way, it had rejected him.

The village was clad in the garments of mourning; even the grey-breasted crows hung their heads in shame. The great sheikh was dead, taken from the trials of this world to the wonders of the next. And so it was that death had called our traveller this way, for news had reached his ears that a successor had been discovered – a very special man by all accounts. His travels and sermons were whispered of in reverent tones, far and wide: in marketplaces with forgotten names; around the embers of dung fires; in the warm belly of dry river-beds. From strangers who took comfort in speaking of miracles, he had heard of this man. He had heard that this son of a boat-builder, whose spirit of devotion shone from his eyes, walked with angels at his side. Words flowed from him like milk from his fingertips.

It was said that a veil of light had preceded him, that throughout the world a new star had been seen burning across the sky to herald the coming of the End. They said that the Prophet himself had spoken in a dream to this humble man, and on hearing this Abdullahi felt a quickening of his heart such as one might feel upon recognising a brother after years apart. He set off in search of this man, finding the route through fits and starts and wrong turnings, and everywhere he asked, the people stared in silence. But here, perhaps, was what he had been looking for all these years.

The village was immersed in a dream; the way layers of heat rest upon the ground in the middle of the day and make it hard for a man to think clearly.

His first sight of the man was truly astonishing. He was lying on the ground at the entrance to the half-finished tomb. He lay there, unmoving, for hours. Abdullahi spent a day and a half watching him just lying there in the burning sun, face down, mumbling prayers. Anyone who wished to enter the building had to walk over his back.

On the second day Abdullahi came nearer. This time the man was kneeling in the mud. His hands were dirty, and the smell of moist earth was like the fragrance of revelation. And the man was small and frail; his neck was not thick and muscular like a wrestler's, but soft and long, almost like a woman's. Abdullahi watched the boat-builder's son work: taking up the bricks from the place where they dried in the sun and placing them carefully, stroking them with his hands, building steadily a tomb of love and devotion for his dead master. How humble was such a sight! True devotion like cool water on Abdullahi's skin after such a long and dusty ride.

The man moved easily, without fear. He did not look over his shoulder except once, to smile. Yes, he smiled with his eyes, with his soul, and the signs were there: the mole on the right cheek and the gap between the front teeth. Abdullahi was speechless. He stepped closer, with the strangled groan of a wounded animal. The man turned to face him and Abdullahi fell to his knees, tears rolling down his cheeks. The man reached out and held Abdullahi's hands in his, and they stayed like that for a while, gripping one another's wrists the way a married couple might.

'Master', he found himself saying, 'I have seen it written in my dreams that you are the Expected One.' And the other man smiled the simple smile by which all men would know him and trust him and he nodded once and said simply, 'yes'. And then the man raised his arms and the others working on the tomb dropped their tools in the dust and came forward: men and orphans, the poor and devoted, women wearing the clothes of beggars. They came from every direction, to gather round the man with the mole on his cheek. In that instant Abdullahi knew that he had not been wrong, that at long last he had found the right place. Here was the remedy for his torment.

The sun moved across the sky quietly and without fuss, and the world went on sleeping, unaware of what had taken place.

1. The White Nile,
12 August 1881

Upon the warped deck, beneath a canvas awning that was the colour of worn sunlight and contained the odour of a thousand dead afternoons, Muhammad Abu Al Saud Bey, notorious slave-trader and assistant governor of the Soudan, sat upon an upturned packing-case that had previously contained rifle ammunition in what passed for his command post. There was a small table which leaned to one side and a bamboo lounge-chair that had collapsed in a state of exhaustion in one corner. The khedive's red flag with the gold crescent hung limply from the stern, disturbed only by soft gusts of wind that crawled over the rails of the boat to bring brief moments of relief from the oppressive heat.

Saud's eyes itched. The air was thick and fetid and his legs were giving him pain again. He tried to ignore the buzz of insects and the sound of men down below, shouting at one another. His eyes were trained upwards at the distended belly of the canvas awning where a cluster of carrion kites flopped about in the heat, falling over themselves, pecking one another viciously. Their incessant cawing rose and fell as new arrivals dropped in from the trees along the riverbank. The small steamer had been motionless for three hours now and the scavengers were beginning to get impatient.

The unstable surface which passed for a desk lurched to one side as Saud lifted his head from his hands and screeched for assistance. A tall soldier, awkward in his stiff uniform, came running up the narrow steps that led from the main deck to the bridge, his dusty *tarboosh* tumbling from his head. Saud wrenched the rifle impatiently from the bewildered soldier's hands and let off a load of grapeshot, barely taking the trouble to aim. The birds flew up in a single cry that echoed across the rippled water. As the sound of beating wings faded feathers drifted down over the head of the soldier, who did not blink an eye.

He took the rifle thrust irritably at him by the Egyptian, and then, impassively, without a word, retreated down the steps.

Hundreds of shafts of dusty afternoon light projected through the perforations in the jaundiced canvas shade. One wounded bird still struggled to understand why its wings had ceased to function, making the canvas twitch spasmodically. With a curse, Abu Saud dismissed the matter and strode to the side of the boat. The craft gave a sudden lurch and he grabbed for the iron railing.

Down below, a bunch of soldiers splashed about and laughed as they tried to free the vessel, which had lodged itself on a sandbank. Then there was a shout and the men at the rail began firing into the water. A muddy shadow shifted beneath the surface and was gone. The soldiers were hauling themselves up the ropes and back over the side into the boat. There was more laughter and cries of mock fright as they collapsed gasping on the deck. Saud turned his back and shook his head in despair. He let his eyes rest on the loamy brown earth of the riverbank. Why had God chosen him for this particular task?

The governor-general, of course, in all his wisdom, understood nothing of what was going on here. If it was left to Rauf Pasha nothing would be done. 'One fanatic does not make an uprising, my dear man,' he had declared in that asthmatic fashion of his, examining his fingernails. Saud had tried to impress upon his superior the gravity of the situation. He, after all, had experience of dealing with unruly types from his days in the south, in the slave camps at Gondokoro, for example. Never show any sign of weakness was the first rule. One could never be too harsh with these people. It did not surprise him, with his experience, to learn that this unremarkable island had become a nest of dissent. The presence of a strange man there had been common knowledge for years. Boatmen, fishermen, even soldiers on the numerous steamers going south would break off to raise their hands to their faces and pray, out of respect for the holy man who resided on the island. But the governor-general's face had wrinkled in obvious distaste as Saud pressed his case, and Saud sighed. If they did not arrest the man right away and force him to come to Khartoum to explain himself to the *ulama* they would be inviting others to defy the authority of the khedive.

'Yes, yes, but what has the poor fool done, apart from preach and make absurd proclamations? You told me yourself that he is surrounded only by runaway slaves and thieves, men of the lowest kind. You cannot start a revolt with beggars and whores.'

In the corner of the large stateroom, the Armenian secretary cackled to himself, obviously enjoying the moment. When Abu Saud shot him a scathing glance this hyaena dropped his eyes back to the papers he was pretending to examine, but the governor was warming to his audience. 'The man is obviously a lunatic, claiming to be the ruler of this land, unless I have unwittingly been transformed into a dirty figure dressed in rags.' He raised his hands theatrically and looked round to examine his condition. The Armenian whined in the corner. 'If you are so concerned,' continued the governor-general, 'then I suggest that you take charge of the matter. Take as many troops as you need and bring this lunatic back here.' With a wave of the hand Saud was dismissed.

So if anyone was to blame for his present predicament it was himself. Still – and at this thought Saud felt a thrill of satisfaction – the khedive himself would probably promote him for his efforts, and then Rauf Pasha would be called back to Cairo with his tail between his legs. Saud turned round, to find the adjutant major in front of him. This, he recalled, was the dim-witted one with the moustache. There were two platoons aboard the *Ismailia*. Saud could only recall that one *bimbashi* was tall and the other short, one slow-thinking and the other headstrong. He drew a deep slow breath on noting that the officer had not bothered to salute him, reminded of the insolence he had glimpsed in the eyes of the soldier earlier. Between the resentment of soldiers and the ravings of madmen his work was truly cut out today.

'Yes?'

'Sir, I am worried about the men.'

'The men? What's the matter with them?' Saud made no attempt to conceal his irritation.

'With all this strenuous work to free the boat they will not be in very good condition for attacking tonight. If,' the officer added darkly, 'we manage to reach Aba island today, sir.'

Gripping his fists tightly behind his back, Saud paced across the deck. 'Are you suggesting that your men might need a little rest, a short convalescence perhaps?'

'Well,' the moustached officer shrugged, 'I simply mean that we might consider delaying the attack until tomorrow.'

Saud sat down heavily upon the ammunition box and leaned his elbows on the table. 'I thought we had agreed that a night attack was best. I need not remind a military man such as yourself of the strategic advantages, surely?' He lifted his eyes: the *bimbashi* was staring at the deck. Saud took a deep breath. 'Of course your men are welcome to take a night's rest. They are under your command. But I would have to ask the others to go ashore alone.'

That settled the question. Naturally, the officer could not allow his men to be upstaged by the other platoon. Saud smiled to himself: two rival commanders on one boat ensured the best results. He congratulated himself on his genius and went back to examining his fingernails and thinking about a certain Syrian girl that had come into his possession recently: fair-skinned and very young. Life was not all hard work, he thought, as he looked at his hands and recalled how those pert little breasts fitted there.

Heavy clouds rolled in as night fell. The *Ismailia* clung to the overhanging leaves, scraped past the long spiny palms as the river bubbled and frothed around its rickety hull. The rain fell in thick sheets, drenching the sullen soldiers who stood at the bow of the steamer, clutching their weapons and gazing out at the wooded surface of the island. All was silent and still but for the rain: not a breath of wind, just the weight of the clouds that seemed to press down so hard it made a man's head hurt. They anchored off the north-western tip of the small island. The men dropped over the side and waded ashore, rifles raised above their heads. They split up and soon vanished from sight, to be covered by the night and the veil of soft warm rain.

◆

From the prow of the *Ismailia*, Abu Saud watched for any signs from the island. He was thinking about the last time he had anchored here. The lonely screech of a parakeet sounded mournfully in the distance.

10

Five days ago he had looked out on this very same view. On that occasion he had arrived with only a handful of men to guard him. They made their way on to the island in an orderly procession, with no attempt at concealment. As they walked along the path which led from the riverbank to the small collection of huts, they were surprised to note that the farmers at work in the fields stopped their hoes in mid-swing and stood upright to watch them, and then, without a word, came drifting from the fields in groups of three and four to drop on to the road behind them. One of the soldiers had remarked on this.

'Pay them no heed,' replied Saud. 'They are just curious goats. They want to know what is happening, that's all.'

Word of their arrival somehow managed to precede them, so that the village was waiting for them when they reached it. A crowd had gathered around a small straw hut, outside which was a low, roughly made *angareeb*. On this rope-bed sat a man, who got to his feet as they approached. He was a man, simple enough, perhaps a little taller than average, although he stooped somewhat which made it hard to tell. He had a pleasant, clear face which was disfigured only by a large black mole on his right cheek. He seemed to smile all the time, displaying a prominent gap between his front teeth. Saud found this increasingly irritating as time passed.

'Are you Muhammad Ahmad?' he demanded.

Still smiling, the man nodded.

'Are you the one who has been calling people to defy the authority of the governor-general?'

Again the man smiled. 'I have only spoken the truth as it is revealed to me,' he replied softly.

Saud wiped his brow with a large cravat and glanced back at the crowd, which now resembled a nasty mob. They still gripped their hoes and axes and herding sticks. Poor, uneducated people who had nothing to lose: exactly what he had expected to find, though he had not expected so many. Where had they come from? What had drawn them here? This man with the look of a mournful goat? There were crippled children and scarred women; lepers with no fingers; old men with grey hair and hands that shook. 'How many of you are

11

wanted by the authorities?' he demanded, raising his voice, turning to survey them carefully. There was some shifting of feet, but no one answered.

The boat-builder's son spoke now, gesturing to his audience. 'These people are gentle farmers. They have done nothing for which they should be punished by you who call yourselves the authorities.' He made a sign of reason with his hand. 'There is no authority here higher than that of God. Not even you with all the soldiers and arms in the world can destroy the word of God.'

Saud sighed. *La illaha il Allah*. We all believe in the same God.'

But Muhammad Ahmad shook his head sagely. 'Many have forsaken the true meaning of the Message and you know this is the case. The people whom you represent have squandered their dignity and corrupted the meaning of the word "Islam". You drink wine and smoke tobacco. You have been consumed by the vanities of the world.' He held his hands out wide, appealing to the crowd to make their own judgement. He indicated Saud's suit and *tarboosh*. 'You wear the garments of the European infidels. We wear the simple clothes of our land.'

Saud's temper flared. 'Who do you think you are? Go back to your fields and goats,' he shouted, addressing the blank faces. Not one of them moved.

The smiling man widened his eyes and said, 'They do not fear your threats for the Prophet has spoken to me and through me to them. They know who I am.'

'And who might that be?' demanded Saud, taking a step forwards. There was an intake of breath, a bracing of shoulders, as a ripple of tension passed through the gathered devotees.

The serene prophet looked apologetic. 'I am the proof that the Final Hour has arrived,' he said simply. 'I shall lead the devoted in the holy struggle, the war against the corruption of power and faith which you and all the Turks represent. Victory shall be ours. The Prophet himself came to me in a dream.'

It was Saud's turn to laugh. 'You are still dreaming. I am here to take you back to Khartoum to explain yourself to the learned members of the council of *ulama*. Let them decide if what you say is

12

part of God's plan.' He took another step forward, signalling for the soldiers to take action. Muhammad Ahmad did not move. The man beside him, small and burly with a face pockmarked by smallpox, put his hand down to rest gently on a sword in a scabbard under his left arm, sunlight glinting on the partially drawn blade.

Muhammad Ahmad was looking at the soldiers carefully, watching their eyes. 'Your most learned *ulama* know little of the true faith,' he replied softly. 'Their understanding is based on academic study. They have never seen the light of God, nor heard the words of the Prophet as I have.' He stopped, reaching a hand out to his companion, who let the sword drop back into place. 'Tell them that if they come and pledge allegiance to me now they will suffer no consequences. God is merciful. If their hearts are true they will not suffer when the time comes. Remind them that they stand in judgement before God as all men must.'

Saud looked about him. He turned to the onlookers: 'Listen to me. What he says is nonsense, and what is more, it is dangerous nonsense. He will lead you, not to glory, but to gaol along with him. If he is who he claims to be then why has no other learned man in the country pronounced his coming? Why should God ask one Muslim to take arms against another?' He saw no response to his appeal. He drew a deep breath. 'There is one law in this country and it is the law of the governor-general, of the khedive who rules these lands.' The weight went out of his voice. 'This is nothing to do with religion.' He stretched out a hand towards them and smiled. 'This is not the end of the world.'

As he turned to leave, his eye latched on to a familiar face in the crowd: a small, wizened old man with restless eyes. 'Wad Awad,' he called. 'You once served me well, in the old days in the south. What are you doing here with this lunatic? Don't you realise what will happen? You will lose your homes, your land, your freedom. The soldiers will come and they will not reason with you as I do. You are an old man, a wise man, think of what you are doing.'

But old Wad Awad shook his head. 'Saud Bey, he speaks the word of the Prophet Himself. It is the will of God,' he murmured, his jittery eyes flickering back to the ground.

'May God have mercy on you, on all of you.' And with that Saud left the island with the sound of laughter and jubilation ringing in his ears.

◆

The hurricane lamp hissed away long past midnight. There had been shots, not many, from far off, all coming together like an animal coughing in the distance, and then silence – an uneasy silence. From the railing of the boat Saud Bey looked out towards the beach. The mosquitoes were closing in now that the rain had stopped; the deck was swarming with them in the stale humidity. Saud Bey paced up and down, impatient for news, until a cry in the distance brought him back to the rail. Another cry. A cold sensation in his spine told him that it was the cry of a man. He moved urgently towards where the crew were huddled together, leaning over the side, looking towards the island. 'Can anyone see?'

'Should we man the gun, sir?'

'What are you going to shoot at?' he snapped, not taking his eyes off the strip of cane and the flat broken outline of the shore.

'There!' cried a soldier, pointing out. Saud cursed his eyes.

Another soldier joined in: 'There's another one.' Five, six, perhaps a dozen men appeared, bursting through the line of tall canes. 'They are hurt. Look, they are carrying that one.'

'Stay where you are,' ordered Saud Bey, watching the figures now splashing into the shallows.

'Crocodile!' came a shout from the bow. The soldiers loaded their rifles and began trying to aim for the long arrow-like swirls of water. 'Fire into the air!' Everything was confusion until the sound of screams from the water told their own story.

One man made it to the boat. Hands reached over the side and pulled him aboard. He lay on the deck, gasping and shivering with terror and relief. The men crowded round, stunned into silence. The soldier was badly wounded; blood and water mingled darkly in the faint glow of the oil lamps. He shook his head from side to side, weeping hysterically. 'They were hiding in the fields around the village, in the ditches – buried like snakes in the soil. There was firing from all sides, and too late we realised that it was our own men firing on us.' He shook his head in amazement. 'Then ten men were dead and others wounded. We stopped to recover our strength and decide what to do, when they came upon us.' Once again he broke off, as though finding it difficult to comprehend what he himself had witnessed. 'They had axes and stones and sticks and machetes and clubs. They beat the men to death, cut their heads off, smashed their skulls to pulp. I saw the *bimbashi* die.'

The loss of the moustached officer made little impression on Saud. He sniffed. 'And you. How did you get away?'

The man looked up. 'A few of us escaped. There was no other way, the rest of them died there.' He looked back over his shoulder. 'It is a bad place.'

'I ought to shoot you for desertion,' snapped Saud Bey in disgust, turning on his heels to stalk down towards the helm, calling to the pilot to haul in the anchor. They would head back downstream to Khartoum and the governor-general. He heard the whispers of the men as they talked of curses and divine intervention. He smelt the thick stench of superstition which covered the small steamer like a mist. As he stood clutching the rail, light was beginning to signal the arrival of dawn. Saud Bey bit his lip. 'Now,' he said to himself, 'now there is going to be trouble.'

2. The Gezira,
1882

After all these years, there were few who might have recognised the thin, hunched figure balanced upon the protruding spine of the skinny mule. The animal came like a sack of broken bones into the small Gezira town, which sat in the crook of the two Niles, south of Khartoum. Its spindly legs knocked into one other until they were scarred and swollen; blood ran down over the grey fur and left a thin dotted trail in the dust.

None of those who had heard him speak when he was at the height of his powers, in the days when his name was spoken in tones of hushed reverence, saw him come. Wise men who might have recalled his inquisitive mind and sharp tongue were nowhere to be seen. Nor would any of those who had known him then have recognised him in this rag-bag of a man. His sunken cheeks and bleary eyes bore no resemblance to the handsome confidence which was once attached to his name. None of those who once came with offers of their daughters in marriage – or the married women, who offered themselves when they ought to have known better – would have considered throwing themselves at the feet of this austere fellow now. Besides, he had refused them all and this had brought him enemies, for how many men could claim to have turned away so many, and for what reason did he do it other than conceit? No man lived without the company of women, not even the noblest of sheikhs. Since there was no law forbidding it, such behaviour could only be ascribed to pomposity, unless the man was crazed. Why, one could even argue on moral grounds that it was his duty to give shelter to these women rather than leaving them to the open road; did he not have a charitable heart? But moral argument was no territory upon which to begin debating with this fellow – a man whose entire life, one might say, was a sacrifice to the exemplary and the aesthetic.

Like many who choose to steer the course of their lives according to ideals rather than accepting the nature of the world as it is, he eventually strayed too far. He began to question the very ideas he was supposed to defend, to talk of a second, hidden message concealed within the holy scriptures. But that was then, and who would suspect this bedraggled figure now of harbouring such lofty notions? The very idea of shaking hands with him invoked revulsion; and as for sharing a meal with him, why, one would rather invite the mule.

The curiosity-seekers would have been surprised to learn that this enigmatic figure of a man was spoken of with warmth and respect in, for example, those fabled corridors of learning at Al-Azhar in Cairo. Indeed, the mention of his name there prompted enthusiastic smiles and invited anecdote after anecdote, fanning the flames of controversy in the countries across the Red Sea and in the holy lands as far north as Jerusalem, Tarabullus, Smyrna and Aleppo, all of which he had visited during his years of self-imposed exile. His reputation had reached every centre of learning as far as Constantinople. They knew of him in the mountains of Persia and on the humid coasts of the Indian Ocean. Traders in the markets of Basra and Mosul recalled his sermons, as did herders gathered beneath the shade of the orange groves in the Atlas mountains. People in all these places would call him friend. What would they say if they saw him now in his torn, dusty garments of the roughest linen – a grubby length of sack-cloth over his head to protect that bald and scabby scalp from the noonday sun? How many would avert their eyes and pretend not to notice?

This village was no different from any other: the children, wary of strangers, hurled stones and pellets of goat manure. Women muttered curses and hauled infants out of his path. Men rocked back and forth with laughter and dogs yapped at the heels of the bewildered and half-dead mule. Curses and taunts followed the man who had once kept kings enraptured with his wit and wisdom, just as they had followed him in a trail that zig-zagged back and forth across the roads and open tracts that brought him here, a trail whose course, if seen from on high, might be found to trace the word 'outcast' – if it traced anything intelligible at all.

The man, whose name was not even remembered by the majority of inhabitants, nevertheless seemed capable of finding his way through the collection of mud walls and shelters, leaning *rakubas* and straw huts, past withered hens and inquisitive goats, to where he was going. He arrived, finally, accompanied by an entourage of half-wits and laughing children, outside the largest and most well-kept house in the village. The gate was painted green and the walls were whitewashed with chalk. And it was here, rather than at any of the humble abodes he might have chosen, that this traveller decided to stop. The crowd, under a spell of wonder, looked on. He slid from the haunches of the mule, managing to lose his footing – his legs being numb from the ride – and deposited himself in an undignified heap in the dust, much to the amusement of his audience. He made a sound that resembled a growl and then, rising painfully to his feet, he dusted himself down and hobbled towards the door.

The servant who answered his knock was a small, muscular fellow with a shiny, well-scrubbed look about him. He regarded the crowd cautiously and examined the stranger with a look of some disdain. 'Who is it?'

'I've come to visit Sheikh Rahman, brother. Is this still his house?' the traveller enquired.

The servant shook his head. 'The master is not at home,' he declared. Nothing on earth would prompt him to admit such a pitiful excuse for a man.

'Please call him.' The stranger was insistent. 'I have travelled a long way.' He spoke with a forthright obstinacy which might have rung a bell with some of his former acquaintants, but this boy was too young to remember. 'I will wait for him if he is not here,' the stranger continued. 'Give me a glass of water and a place to sit.'

The boy waved a hand, 'Go and beg in the marketplace, God is generous.' He could be resolute too. He made to close the door, but the stranger stepped forwards to place his foot in the way. There was a rumble from the crowd.

'I asked for a drink of water,' explained the stranger. 'Does your master teach you that only those in fine clothes will find a place in paradise?'

'Old man, you must be deaf. I told you that the sheikh is not here.'

The traveller wiped sweat from his forehead. Behind his back, he sensed the crowd growing nasty, as though they suspected him of having come to cause trouble. How things would have developed it is hard to say, for at that moment a voice of authority was heard from within and the crowd seemed to heave a sigh of collective relief.

The half-closed wooden door swung aside and in a rustle of freshly laundered cotton the sheikh himself appeared. He had a warm benevolent presence, confident and calm. The two men stood face to face, both transformed almost beyond recognition by the years: one swollen and content, the other worn like old wood by the ravages of time. The furrow in the sheikh's brow deepened as something stirred in his recollection.

'Are you a beggar?' he enquired after a moment. But then he fell silent. The wind rustled in the trees. He took a step backwards. 'In the name of God! Is it you?'

Weariness descended on to the stranger's shoulders. The sun pressed like a boulder on his head. His feet burned from the sand. For a moment he swayed back and forth, until the sheikh stepped forward to embrace him. 'Hawi, is it really you?' he repeated, as though astounded by the facts. He made a dismissive gesture at the crowd. 'Go on, go away,' he called. 'You have seen what you wanted, now go about your business.' And reluctantly they obeyed, leaving only one fool standing alone, his head tilted to one side and his tongue hanging out, until a child took his limp hand and led him gently away.

Hawi entered the house with the sheikh's hand on his shoulder. 'Please, please come in. My house is your house.' He clapped his hands and issued orders to his servant to fetch this and that, water and refreshments. The boy scuttled away with his head down. The yard was peaceful, green and shady. A pleasant breeze ruffled the uppermost leaves of a tall neem tree – a grand old tree that towered over the low brick house. Two clay water-pots rested in its shade, their sides damp with perspiration. A long prayer-mat was rolled up against the wall. Otherwise the yard was bare. The doorway to the house was open and through it one could see a rectangle of light from a small yard at the back of the house, where the cooks and servants went about their business. Pigeons flew up from a conical clay construction at the side of the house to perch on the eaves, cooing to one another in their sultry, echoing way.

'Sheikh Suliman, may peace be upon his soul, loved pigeons,' explained Rahman in an obsequious manner which the other man now recalled with slight distaste. The world outside, the long hot road was gone; for the moment Hawi even forgot why he had made this journey here in the first place, so that when Sheikh Rahman asked him casually what he was doing in these parts, he replied with a wave of his hand, 'Just passing through.' The sheikh did not question him further on the matter. Instead, they both sat upon the raised veranda in the shade as the servant brought jugs of apricot juice and bowls of nuts, dates and honey. Rahman ordered the boy to prepare roast pigeons for their lunch. Hawi's mouth watered at the mention of food. For weeks he had been living on stale *gorassa* pancakes and tepid water, or whatever people could spare him. He was tired and had a fondness for roast pigeon. He put aside his reservations and smiled amenably.

The sheikh propped himself up on his elbow. 'So, old friend, what have you been doing all these years? No one has seen or heard from you in ages. Where have you been?'

Al Hawi smiled, and bit into another date. 'These really are delicious,' he said, holding the stone up before tossing it over his shoulder. The sheikh concealed his exasperation with a shrug. Hawi gestured round the yard self-consciously. 'A fine place this is.'

Another shrug. 'God is generous indeed. I remained with Sheikh Suliman until he died. It was his last wish that I should stay on in his place.'

'May the Lord have mercy on his soul.'

'He was a good man.' Rahman fell silent for a moment, turning the beads of his rosary in his hand. 'He never forgot you. Sometimes he would say, "I saw a face in the market today which reminded me instantly of Hawi."' Rahman gazed off over the trees, recalling their old master. 'Once he said he had a dream in which he saw you in a town where the streets were made of water. He was very curious about that.' Sheikh Rahman laughed. 'It was a mystery, he said, because, of all the people he knew, you were the only boy who had never learned to swim.'

Hawi stopped chewing to recall the wind as it blew the rain across the plaza of St Mark in Venice. Rahman was watching him with close concentration. 'How long is it since you left? Fourteen, fifteen years?'

'Sixteen,' nodded Hawi. 'I left in the month of Rajab, the year 1283 of the *hegira*. Sixteen years.'

The other man nodded slowly. He looked out at the simple splendour of his home. Turning back to his guest, he repeated his question, 'And, after all this time, what brings you back now?'

The servant arrived at that moment with the pigeons on a tray. Sheikh Rahman told him curtly to place them on the table and go. The boy hurried away, muttering to himself about injustice. Rahman was waiting for a reply. The contrived geniality of his tone was beginning to wane in proportion to his rising exasperation. Hawi was busy examining the craftsmanship of a small table between the two divans on which they were seated. Impatient, the sheikh got to his feet and paced to the edge of the veranda and back. 'You left here in disgrace, your life was in danger. You were lucky get away alive.' He shook his head. 'You did not come back here after all this time just to pay your respects.'

Hawi cleared his throat and looked up. 'I was in Cairo, and I heard that something had happened. You must know, this man who calls himself . . . the Mahdi. I wanted . . .' He did not have time to finish what he was saying, for Sheikh Rahman broke in with a hearty peal of laughter that rocked Al Hawi back on his tail. 'What?' he repeated, a look of disbelief on his face, 'You came for this?'

'I . . .' Hawi was at a loss. He let his shoulders slump.

'Truly, you came back to find this fool, this trickster, this market-place scroundrel?' Rahman shouted, getting to his feet and waving a hand in the air above his head. 'In all the years we have sat and wondered what happened to our old friend? Whether he was still alive?' The scholar paced the floor, turning the rosary beads furiously in his fingers. 'Not one word, no letter or message; nothing. And our master, may peace be with him, dies wishing he could have one more chance to speak to his favourite student; the best student he ever had, the most diligent, the most intelligent – just one chance. But no one knew where you were. And now you come back for this?'

Hawi stared blankly into the air, unable to think of anything to say. Rahman stepped to the table and jabbed a hand at the tray of pigeons. 'Eat!' he ordered. 'At least you might do us the honour of eating what was prepared for you.'

Hawi licked his lips and stretched out a hand. He bit into the blackened meat. It was good. He tore off a small strip of it with his teeth and went on chewing.

'Perhaps I made a mistake in stopping here to visit you,' he ventured after a time.

'He's a fool. I met him once, so did you, many years ago.'

This new piece of information took Hawi by surprise. 'I met him?' he asked, in such a reverent tone that Rahman rolled his eyes in despair.

'Very surly,' continued Rahman. 'Caught up in his own thoughts, somewhat like you once were, but,' he paused to tilt his head, 'without your wit.' Their eyes met on this note and immediately diverged again. 'He comes from Dongola. His father was a builder of boats. They are simple, ignorant people. They still bury their daughters alive for want of a son.'

'They say he defied the Turks.'

'A small group of soldiers were clubbed to death by farmers, and besides, I heard the soldiers were drunk.' Rahman shook his head. 'Not a military victory. He claims to have been informed by the Prophet himself in a dream that he was the Expected One and that he was to raise an army of the faithful and drive out the Turks.'

'But if this is not true, it is outrageous.'

The sheikh yawned. 'He will pay the price when his time comes.'

'So you think he is an impostor?'

'Either that or a fool. It will take more than a few farmers with clubs to defeat the trained armies of the khedive. Where would he find enough men and arms? No – ' Rahman shook his head, 'The khedive will send a small army and they will cut off his head and then we can get back to normal.'

Reaching as unobtrusively as he could for another pigeon, Hawi nodded. 'You don't think he is right then to oppose the Turks?'

'All I know is that he sheds a bad light on all the schools.' Rahman tapped his chest. 'On all of us.'

'But if it is true,' Hawi insisted, 'then surely he will bring a new age, a piety and purity to the land; cleanse it of corruption and vanity, as he says in his proclamations. No one can say that the taxes are fair, that the people are not poor, surely?'

Rahman waved his hand like a fan. 'Please don't lecture me on injustice – it is so boring. All cannot be equal in this world. You will see, it will all come to nothing.'

Hawi reached into his pocket. 'I found one of these. They have them in every marketplace. His agents have been busy.'

Sheikh Rahman ran his eyes over the printed yellow sheet of the proclamation and then tore it into shreds. Hawi carried on chewing without saying a word. The sheikh held up the torn paper. 'If the soldiers caught you with one of these they could hang you,' he said, adding, 'It would be very embarrassing if it were to be found in my possession.'

'There are certain signs, markings. One would know it if one met him face to face,' Hawi urged.

'No,' snapped the sheikh, dismissing the idea. 'I don't need to see him. Listen, I will not take lessons from you when you come wandering in here like a stray dog after all these years.'

'But they laughed at the Prophet at first, they called him an impostor too.'

The sheikh shook his head. 'I am appalled. You truly have no shame.'

'They too refused to listen,' continued Hawi.

'Enough!' shouted Rahman with vehemence. 'I know what you want and here is your answer: I will not go with you. You want to find out the truth then go and find him, this Mahdi of yours. Go to Aba and go to the Nuba mountains where he has led his followers – with the audacity to call his journey a *hegira*. His followers name themselves *ansar* after the followers of the Prophet. They should hang this man as an apostate, a blasphemer, for making such claims. This at least you have in common with him.

'Go to him by all means, but whatever you do, do not sit in-judgement on my abilities. Sheikh Suliman, may God bless him and give him peace, treated you better than his own son. He died wishing that he might have had a chance to speak to you one last time, and he loved you despite the fact that he never understood your reasons for abandoning the teachings in the pursuit of your own vanity – all your talk of hidden meanings in the holy scriptures.' A shudder went through Rahman, and Hawi glimpsed once more the figure he had known in his youth. 'He never forgave you for that.'

Hawi stood up and wrung his hands. 'I didn't come here to argue with you, old friend. I came to find the truth.'

'You are my guest and you are always welcome in my house,' Rahman said finally.

'Thank you,' said Hawi, and he meant it.

Rahman was watching him closely. 'Where will you go from here?'

'I'm not sure. I thought about Abbas.'

Rahman sighed. 'If he is still alive. Go to him by all means.'

He placed a hand on Hawi's shoulder and led the way. 'But you will stay here tonight and when you are ready to leave we will give you another mule. God knows, yours is less use than a rug.' He paused to smile at his own humour and then added, 'And we will ask God to guide you.' Then he shrugged his shoulders as if shaking off a shawl and stepped off the *rakuba*, saying, 'Now it is time to pray.'

3. The Western Plains,
July 1882

And someone had smelt rain. It fell thickly in a grey veil over the land. The air was clammy and warm: a net cast out over all the thin-limbed trees; the web of some huge spider drawing them inwards. And through the stunted acacia, the thorn trees and the mesquite bush came pencil strokes that moved like shaved shadows. A stench of dead meat preceded them – a scent that made the gazelle run from their shelters, stopped dogs in their tracks and pulled hawks down from the sky to perch in the crooks of ashen branches and wait.

The horses plodded on through the night with their heads down. The first drops spat up the dust in bubbles that swelled and burst like sores. It was that odd hour between dawn breaking and the coming of day, and Kadaro was asleep on his feet. When the call came for a halt they were making no actual progress at all. Up ahead, Juma and Wahab were engrossed in an argument, too far away for any of the men to catch what was being said, though they looked on sullenly and in silence.

'Not even God's dumb beasts like him,' muttered Abd al-Tome one day when Juma received a kick in the leg from one of the pack-mules. If the two men had fallen upon one another with bayonets drawn not one of the soldiers would have raised a finger to stop them, for it was more than likely that Wahab would be the victor.

◆

Hooves clatter nervously upon the rocky carapace of the plateau. The men are in a ghostly, somnambulent state, having been moving for over two months now without proper rest. They come dragging their heels, stumbling over pack-mules and worn-out ponies with pots and pans clattering. Men dressed in all kinds of rags and wretched garments. The Ninth Company of the *Bash-Buzuq*, the governor-general's Irregular Cavalry; a motley, misfit crew, never despised so much as now. The khedive's power is on the wane and so are they. Everywhere they go they are spat upon.

It is the Year of the Comet. The yellow fields of millet are so dry that wisps of smoke can be seen rising from them in the midday heat. The stalks are shrunken and emaciated. They gather acacia pods and boil them for days before eating them. When they come, without warning, people lift their children and run; women drag their daughters inside, out of sight; men stand silently, bracing themselves. The soldiers are irregular by name and irregular by nature. Some years they are late; this time they are early.

In every village they come to it is the same thing: they round the villagers up to form a circle for the registering of names and the listing of property. Most have nothing to give. They shuffle forwards with their heads bowed, knowing that the heavy lash of the *courbaj* awaits them, for this is not the first time. Some years are good and others are bad, and this is the way God made the world.

Ten days ago Major Hantoub died in a village much like this one, further north, among the Zaghawa. A group of men had assembled, proclaiming themselves spokesmen for the others. No taxes would be paid to the servants of the infidels, they said. Hantoub tried to reason with them. And then a strange thing happened: one of the men engaged in the argument simply drew a knife from under his clothes and plunged it into the major's belly. The old man took hours to die. Kadaro watched the process: when the end came the man was whimpering and crying, his clothes soiled, blood frothing from his mouth. The culprit made no attempt to get away, but when they came for him he began shouting – religious words, proclamations of faith. It was Juma who shot him. Holding him down on his knees, he put the rifle to the man's head and pulled the trigger. The dogs scurried forward to lick at the dust-coated brains.

◆

'Not even God's dumb beasts like him,' muttered Abd al-Tome, recalling the day when the *sanjak* had received a kick in the leg from one of the pack-mules. Kadaro wondered to himself what this meant. He was twelve years old and this unit was the only family he possessed. Abd al-Tome took a deep breath and rose to his feet. 'This is my last tour. It's been too long, too many killings.'

'It wouldn't be so bad,' ventured the boy, 'if old Hantoub was still here.'

Abd al-Tome did not look down at the boy. 'You be careful who you speak to about things like that, boy. Juma would eat your kidneys for breakfast.'

'But you know it's true,' protested Kadaro.

Abd al-Tome swore into his tunic. 'Sometimes I think you haven't learnt a thing since the day you came to us!' His anger surprised the boy. 'Truth has never had anything to do with anything.' The old man slapped his hand against his side. 'Where would we all be if we all went round doing that, eh? Dead is where we'd be.'

Kadaro shrugged and tried to spit, making a mess and drooling down his chin. He looked away and rubbed at it with his hand. The other man gave a snort of disgust.

Wherever they went it was the same: the men of the *Bash-Buzuq* found themselves unloved in an unforgiving land. They were fired upon, spat at. Wells were sealed up and even, in one instance, poisoned. When they finally reached the sanctuary of the garrison fort at Al Tayarra, they found it in the hands of the Mahdi's *ansar*, whose black banner, covered in words of holy devotion, fluttered in the wind. 'As if our faith were not the same,' they cursed. 'We are all of us Muslims, God damn them.' What had become of the world when soldiers had to sneak through the dark like common thieves?

They no longer had anywhere to go. They survived on whatever food they could beg, steal or catch. There was some talk of stripping off their uniforms and going home to their villages and families. 'This is a bad business,' they muttered when they gathered round the fires at night. 'These fanatics are everywhere.'

'They are no more fanatical than my mother is a whore.'

'Maybe he truly is the Mahdi – did you think of that?' Any man found talking openly about the matter risked the *courbaj* or worse.

27

Wahab stalked around at night telling them to shut up. He was a large, broad-shouldered fellow with two wide streaks cut into each cheek. He had a wide face and skin as hard as leather – thick as the hippopotamus hide of the lash which hung loosely from his powerful wrist. It was clear to him that he was protecting his men: *Sanjak* Juma would shoot anyone who broke the rule without giving it a second thought.

They had been planning to circle round from the south-east to reach the town of El Obeid. But three days ago they had crossed paths with a trade caravan carrying wives and wares to the north, who told them that the town was under siege. 'What's the point,' the men grumbled, 'of getting ourselves there just in time to be massacred?' And Wahab had somehow managed to convince the *sanjak* that the best policy was to pull back towards the centre – towards the Nile.

The tail of the *Bash-Bazuq* was dragging in the mud. Some of the riders pulled blankets over their heads while others removed their tunics and tied them around their skulls. The rain hissed down upon them, smelling of dead centuries and the breath of drowned birds. The forest closed in, pushing the men apart, breaking up the column. The mules hesitated and sticks came down on their flanks. Listlessly the men dropped to the ground to walk as the trees grew thicker. They rode on through the night, not daring to stop.

◆

They emerge from another sleepless night. They are haunted by the vision of the sky erupting into light in the dead of night: the silver-tailed *jinn* which has left its impression on the retina of every one of them. Soldiers do not understand comets. This sign was not for them, they thought; but they hear it now, whispered in the grains of sand crawling over the rock. They sense it in every broken saddle-strap, every horse gone lame, every water-hole filled in along the way. They are tired and far away from home. The land has changed, like a scar never spoken of, now laid bare in this hour between darkness and light.

◆

The pilgrims were in a pitiful state. Dressed in rags, many of them too weak to walk, they seemed to have simply sat down in the sand to wait for death. They had one goat, which was over-milked and limping. The women drew their black wraps across their faces as the company led by *Sanjak* Juma came across the red plain in a cloud of dust. Horses staggered and reared up. The pilgrims cowered together in a close circle as the cavalry struggled to sort itself out. Their bundles of belongings were scattered on the ground.

'Wahab!' the *sanjak* yelled over the noise of horses and men. 'Pull the men back to form a circle.' With a sigh Wahab began to move round, slapping the horses on the rump, grabbing soldiers by the arm, nagging and coaxing until the ragged unit was in something resembling a circle, at something like a respectable distance. Juma stood up in his stirrups and surveyed the result. He nodded his approval and sat down. He swung his horse round and walked forwards until he reached the pilgrims. 'Who is the elder here? Who is in charge?' He pointed with his rifle. 'You, come over here.' A man, who was perhaps twenty, perhaps thirty years old, came forwards. He stood upright with his back straight and looked into Juma's eyes. 'Where have you come from?' The man turned and raised his arm, pointing towards the horizon.

Juma looked in the direction of rocks and dust. 'Where are you going?' The man, dropping his arm, now raised the other and pointed in the exact opposite direction. Juma nodded his head, dug his heels lightly into the flanks of his mount and stepped closer, then, raising the stock, he swiped the man hard across the head. The man fell to his knees, both hands clutching his left ear; a trickle of blood seeped out through his fingers. Juma grunted. 'You will answer me when I speak to you,' he said.

A woman dressed all in black rags, thin ankles protruding from the hem, stepped forward. 'He cannot answer you any other way. They cut his tongue out.' She pushed the cloth away from her eyes and they glinted in the sunlight. The breeze pulled at the uneven edges of her garments.

Juma looked at her for a moment. 'Who?'

'Soldiers, bandits, what difference does it make? You are all the same.' She stood there, no stronger than a dry twig, talking to an officer of the cavalry as though he were a peanut vendor in a marketplace.

'She's not afraid,' thought Kadaro to himself in wonder.

Juma stabbed at the woman with his stock. 'Well, since they decided to spare your tongue, perhaps you can tell me. Where are you going?'

Again she stood her ground, holding her braids and tugging her scarf around her head. 'We are going to join the Mahdi, for he has spoken.' She half turned to indicate the people behind her. 'We have no belongings, everything has been taken from us, but he says that we may come into his family if we join him at the holy mountain.'

Juma snorted a laugh. 'The holy mountain, eh?' He shook his head, 'I must have missed something. What holy mountain is that, sister?'

The woman explained patiently. 'The Mahdi has renamed the mountain Massa, after the tradition of the Prophet Muhammad. He was told to do that by the Prophet himself,' she added with a nod of conviction, 'in a dream.'

'Well,' said Juma, leaning forwards, 'that's all very fine, with your holy mountain and everything, but you are a long way from anywhere and you will probably die out here.'

'If we are to die here then that is the will of God. Otherwise he will oversee our safe arrival at the mountain where we can join him.'

Juma shook his head. 'You won't get anywhere. You will die out here like dogs in the sun. Look at you,' he laughed in amazement. 'You have no mules, no horses or camels, only that dog which looks more dead than alive.'

'That's a goat,' the woman corrected.

'You'd get more milk from a dog.' Juma swung round to see if the men were amused by his wit, but the men were enthralled by the pilgrims, and an air of silent wonder had descended on the company.

'God will guide us and watch over us,' repeated the woman.

Juma moved closer. 'You know who we are?'

For the first time a look of concern crossed the woman's weary face. Her lips trembled as she took another look at the assembled soldiers with their bizarre collection of uniforms and weapons. '*Bash-Buzuq?*' she whispered.

Juma smiled thinly. He raised his voice to address the others in the

30

small party. 'And how many of you are going to fight for this Mahdi of yours, eh? How many of you are going to join the *darawish* so that you can kill soldiers like us?' The faces of the men and the women, the old ones and the children stared sullenly back at him.

At this point something unforeseen occurred. A young soldier named Razig, a timid fellow but with a good heart, dropped from his saddle and walked towards the wretched group. He carried a small sack which contained all the food he had: some stale bread, a few handfuls of flour, some dried dates. He deposited the sack in front of the pilgrims. He hardly seemed to stop to consider the consequences of his actions. It was just something that had to be done. Kadaro looked across at Wahab and saw the big man look away, muttering to himself under his breath. Juma watched the whole thing with disbelief on his face.

'Soldier!' he roared. Razig stopped in mid-step and looked round with a look of genuine surprise. 'Soldier, what do you think you are doing?'

Razig gestured empty-handedly towards the pilgrims and then shrugged. He turned to look back towards the line of soldiers and horses. Juma spurred himself forwards suddenly and struck Razig in the back with his full weight, sending him flying to land on his face in the dirt. All around him, to left and right, Kadaro could feel tension growing. Juma dropped to the ground and began whipping Razig about the head and chest with his riding switch. The pilgrims looked on in amazement. Wahab, moving with slow deliberation, dismounted. 'Sir,' he began, 'I think he has had enough.'

The *sanjak* rounded on him, his eyes red, his face like thunder. 'This man is guilty of feeding the enemy. I call that treason, would you not agree?' Wahab looked away without saying anything. Juma indicated to the two men nearest to him: the mute and an old man. 'We shall set an example of these people to those who would follow this madman. Sergeant, despatch two men to fetch some wood.'

Two soldiers set off towards the trees. Everyone stood in the dust to wait, while the sun climbed through the sky. When the men returned with wood, two large crosses were constructed, rough and uneven like two deformed trees in the middle of the sandy plain. The old man and the mute were nailed on by their hands and feet, their waists bound to the stakes with rope to carry some of their weight, so that the nails should not tear through their flesh. The women wailed and screamed, but Juma was unrelenting.

'Let them try to enter paradise fastened to the crosses of the unbelievers. May that be a lesson to you all. This Mahdi of yours is nothing but a petty fool.'

At this point a young boy, with bright brown eyes that shone like pools of rain, stepped forwards from behind the flock of crow-like women squatting on the ground. He stood in front of Juma. He was no more than nine years old. He pointed a finger. 'There is no God but God and Muhammad is his prophet, Muhammad Ahmad is the Apostle, who will deliver us from the tyranny and vanity of the Turk. You cannot resist the power of God, not with guns nor any kind of sword.'

The soldiers were smiling – at the audacity of it, at the clear tone of conviction in the boy's voice. They admired courage when they saw it. A shot rang out, singular and complete, over in a second. The boy crumpled to the floor, his blood spilling across the sand. Wahab stepped forwards, reaching out as though to catch the boy, but much too late. He turned in disbelief and Juma, who must have read what was written plainly in the big man's eyes, stepped back and raised the pistol again. No one spoke, and for a brief instant nobody even breathed. Then a rifle exploded and the moment was shattered: Juma lay on the floor kicking his legs, writhing and cursing in pain. Wahab reached down and quietly retrieved the fallen revolver. He tucked it into his belt. Juma screamed obscenities and orders, but no one paid any attention. It was decided, without a word being spoken.

'Bury your son,' Wahab said to the women, 'and bury him well.' He turned to the soldiers, indicating the men on the crosses. 'Cut them free. Razig, collect what food you can from the others and give it to these people. Whatever can be spared.' He pushed past the men, who now began to move as though waking from a trance. 'Rig a litter with blankets and sticks for the *sanjak*.' He approached the soldier who had shot Juma. 'That was a foolish thing to do, old man.'

Abd al-Tome said nothing as Wahab lifted the rifle gently from his hands. Wahab climbed on to his horse and addressed the crowd: 'Go towards the south from here and if you are lucky you'll reach a good well by nightfall. From there the road will take you to Bara where you will find what you seek.' The pilgrims said nothing, but stared as if they did not believe what they were witnessing.

'It's true,' said the woman who had spoken back to Juma, 'there is a miracle in this land. May the Lord bless you and may He guide you,' she cried with joy.

Wahab snapped his reins impatiently. 'Give them a mule,' he said, 'and then let's get out of this cursed place.'

So with Juma strapped to the makeshift stretcher, and men tailing along in an unruly line, the column moved off towards the east. Juma struggled to raise himself up in a sitting position and then with a curse on his lips fell back into unconsciousness.

4. Khartoum,
July 1883

The peacocks unfurled their tail-feathers like fine ladies surveying their hands in a round of after-dinner bridge. In their eloquent blues and greens they strutted along between the arches of the stone veranda, taking long elegant strides as though impervious to the dust and the guns.

Suddenly startled, they leapt out of the way, their feet skating on the tiles as they vanished, only narrowly escaping the long stream of acrid tobacco ejected in their direction by Medani, the old palace cook. He was rumoured to be the governor-general's most trusted man – a gnarled old figure with the scars of the Berbers on his face and a moustache that bristled like steel wire. The peacocks unleashed their exasperation among the clutter of chickens that inhabited the courtyard of the governor's seraglio, causing feathers and dust to erupt into the air, along with a squawk of alarm. Then, with a shudder, the peacocks recovered their poise and resumed their stroll in the sunlight.

In the indigo shade of the wall on the far side of the palace yard, a soldier yawned and leaned against a gun carriage. Over the perimeter wall came the distant sounds of the town shaking off its sleep: street vendors and hawkers, boys driving their herds of sheep to market, bow-legged farmers struggling under heavy sacks, out of which protruded aubergines, curly cucumbers and bright ruby peppers, merchants counting their coins and chatting idly about the future. To the people of the town, the coming and going of the soldiers only bore witness to the security of their situation. Rumours of skirmishes in the remote west were of little concern.

Medani passed the archway that cut through the long building and framed a gentle view of the river. Beyond the unelaborate structure of the seraglio, there were low-shouldered banks and a string of palms with long fronds like green razors reaching towards the swirling water. Somewhere in the fields a donkey was braying over and over, malodorous and discontented. The river hummed by slowly beneath whitewashed walls now streaked with rust from the previous rains, as if the veins of some strange tree were trying to break through the bricks and mortar.

In the governors-general's reception chamber, a long silence was broken by the shuffle of Medani's approach. He carried a silver tray upon which a selection of his formidable pastries reclined. Behind him a small procession of young boys wearing white cotton uniforms and gloves, with green *tarbooshes* balanced on their heads, followed on carrying the tea. Medani always delivered his pastries in person, despite the distaste that his dishevelled appearance aroused at times in the governor-general's visitors. His reputation for skill with pastry, however, was enough to allay the concerns of all but the most jittery – and they, quite simply, did not deserve a taste. Why, it was an honour to be served by the man in person. Rumours of his culinary skills were said to have reached Cairo and Damascus. His own secret recipes. He did not trust the clumsy servant-boys to carry them from the kitchen lest they should drop one of his precious jewels – or, more probably, *dare* to wolf down a couple on the way upstairs.

As Medani entered the chamber he ignored the officers seated beneath the exquisite tapestries and paintings that decorated the walls and made his way towards the governor-general himself. Displaying the wares with a short bow, he placed the tray on a low table between Colonel Hicks and the old lizard of a Circassian general, who was reclining on the divan opposite. The governor-general, whose once-muscular frame was now softening with age and lack of exercise, stroked his moustache with two fingers while the other hand drummed on the top of the wide teak desk. The sight of the pastries was akin to that of a pool of water to a thirsty camel, for the fact was that Ala'adin Pasha Siddiq was bored. Medani straightened up, saluted with a flourish – the irony of which was not noted by any of the military men – and then, swivelling on his heels, he left the room. The governor-general made a mental note of this insubordination and reflected briefly on the fact that his mission here afforded him very few moments of real pleasure. He noted too that Hicks was tapping

35

his switch against his knee in an irritating manner in order to draw attention to the fact that in his esteemed opinion this was not the time for tea-drinking: the tapping business usually came in advance of some facetious observation. Ala'adin decided that he would never really understand the English, not in a thousand years. Deciding that it was time to intervene, he stood up, and putting on his most charming smile, for he was indeed capable of great charm, he drew their attention to the refreshments. 'Gentlemen, please: tea.' He signalled with a snap of his fingers for the boys to serve. The officers seemed reluctant, but the chinking of porcelain and the purr of tea being poured appeared to soothe them: there was a good deal of stroking of moustaches. Evans and Forestier Walker had just returned from the morning drill – they, the governor-general anticipated, would be the first to move forwards to accept a cup. He was right.

There was another young officer present. A clean-shaven captain who looked too young for his rank. Too young to be away from his mother, thought Ala'adin in a moment of weakness. His green eyes seemed to catch the reflected light from the river that filled the open window, in a rather romantic fashion. His name was Hamilton Ellesworth and he was something to do with Intelligence, seconded from Cairo; and assigned to Lieutenant-Colonel Stewart; apart from the main body of the expeditionary force though having travelled with them. This detachment seemed to suit his rather aloof mood. He did not seem to have noticed the tea but was staring out of the window with a glazed look. Ala'adin Pasha, strolling round the room like a good host, lit himself a cigarette and gestured to the serving-boy. 'Tea, Captain. One must never underestimate the body's need for refreshment in these climes.' Ellesworth started as though he had been stung, dropping his hat in the process. The governor suppressed a smile and turned back to the room, trying to calculate how many of Medani's pastries would be left when the officers had finished. It was the Syrian, the old Circassian, who was the most trouble, for he had the manners of a pack-horse, and was helping himself to a third one already. His tunic was splattered with pistachios and flakes of pastry. He wiped his sticky fingers unself-consciously on the divan.

At least the ice was broken. Major Martin was discussing aspects of the day's drilling and conferring with the other two captains about the Nordenfeldt machine-guns which seemed to be posing a problem to the Egyptian conscripts. The tone of their voices grated somewhat on Ala'adin's nerves and he cursed the humiliation of having the British here at all. It was only on account of Urabi and the riots in Alexandria that they had been given the excuse to step in and take charge. Since they had landed at Tel-el-Kebir, a certain element of absurdity had entered the proceedings. This Hicks, for example. He knew nothing of the region, had no experience, and he was about to embark with an army made up of the very same fellaheen who had fought alongside Urabi in the uprising. Where was the sense in that? Ala'adin smiled and gestured for the officers to help themselves to Medani's pastries. On the other hand, sending one group of rebels to put down another had a certain panache about it, he had to admit. Using British soldiers was out of the question – too costly and too risky. That had always been the way, had it not?

Colonel Hicks was holding forth. Once they departed from the capital to head south-west into Kordofan literally anything could happen. 'Once you take out supply transport and provisions on the march, I will, by my estimate, have an effective fighting force of less than three thousand men. This Mahdi chap of yours has around seven times as many.' He paused and brushed an imaginary crumb from his chin. 'Rather unappealing odds, wouldn't you agree?'

The governor-general nodded in time with this lecture. He knew these figures. He knew also that Hicks had relayed his views to the consul in Cairo and that the news from London was that Lord Granville would never dare to ask the British tax-payers to underwrite the cost of such an operation. If and when any reinforcements turned up they would be nowhere near the ten thousand men requested by Hicks. There was another more immediate problem facing Colonel Hicks, Ala'adin Pasha noted: the Syrian, Suleiman – the Pastry Eater.

Colonel William Hicks gave up tapping his riding switch against his leg and now sat staring, arms crossed, at the open window, perhaps trying to impart a sense of urgency. The governor-general sat back down behind his desk and puffed away at his cigarette. A plan had just occurred to him, but it would take a little time to arrange. He locked his fingers together on the desk and smiled. 'I understand, Colonel, that the drilling is showing some signs of improving the men's ability.'

The colonel snorted. 'Improving? Hardly. That rabble will never make a decent fighting force. Passable at best perhaps, and for our sakes we had better be damn sure.' He gripped the sides of the chair as he barked into his small beard. 'When we get out into that godforsaken patch of dust, these little buggers may be too busy slitting our throats to notice the enemy. They know the country no better than Queen Victoria herself and personally I would rather rely on her help than theirs.'

Things had obviously been very different for the colonel when he served with the Indian Army. Ala'adin Pasha reconsidered the ground ahead. Suleiman Niyazi was officially commander-in-chief here; Hicks was officially seconded to Niyazi as chief-of-staff. This in itself was enough to cause animosity between them. Pasha glanced across at the old Circassian, for whom he felt a degree of sympathy and even affection, not only because he reminded him vaguely of his own grandfather, but also because age comes inevitably, if we are lucky, to us all. But the old war-horse was snoring away peacefully, oblivious to the discontent that surrounded him. With his eyes half closed it seemed as though a long white furry centipede were crawling across his brow.

The governor-general swatted a fly away from his face. Since taking up his post six months ago, he had known only frustration. His hands were tied, both by the khedive's debts to the British, which undermined his authority, and by his basic lack of knowledge of the lands to the west where the Mahdi was holding out. The thread of the Nile curled down the map on the wall from Cairo to culminate in the elephant's trunk from which Khartoum drew its name. The line of the Blue Nile turned eastwards and south while the White Nile flowed straight down, past the innocuous shape of Aba island, to vanish into the papyrus swamps of the Sudd. Ala'adin rose from his seat and crossed the room. His finger traced a line: southwards down the White Nile to Dueim and then south-west into the region of Kordofan, curling across the Nuba mountains, to the town of El Obeid – the seat of their little problem. A distance of perhaps two hundred miles as the crow flies. The bowl of land east of the river was pockmarked with defeats, stretching far out to the wilderness of Darfur. He turned back to his guests. 'Gentlemen, I have a suggestion, a mere idea.' His finger traced a circle around the area just south of the capital: the Gezira, a wedge of fertile land bounded east and west by the rivers. 'Perhaps we ought to give more serious consideration to Lord Granville's suggestion that we restrict our efforts to the Gezira area?'

Hicks was clearly against the idea. 'We must go for the head of the serpent and strike it clean off.'

The governor put his case: the distance involved; the difficulty of the terrain; the fact that there had been a series of uprisings in the Gezira area over the past year. Stretching themselves beyond that, all the way to Kordofan, was not the wisest of plans. But his suggestion was overruled.

'I am in no doubt,' continued Hicks, 'that while the Mahdi may not dare attack us here today' – the memory of the ferocity encountered on their journey across the desert from the Rea Sea was still fresh in the British contingent's memory – 'he will surely come round to the idea.' Hicks got to his feet and began to stroke his beard. 'Since the fall of El Obeid, I have no doubt that he intends to go on until he meets his match. It is imperative, therefore, that we go out and give him a sound thrashing.'

Murmurs of 'hear hear' issued from the junior officers at the back of the room. 'Religious fanatics,' continued Hicks, getting into his stride, 'cannot be reasoned with, but they can have the fear of God put into them.' He snickered into his whiskers. 'If you'll forgive me my little pun.'

The governor wondered if anyone ever had forgiven the colonel his efforts at humour; it seemed unlikely. His answer, however, was discouraging. The town of Khartoum was well fortified and could be defended for months; by then the fervour would have died down. The Mahdi's followers would be missing their families and homes and be tired enough of the war to give up and go. To venture out into Kordofan now seemed an unnecessary risk.

The old Circassian was still snoring. He rolled about on the divan trying to get comfortable, in serious danger of perforating himself, or someone else, with the sabre that he insisted on wearing at all times. A long drawn-out rupture of escaping gas thundered through the room, followed by a smell like a swamp rotting in the heat after heavy rain. There was a snigger from the young officers.

39

Ala'adin sighed. The grey-lidded eyes fluttered open and alighted, as luck would have it, on the tray of pastries. 'Ah,' breathed Suleiman Niyazi asthmatically, 'tea.' His face was the colour and texture of an old rifle butt. He cleared his throat noisily and spat towards the copper plate on the floor, managing to strike his own scuffed riding-boots. Colonel Hicks had seen enough. He leapt to his feet, threw salutes all round and charged out of the room. Unperturbed, the old Circassian helped himself to the last pastry while slurping noisily from his glass of tea. 'He'll give himself indigestion if he carries on like that,' was his only comment.

'He finds himself in an intolerable position,' reflected Ala'adin, moving towards the window to gaze out at the quiet labours of the fishermen and the farmers in the fields. It was timeless and beautiful, the river. He had learned to love it far downstream from here, where this place was a distant ancestor, a forgotten relative, lost in the haze of time. Those in Cairo had no idea what they were dealing with up here. This land took time to learn, time to love, but it had its beauty: the raw charm of nature itself, something rare and unfouled by the ways of men. No wonder the people were given to mystical flights of fancy; no wonder there were seers and madmen, dervishes and prophets. If a Mahdi was to make an appearance in the world, he could hardly pick a better place.

The governor-general turned back towards the commander-in-chief. 'Sire, I have recommended that you be transferred to the eastern coast,' he informed him gently.

'Suakin?' The old man raised the white furry caterpillar. Ala'adin shrugged, hands behind his back. 'If we are to have any chance of winning this campaign I must have Colonel Hicks's complete cooper-ation and trust.' He made himself clear. 'He doesn't like serving under you.'

The Circassian warrior sighed and set down his cup. 'He's a pompous ass. A danger to his men because he thinks that being in command is about talking loudly, instead of listening.' He got unsteadily to his feet. 'You know, I heard that in India the British used to coat their bullets with the fat of pigs to scare the Muslims. Ask your Colonel Hicks what he knows about that.' He raised a knowing finger. 'If that is modern warfare, then you can keep it. I'd rather die with honour in the arms of an old whore.' And with that he walked from the room, signalling to the silent, stone-faced body-guard who went everywhere with him. 'Send me to the coast,' he called over his shoulder with a wave, 'I could do with some fresh sea air. This place has a peculiarly rotten smell about it these days.'

Ala'adin Pasha Siddiq smiled to himself. He would miss the old reprobate. But the question really was a matter of whether he would be an asset or a liability in Kordofan, and the facts of the case went in favour of Hicks. Suleiman was only a token figure despatched from Cairo to even the balance. He reached into the sandalwood box inlaid with mother-of-pearl and extracted another Turkish cigarette. The old Circassian was something of an ancient species, soon to be overtaken by progress.

The signs were obscure; with the rise of tribal conflicts and superstition, there was something unsettling about this Mahdi and his call for a return to the golden age of Islam. Whether or not he was sincere, his words contained a grain of truth. The belly of Muhammad Ali Pasha's empire had grown plump. When the Mahdi called for piety to replace vanity he struck a chord. Something would have to give.

Looking out at the calm of the river, beyond the red flag fluttering on the steamer moored below, he saw a fishing boat drifting aimlessly along, carried by the current. A man raised his hand and waved to someone on the bank. He could hear the sound of the wind through the palms; the sound of voices in the marketplace speaking, as always, in riddles and rumours; the groan of the waterwheel turning one more time. And what were the signs so far? A comet crossing the sky; a gap in the front teeth and a mole on the right cheek of a soft-spoken man given to smiling. Ala'adin had the idea that he would never come face to face with this mysterious character; never be able to judge for himself whether his claim was true or false. He longed to see with his own eyes, for there was something intriguing about a man who dared to speak his dreams out loud. Suddenly, on the river, a flash of sunlight on broken ripples unfurled like a handful of dust thrown into the air out of which, as if by magic, a flock of yellow-tailed sparrows seemed to fly. A trick of the light, or something more portentous?

5. Anglo-Egyptian Garrison, Khartoum

Miss Amelia Tamarind Walden
Care of Sir E. B. Walden of Dovecote,
Derbyshire at Redcote House

Khartoum, August 2nd 1883

My dearest Amelia,

My darling, I hope that this letter finds you well. The very
sight of your name written upon this rather shabby scrap of
paper is almost too much for me to endure. I keep my thoughts
of you locked well within my heart, for I can hardly bear to
think of when we shall meet again. I was a fool to come here,
Milly; I realise now that I had no idea what I was doing. I
should have listened more carefully to your wise words. This is
indeed a wretched excuse for a place on God's earth.

The desert across which we came from the Red Sea coast is a
barren tract, inhabited by savages of the most unwholesome
race. They resemble strange two-legged animals; their skin is the
colour of saddle leather and they are as agile as monkeys, strong
too. They fight like the devil himself and they know every thorny
patch of scrub by heart – even give them names. The way they
treat animals is a scandal, not to mention the practice of human
slavery which is widespread outside our protection. If we could
extend and protect the honest traders, this inhumane practice
would be stopped.

I feel like old Livingstone preaching commerce and
Christianity, but this is the only way forward for these wretches.
It is hard to explain, Milly, but their world here is so different

that we can hardly be expected to understand their way of thinking.

This Mahdi fellow holds great sway over them. Some say that he claims to be the mysterious and long-hidden Twelfth Imam, which is a kind of saint or something. Others say that such beliefs are only prevalent among a particular sect and do not strike a common note. All is confusion. We have no idea. All we know is that his followers gladly lay down their lives for him. It is hard to understand the kind of devotion which will turn a simple, apparently peaceful people into a rabid mass, thirsting for the blood of any Christian. Do not be alarmed, my dear, for we are better armed and have the edge on them in terms of discipline and strategy.

I see that I am carrying on a bit. I hope you will forgive my confession to you, my heart, my beloved. Here I am, thousands of miles from civilisation, engaging an enemy who is only doing what any decent fellow would, namely, defending his country. One cannot blame them for being misguided.

What news do you hear at home? Our papers are always out of date by the time they reach us. How is Gladstone describing our efforts? How I would love to stand in the public gallery and listen to them debating our fate in Westminster.

This town, however, is a little green jewel in an otherwise dull-brown, monotonous tract of land. Our spare moments are spent strolling in the fine little gardens where the temperature in the shade with the breeze from the river begins to approach the tolerable. Your father would be delighted by the botany, I am sure. I am surrounded by your namesake: delicate little pods, though the fruit is a little on the bitter side, which makes me wonder whether your father was right in his choice of name for you. I would have chosen Hyacinth, myself, which has lovely papery petals whose subtlety reminds me of your nature.

However, the town is swarming with spies who would sell their old granny for a loaf of bread, so we have to take great care. They say that the enemy are so well informed that if the governor lights himself a cigarette, our Mahdi knows of it.

As for my fellow officers, well, they have their work cut out in

getting those thick-headed fellaheen fellows to learn which end
of a machine-gun is which, but they are for the most part good
chaps, with plenty of fine stories to while the evenings away.

At the mention of his fellow officers, Hamilton Ellesworth found his
mind distracted. He looked up from the table where he sat to find a
small weaver bird perched on the window-sill. Beyond the compound
wall he could make out the squat outline of the cartridge factory. It
was mid-morning and the soldiers were resting after their training. As
usual, they had been up at five that morning and then down to the
river where they boarded the steamers to sail past the confluence of
the Blue and White Niles. The muddy streams coming joyfully
together formed a ridge on the surface which never ceased to delight
Ellesworth. Although he was not required to take part in the training
every day he nevertheless offered his services, simply for the pleasure
of riding on the steamers. The river was cool and calm at that time of
day and blew the cobwebs from his head. It was hard to recall that
beyond its low, tranquil banks and lazy palms there was a battle
waiting to be fought.

Each day they disembarked at a different spot and began drilling. It
was important that they were seen to occupy as much of the region
around the town as possible – not only in the hope of giving the Arabs
a confused impression of their strength and numbers, but also to press
home a strategic point about how swiftly troops could be deployed
by steamer. Day after day they went through the routine with the
Nordenfeldts: assembling the tripod and attaching the feeder boxes
through which the cartridges dropped. On a good day one could
begin to see the strands of a fighting unit being drawn into place.

Today had been nothing less than a disaster. It began with the
arrival on the scene of the newly promoted General Hicks. They were
one horse short and their haste to impress the general soon turned to
panic. Colonel Farquhar was busy trying to blame someone for the
oversight, while the beleagured sergeant, crying 'ma'alish, ma'alish,'
tried to persuade the colonel to use a mule instead. Throughout these
proceedings, a group of fellaheen had been setting up one of the
Nordenfeldts. Men scattered like flies when the gun leapt into life, as
bullets flew everywhere. Some soldiers dropped to the ground; others

ran screaming to jump into the river. Luckily no one was hurt – apart from a withered-looking mare which received a bullet in her rump. Hicks was furious. He hopped up and down, cursing Farquhar in front of the men, while the sergeant went on with his apologies. '*Ma'alish* yourself,' the general had retorted. 'These men couldn't fight off a troupe of dancing girls, let alone a horde of screaming savages.' Ellesworth smiled to himself at the memory of the day's events – there would surely be plenty of banter that evening in the officers' quarters.

From the window, if he craned his head sideways, he could see the dockyards west of the city at the Mogran, surrounded by the squalid quarter where the workers lived. To the other side, in contrast to the surrounding mud and wattle, was the noble architecture of the Roman Catholic mission in solid brick. On his desk, meanwhile, lay numerous intelligence reports to be examined, none of which, he felt certain, would contain anything significant or even reliable. When he had finished applying his weak grasp of Arabic and had wrestled his way through yet another obtuse translation, the results hardly seemed worth despatching to Cairo. He was almost embarrassed by the degree to which one account was contradicted, almost before the ink was dry, by the next. The informants who came in were just as likely to be double agents as anything else. They seemed to oscillate between camps, exchanging words for money. Like modern-day storytellers or travelling minstrels, they were valuable only so long as they had a yarn to spin. It was hard enough to trust the translators; sycophantic merchants, Coptics and Greeks, Syrian horse-traders who would prefer to tell you what you wanted to hear than what was accurate or true.

'Pondering the mysteries of life again, I see.'

Ellesworth spun round to find the rotund, slightly comical figure of Sherwood Louth standing in the doorway. He was wearing, as usual, the silly, lost kind of smile on his face which passed for amiability, but which Ellesworth suspected was designed to conceal his lack of intelligence. He was clad, again as usual, in a loose-fitting beige suit, of which he had apparently a fair number, stitched by some clumsy tailor in the Cairo bazaar – Ellesworth could distinguish them only by the various stains which adorned the rough linen. A thin trail of grey-blue smoke dribbled from Louth's fingers past the unruly mop of curly hair towards the ceiling rafters. He squinted his eyes and drew on the cigarette. 'Any crumbs today?' he asked laconically.

Ellesworth leaned back in his chair and grinned. 'Are all you writer chaps this nosey, or is it just a personal trait?'

Louth waved a distracted hand in the air. 'No news,' he announced loftily, 'is too insignificant for the readers of *The Chronicle*.' Yawning now, he raised a hand to cover his mouth while leaning further forwards. Ellesworth, realising what he was up to, casually shifted a sheet of blotting paper.

'Your young lady, I presume?'

Ellesworth got to his feet, gathering up his work with unconcealed irritability. 'I must say, Louth, you can be particularly uncouth when the mood takes you.'

'Uncouth Louth, that's me. I'm sorry.' The journalist turned away from the table to glance around the room. 'It is an unendearing habit,' he mused.

Ellesworth hesitated. 'How did you know my letter was addressed to a lady?'

Sherwood Louth shrugged his shoulders. 'If it had been official business you might have let me have a peek. I'm no security risk. But matters of the heart . . .' He wagged a finger in the air, and then catching Ellesworth's eye he stuck his hat on his head. 'How about a stroll down to the river?'

'Why not?' sighed Ellesworth. He pulled on the red tunic and picked up his white helmet. As they wandered down the long, cool corridor Ellesworth asked, 'You're from Cheshire, aren't you?'

Louth gave a cackle. 'Good grief, no. Gravesend, I'm afraid. Father was a wholesale merchant – timber, mostly. Although, I hear it is charming.'

'What is?'

'Cheshire,' smiled the correspondent. 'Not far from Derbyshire, either.'

The sun beat down hard upon the dry parade-ground and they had to squint against the sudden intensity of the light. A soldier was busy polishing the barrel of a cannon. The brass gleamed like gold. They turned away from the wealthy areas around the high, whitewashed walls of the governor-general's *serail* and, passing the armoury, began walking towards the collection of brick walls and boulevards that marked the centre of town.

A man driving three donkeys laden with firewood cut across their path, and a smell that was a mixture of excrement and dust filled their nostrils. 'I love the smell of this place. It's like the essence of life itself, something honest,' declared Sherwood Louth, throwing his arms out wide and almost knocking a basket off the head of a small girl walking alongside them. Ellesworth shook his head in despair. He had the sense that half of what Louth told him was made up and the other half was just plain lies.

'I feel free here,' continued Louth, turning to look at Ellesworth. 'Isn't that strange? Thousands of miles from home, surrounded by pagan ritual and fanaticism and not speaking a word of the cock-eyed lingo and yet I feel such a sense of liberty.'

Ellesworth tilted his head to one side, not quite sure whether his leg was being pulled. 'You're lucky,' he sighed. 'You don't have to worry about writing reports and interrogating spies.' He waved a salute at a passing soldier.

Louth had swivelled on his heels and was now walking backwards, hands in his pockets. 'Listen to me, now. I'm thinking of doing a series of profiles. You know the sort of thing: the soldier's story. I mean, take you, for example. You are young, physically in your prime and you're a soldier. Here you are on the verge of the greatest adventure of your life. The opportunity to test yourself against the enemy.' He punctuated his words with vigorous arm gestures, swatting the air here and slicing there. 'Let the readers know how it feels. Up against the heathen, wild savages and your sweet girl waiting for you at home. You're the perfect candidate.' Ellesworth was shaking his head, but grinning at the same time. With a sigh of resignation, Louth turned round and continued walking. 'At least give it some thought,' he said. By now they were winding through the narrow streets past the older houses where the merchants lived, with their high walls and their projecting *mashrabiyya*s, whose carving was as fine as any that could be found in Cairo or Damascus. Then they turned a corner and Ellesworth realised they were heading into the notorious Salamat al Pasha, where the brothels thrived.

'I thought we were going to the river?'

Sherwood Louth waved a hand. 'The thought of the river made me thirsty.'

Ellesworth stopped to examine some lamps. He laughed. 'Look at that. This is what they do with old shell cases: slice them up and engrave them and there you are – half a dozen magic lamps.'

Louth was unimpressed. 'Necessity breeds innovation.'

Ellesworth addressed himself to the matter uppermost in his mind. 'I think that sometimes you forget the serious nature of our task here.'

'Your task is to kill this Mahdi fellow and restore order.'

'Well, perhaps, but it's more complicated and a lot more dangerous than you make it sound.'

The man from *The Chronicle* drew himself up. He leaned in towards Ellesworth until their noses almost touched. 'Don't patronise me, officer. I know what's going on around here. I'm probably better informed than you are.'

Ellesworth, somewhat taken aback by the vehemence of this, made a slight bow. 'You probably are,' he conceded. They went on in silence for a while, as the sun beat down and dust rose up in bands like thick waves. A mule dragged a heavy cart. Carcasses hung from the hooks of butchers' shops. For the moment there was enough food, but in a month, six months, a year, who could say? They were moving southwards towards the mud-lined alleyways where the houses were smaller and less solid. There were fewer soldiers here and Ellesworth as a rule did not like coming this way. Sherwood Louth, he knew, had a better knowledge of this part of town, in which the majority of the population of thirty thousand or thereabouts lived huddled together. It was hard to tell with whom these people were allied and an officer had to watch his step. Loyalty aside, there were still plenty of people who would be prepared to jump a lone officer for the simple honour of owning his revolver.

Beyond the farthest streets there was open ground leading to the cemetery, and beyond that more open ground and the squat walls of the fortifications to the south. A boy carrying a tray of bread went by. He waved a hand in mocking salute, accompanied by a wide grin.

'The children are really charming, don't you find? Very sweet.'

'Yes, especially when they aren't suffering from enteric or leprosy.'

Ellesworth stopped. 'How did you get so hard-hearted?'

Louth kept walking. 'I'm not,' he replied. 'I just can't stand pity.'
As they went on, Ellesworth reflected how little he really knew about
this man. He had heard rumours around the officers' mess that Louth
did not in fact represent any paper, but had come out here of his own
accord, on money gained from some kind of trust-fund, or fraud, or
something. They said that he was a political radical who believed that
all property was owned by no one and everyone at the same time.
Lieutenant-Colonel Stewart had earmarked him as a subscriber to
radical forms of socialism and had actually warned Ellesworth to
steer clear of him.

They turned a corner and Louth stopped. He looked round and
scratched his head. 'This is wrong, we should have taken the last
turn.' As they began to go back, they saw a small child sitting outside
a house stuffing earth into his mouth. Louth went over and knelt
beside him, taking his hand and shaking his head. 'No, no. Not good
for you.' He looked up at Ellesworth. 'How do you say that in
Arabic?'

Ellesworth shook his head, recalling instantly that he was supposed
to be somewhere else, that he had a language class that afternoon.
'Come along, Sherwood, he doesn't care – probably been doing it all
his life. Just slap his hand a bit and then let's go.'

Sherwood did this and the boy began bawling at the top of his
voice. A woman appeared in the doorway and began screaming at
them, sweeping the boy from the floor to her hip in one move. Others
gathered round the woman and tried to calm her, looking nervously
at the two men. Some began to shout and one waved a blow at them
with a broom she was holding. Sherwood and Ellesworth backed
away, bowing their heads and nodding as they went. A crowd was
beginning to collect as passers-by were caught like leaves in a corner.
The two men pushed their way through, with Sherwood raising his
hat in apology and Ellesworth ordering them as loudly and firmly as
he could to clear the way.

They ran up towards the square and turning a corner soon found
themselves breathless and laughing outside the Italian consulate.
Sherwood wiped his brow with a handkerchief that could conceivably
once have been white and clean. He took Ellesworth by the arm.
'Come along, captain, time for a little refreshment I think.' Ellesworth

concurred and Louth led the way to the bar – an unambitious little watering-hole in the shady corner of the square whose chairs and tables were occupied by the odd cleric drinking a glass of tea, or merchants discussing business. Louth dropped his hat on to the nearest table and the proprietor, a Yemeni, came forwards hurriedly to give the table a swipe with his dustcloth. The hat was a floppy goatskin affair which Louth had constructed himself as protection from the sun. For some obscure reason he regarded the thing as a mark of individuality and guarded it zealously.

The Yemeni deposited two chipped glasses and a bottle in front of them. 'Hennessey's Three Star Cognac,' read Sherwood, rolling a cigarette between his fingers. 'Good thing Mr Hennessey can't see us. Probably give the old boy a heart attack to be made aware of the travesty being perpetrated in his name.' The brandy was manufactured locally and not under any known licence, and was apparently the only one of the many spirits on display behind the bar not in short supply. Ellesworth sipped cautiously at his glass. He was not a drinking man; indeed, if there was one thing that seemed to create problems in his relations with his fellow officers it was his restraint during their evening sessions on the veranda of the officers' club. In a few hours, he smiled to himself, Louth would be lying on his bed in the hotel, clutching the remains of the bottle, while he was once again at his desk, thumping his head against the brick wall of ignorance. His heart gave a lurch as he remembered Amelia and the letter he had not managed to complete, and with a sudden rush he drained his glass.

'Steady on, old man, you're putting me to shame.'

Ellesworth sighed and loosened the top button of his red tunic. 'I don't suppose it makes much sense to you, Louth, but I take pride in carrying out my duties.'

'There you go again. I don't doubt it for a minute.'

'What do you mean?'

Louth leaned his elbows on the table. 'Getting on your high horse.' He poured another drink and pointed a finger at Ellesworth. 'You mark my words, young man. Carry on like that and you are going to wind up a distinct bore.'

Ellesworth pulled a cloth from his tunic and dabbed his forehead.

'I'm sorry, it's just so damn frustrating when nothing seems to be moving on our side.'

Louth did not agree. 'With old Suleiman out of the way I hear that Hicks will be making his move pretty soon.'

Ellesworth stared. 'How is it that a damn columnist knows more than an officer of the intelligence department does?' He shook his head at the offer of another brandy and snapped his fingers to attract the Yemeni. 'I think I'd better have a coffee.'

'Yes sir, coffee sir,' nodded the proprietor, slouching away.

Louth shook his head. 'You ought to relax, you know. Once you get out there among the screaming savages you'll be glad of every drop of this you can get your hands on.'

Ellesworth leaned forward and lowered his voice. 'We defeated the Makshif, which means the road is open as far as Sennar. That's half the distance to El Obeid.'

'That was a small local uprising, nothing more. There is no guarantee that Hicks could repeat the same trick out there. The Mahdi would be prepared at El Obeid and besides, we don't have enough men and those we do have are badly trained.'

'You and I know that, but the Mahdi doesn't. He'll think the wrath of God is coming down on his head when our boys start firing those Krupps guns into his harem.' Ellesworth glanced at the nearest table, just by a small fig tree, where two men were talking. This was probably not the best place to be talking so openly about such things.

Louth watched with amusement. 'There are no secrets here. If I know, then everyone from here to El Obeid surely does. It's their country.'

Ellesworth looked up sharply and then dropped his eyes back to the table. 'Either way, it will be quite a battle. He has upwards of twenty thousand men, I understand.'

'Untrained, and more to the point, unarmed – except for old muskets and rusty swords. No match for Remmington rifles, as proven with the Makshif.'

Ellesworth rubbed his chin. 'It will be good to get out into the field.'

The rotund journalist laughed loudly, causing the whole square to turn in their direction. 'It's damn hard country to go for a Sunday ride in.'

'You don't have much faith, do you?'

Sherwood shrugged. 'Those are the facts. The people out there fear the slavers more than they do your toy soldiers. They are familiar with the land and the people, which is more than you can say for your officers.' They rose to leave and as they walked in the sunshine Louth grew red-faced, sweating out the cognac so that another circular stain appeared in the armpits of his jacket, which were already a crumpled calendar of sweltering days.

Ellesworth persisted in thinking positively. 'Let's see what we can do with this expedition. Hicks is a fine commander. We'll put a stop to that Mahdi fellow.'

'If you can find him, that is,' murmured Louth, but then, relenting, he slapped Ellesworth on the back. 'However, spoken as always like a true soldier. I only hope for all of our sakes that you are right.' And with that he waved a limp salute and staggered off towards the hostel, the half-empty bottle projecting from his pocket.

6. *Kordofan Province,*
1883

And everywhere Hawi went, he heard the same story: people spoke of this Mahdi as though they knew him well. His presence seemed to pass ahead of Hawi like a ghost on the dust-laden wind. He brought relief to sad faces, dried the tears of those in despair, drew serious looks from the light-hearted fellows who joked in the market squares. People invoked the name of the Prophet and called for the blessing of the Lord at the mention of his name. They pointed out places in the sand where he had stood. They produced wooden spoons with which he had eaten when he passed this way, cups which he had lifted to his lips to drink. Everything was preserved in his sacred memory; he had passed into the realm of legend. He was everywhere and nowhere at the same time.

Perhaps some of the enthusiasm for the Mahdi could be explained by his notoriety: he had established a name for himself as a wanted man, an outlaw who had dared to defy the hated Turk. In this he could claim to represent the poor and the dispossessed. He astonished them with tales of simple clerks who lived in palaces by sparkling rivers, with servants at their beck and call, and where food enough to sustain a village could be produced for one evening's entertainment. He drew the support of the wealthy too: the *jellaba* of the Gezira and the merchants in the big towns. Weary of taxes and tributes, they were ready to support anyone who called for change.

The Mahdi's agents had been busy, travelling widely, spreading the fever throughout the land. The stories Hawi heard were many, but each one was told with such conviction that it soon became clear to him that these people were not simply admirers, they were devotees, all of them. This was an interesting phenomenon in itself. Surely no man who truly claimed to represent the Lord and to be the successor of the Prophet Muhammad would allow such a cult to arise around his personality.

Whatever the truth, in these south-western regions it suited Hawi to travel in the guise of a pilgrim, for the very mention of the Mahdi's name to the peasants or traders of any village would immediately provoke great displays of generosity: offers of places to sleep and food to eat. People would crowd round eagerly, even in those towns still occupied by the khedive's soldiers. And it seemed then as though the Mahdi were not one man, but many, capable of being in several places at the same time.

'He came walking through here light as a feather. A year back, perhaps longer.'

'He was dressed as though he were the poorest man in the world, with fewer possessions than a dog. Only his holy scrolls and his ink-wells, so you could see he was a scholar, a very learned man.'

Another would interrupt. 'Everyone took pity on him and his bowl was filled several times a day.'

'It was never empty, not for a moment. When he began to speak, people stopped to listen. As though by magic, they came wandering towards him, unable to help themselves. Amazing sight to behold!'

'Right here. Right where you are standing, he stood and talked of the holy words spoken by Muhammad and of the way in which time had allowed His message to be corrupted. Of course everything he said was true, we all knew that. We only have to look towards where the governor lives and we can see what justice there is in this world today.'

'He spoke fairly,' interjected another, 'never said things that were not true.'

Sometimes people argued over details. 'He was a small man,' one would say. 'Small?' another retorted. 'You don't know small because your neck is longer than a giraffe's. He was tall, and thin too, but he had a softness about him – in his smile and his eyes, which were dark but carried inside them a light that was stronger than the sun. He blew in across the sand when he came, and we all stood and stared in amazement.'

'Like the light of a very bright star, like gold.'

Sometimes there would be laughter when someone became carried away in trying to describe events. 'Too many poets around these days. He was thin all right, hardly any meat on his bones, but not thin like a lizard. And his eyes were warm, but not burning like the sun or any of that nonsense, and he spoke clearly.'

'He spoke in rhyme. Real poetry, from the soul. It flowed through him so that you could feel it was true, like the words of the Prophet himself.'

'He spoke in riddles. Most of the people round here couldn't understand a word of what he said – they just nodded and smiled like a bunch of goats.'

Fights would break out because this was a matter as personal as faith.

'He spoke in plain words, so that even a child could understand him. Why, he said it himself: "The truth is clearer than the brightest hour of the day." His words shone like the sun, not his eyes.'

Gradually, as the days became weeks and the moon grew and swallowed the months, a picture began to emerge, of a man who came quietly, without fuss, asking nothing but a few scraps for his begging bowl, a place to shelter from the rain for the night. He was dressed in rags, a simple *jubba* covered in patches and thin sandals. On his head was a cap made of sack-cloth. Women chattered, balancing infants on their hips, waving their hands and snapping their fingers in the air. He was surrounded by a flock of white doves which made a circle of shade beneath which he walked. Perhaps it was only in hindsight, but there seemed to be a pervasive sense that he had been recognised instantly. It was almost as though they had been waiting for him to come.

In Jebel Shekedah Hawi met a merchant who told him this story: 'It happened like this,' the man began, speaking with the authority of a scholar on the matter. 'He disgraced himself with Sheikh Muhammad Sharif. The Mahdi was his student. He criticised his own sheikh for being too frivolous in celebrating the circumcision of his son.' The merchant sat cross-legged, reaching out from time to time to wave the flies away from his pile of dates with a woven fan. 'The sheikh called him a traitor and struck him from the *tariqa*. The Mahdi returned on his hands and knees, his head covered in ashes. He wore a wooden yoke, a *shubba*, around his neck like a slave. He wore no clothes, only a goatskin round his loins. Where was he to go? What was he to do if his master banished him? The sheikh was unrepentant, he would not listen. So Muhammad Ahmad went instead to Sheikh Qurashi nearby. When Sharif heard this, that his student had gone to the house of his rival, he sent a message forgiving him.' Smiling, the merchant wagged a long bony finger. 'But now he did not need Sharif, so he returned the message saying, "I do not need your forgiveness, for I have done nothing wrong." And so the story began to spread, that this man had refused the forgiveness of such a great man as Sheikh Sharif.' His eyes grew wide and his head nodded from side to side. 'They said he was the *Zahed*, the Renouncer. That he spoke the truth and that the sheikhs have all been living much too good a life. That was when he began to call himself the Mahdi, the one who is expected.'

'How did he do it? How did he reveal his mission?'

'He did not need to. There is a new star in the sky, very bright. Have you not seen it? It was a sign.'

Hawi looked at the ground where the ants crawled. 'There are many stories in the world,' he said.

But the merchant was not to be swayed. He shrugged briefly and continued his tale. 'He was known here, long before that. Some say that he reached as far as Jebel Marra in his travels. Everywhere he went his begging bowl was always filled. They listened to him speak of injustice and the true meaning of the faith. He was a gifted speaker. And although he never revealed his true purpose, they waited. Then the star came,' he waved a hand above his head, 'burning across the sky, filling the darkness with light, and so they knew that he had come to the world. We have been waiting for a long time.'

The two men fell silent. This, thought Hawi, this is where it begins. He felt it in his bones, sensed the spirit of the man he was pursuing in the very rustle of the thorn bushes. Like the tread of small insects crawling through the grains of sand, something had stirred here which had disturbed the calm surface of the world. And for the first time in his career as a scholar, for the first time since he bent his head over the whorls and scrawls of words that would become ingrained in his soul, he felt what it must have been like at the beginning, in the moment of transition when religion was born, when the words of

God were revealed to man. He was terrified. In all the years of devotion he had never felt anything as real as this. He shut his eyes tightly and drew a deep breath. This then was to be his test. This was why he had returned.

PART 2

Shaykan

7. Dueim Fort, The White Nile, September 1883

The evening fires burned smokily, flickering within the dark arches of the fort. The smell of burning dung and the crackle of dry wood permeated the whispered conversations between the men scattered in and around the offices and barracks. With the gates to the fort open, the expeditionary force stretched out across the parade-ground into the star-strewn plain outside the town. After three days here there was little sense of order to the crowd of soldiers, merchants and various suppliers and camp followers.

Captain Hamilton Ellesworth was accompanied on his rounds by his adjutant, Spratling – a small, compact fellow, though becoming stiff where once he had been lithe and supple. As a young man, Spratling had been a boxer of champion potential, and his reputation preceded him through the army. 'Old Ropey', he was affectionately called, though the reasons for this – some reference to the skills of the pugilist – escaped Ellesworth. The two men had little in common, neither background nor interest. Spratling was a tough and respected lance-corporal. Officers to him were another breed. His appointment to the lame task of nursing an officer of the intelligence department with no experience beyond the parade-ground was one of Spratling's grievances. As the two men walked side by side under the stars he made no attempt to respond to Ellesworth's incessant nervous talking. Spratling nodded and grunted as quietly as he could, taking every opportunity to vent his frustration on the enlisted men. 'Get that thing off the ground, soldier!' he barked. 'It's a crying shame to get dirt into a piece of craftsmanship like that. And don't you bloody "*ma'alish*" me, son.'

One of the fellaheen said something loudly and the others laughed. For a brief flicker of a moment Ellesworth saw it again: the sense that all that held the whole circus together was a slender thread of mutual incomprehension. Spratling shook his head. 'Bloody bunch of nanas the lot of them.'

'They are our only hope, Spratling, so let us pray they can fight.'

'Three more months we need. Three more months of drilling and we could be getting there.' Spratling punched a fist into the palm of the other hand. Empty words, it struck Ellesworth, though such a thought would never have crossed his mind a couple of months ago in Khartoum. Spratling was a walking history lesson, as Sherwood Louth had wryly remarked: he was looking forward to the fight.

In places, people were gathered around the glow of fires, singing songs, drumming on beaten tin. Tents stretched out white and billowy towards the dark periphery where there was nothing but open scrubland and thorn bushes that could tear a man off a horse and rip him half to pieces in the process. How Ellesworth longed for green vales and copses and the sound of clear water trickling gaily down a brook! Beneath the scorched brick of the veranda a soldier was sleeping underneath a cannon and a scrawny dog was picking at the remains of some misshapen bone lying in the dust. Ellesworth and Spratling passed the sentries at the wide portico and entered a smaller yard at the rear of the parade-ground. The stone arches were illuminated by torches planted in the sand. A group of officers had assembled at the centre, beside an incongruous white tent: General Hicks's private sanctum. The officers were talking in twos and threes, and the smell of tobacco-smoke and the rolling deep voices of men who have been drinking filled the starry patch above their heads. It was easy to distinguish the Europeans, for they kept apart, not by any rule or regulation, but through habit. The Egyptians stood sullenly to one side, unable to comprehend the nostalgic British recollections of home.

Spratling made his excuses and vanished. Ellesworth looked round, to see the familiar figure of the general strolling over, a cigar in one hand and a glass of brandy in the other. He nodded here and there, exchanged a few words; then, reaching what was the centre of the square, he raised his hand for attention. 'Gather round, gentlemen, please.' The officers shuffled forwards. When he was sure he had them all within earshot he raised his glass, which glinted in the flames. 'Well done, gentlemen, for today. With the unification of the governor-general's troops and my own, our expeditionary force has full strength. We intend to press on without delay.' Never a good speaker, Hicks paused, awkwardly.

'We have at our disposal a total of seven thousand infantry, five hundred cavalry and four hundred from the irregular cavalry, plus around two thousand assorted odds and ends.' His voice tailed off and he smiled for no particular reason, remained staring for a moment at his boots, as though he had forgotten something, then he looked up sharply. 'Sergeant Bradley, where are you? Ah, yes.' The sergeant was there, as ever, right under his nose. 'Sergeant, how many camels at the last count?'

Bradley braced himself, arms by his side, and bellowed: 'Five thousand, four hundred and fifteen, sir.'

A look of amusement crossed the general's face. He raised his glass and smiled. 'There you are, gentlemen: the sum total of our resources.' The darkened faces grew subdued as they absorbed the logistics which contained their fate.

Taking a deep breath, Hicks glanced over at Ala'adin Pasha Siddiq, who stood to one side, calmly smoking a cigarette. 'The governor-general and I,' he began diplomatically, 'have been discussing the matter of the route by which to proceed from here. It seems that there is a seasonal watercourse named . . . something or other.'

He gestured to the Egyptian senior officer, Hussein Mazhar, who dutifully provided the name: 'Khor al Habil'.

'That's the fella,' quipped Hicks. 'Anyhow, we proceed along this southerly route, which will keep us well provided with water, I am assured by the honourable governor-general. It's a longer route by about a hundred miles and it is difficult ground. It is also inhabited by tribes known to sympathise with our friend the Mahdi. It will, however, bring us in towards El Obeid from the south and this should give us an element of surprise.' The general looked up hopefully, as though half expecting to hear the sound of applause.

It was Sherwood Louth who stepped forwards with the obvious: 'If the route is longer and more difficult, what is the real advantage? Surely a swift run over the open ground to the north would be just as effective in terms of surprise?'

Hicks smiled sweetly, as if this question was exactly what he had anticipated, and turned towards Ala'adin Pasha, holding out his hand as though asking for the next number in an obscure dance hall: 'Sir?'

The governor-general stepped into the centre of the circle of officers, dropping his cigarette to the ground. Since he would address his officers in Arabic, he beckoned his translator forward, placed his hands behind his back and stood with his long riding-boots braced apart in the sand. 'Let there be no doubt among you, the choice is not an easy one. But at this time of the year the wells of the northerly route via Bara will probably be dry – at least it is unlikely that they will have sufficient water for the needs of such a large force. The southern route ensures us better chances of finding water.' The governor spoke with confidence, and despite his unfamiliarity with the country, he spoke with a respect for the terrain which struck a cord.

Ellesworth looked towards Sherwood Louth, but the correspondent was retreating backwards, furiously scribbling into his notebook, clumsily stepping on toes. There had developed a distance between them since they had left the relative security of Khartoum – something to do with the fact that a good deal of Ellesworth's time was taken up with his daily duties, but more because their opinions concerning the purpose of the mission and its chances of success were very different.

Ala'adin, speaking plainly, had the last word. 'Neither route assures us total security, or a definite and reliable source of water. We must proceed cautiously.' He saluted the men. 'May God go with you, and let Him guide us to El Obeid,' he added, without a trace of irony.

The night was cool now and the fires were down to a glow of warm coals. The wind circling the square spat white ashes and embers up towards the dark sky. The crowd of officers dispersed in whispers. Outside, the men were still singing; tireless fingers strummed and drummed. Up above, the stars seemed to peer over the rim of the universe, making this expedition of men at arms suddenly seem small and insignificant. These were the last thoughts of Ala'adin Pasha Siddiq as he lay on his cot and tried to sleep.

8. El Obeid Town, 1883

The city walls rise up wearily with the dawn. The sun tilts upwards; shattered rocks creak; the air begins to swell. Crows circle in the sky, their untidy wings fluttering like black and white rags. Every man is made of rags, says the Mahdi.

Far below, a tiny clump of shrouds begins to move. Their limbs are stiff and frozen from the cold night and the hard bed of rock and sand upon which they rested their bones. Children, still hungry, rub their eyes, and the dust pricks tears from them. The pilgrims wrap thin clothes across wind-scarred faces and reach with long fingers for mothers, fathers, sons and daughters to shake them and see whether love still breathes, or whether life has escaped while they lay dreaming. Ahead of them, at last, their quest is in sight: El Obeid sits like the disappointing answer to their prayers, forlorn and incomplete. They stopped walking well after dark last night, for there is no point in stopping when you have no food to prepare, nothing to look forward to but hours of waiting until morning comes again. They spread themselves around in the dust like a handful of feathers dropped by a crow, too tired even to talk, silent beneath the lattice of stars, not daring to speak their worst thoughts.

Dawn has delivered the eleventh day. The mystery of God's plan deepens. The road is long and they are hardly prepared. They have nothing but their faith to sustain them, and nothing but their faith to lose. They recall that the first believers also made a journey across desert wastes, and so they mutter thanks for each day, for every step they take. God will guide them. God has provided them with a goat whose milk runs sour, with children who fall cold to the burning ground with eyes staring upwards. They bury these children quickly, scraping the hard ground away with their fingers, with any piece of wood that comes to hand, for God has provided packs of wild dogs

65

that lope along behind them howling in the dark, pawing at the piles of stones left to mark burial-places. There is a reason for all of this, for God knows all and sees all.

Hawi sits up and wraps the grubby brown head-scarf around his skull. He is a pilgrim, making his way towards the city of light. He moves up and down, folding and unfolding his arms to try and restore some semblance of warmth.

The city draws near, an outline etched against the sand. The mud ramparts that defended the city have been softened by the season of rains. It is nine months since the city fell, or was liberated. The gates to the fort stand open and anyone is free to come and go. The captured cannon are manned by the same soldiers who aimed them at the *ansar* when they attacked, but this is because they are best suited to use such weapons. They have taken the oath, sworn their allegiance; they are welcome.

Men carrying spears and shields are gathered around the entrance to the city, loudly talking. Some of them bear the marks of battle: scars on the face and soul. One has an arm missing. Surviving such a wound is a miracle in itself, Hawi thinks. They are clad in the patched *jubba*, the simple smock that brings the garb of the wandering mystic to the common man, raising him in turn to the ranks of the nobility. They wear their devotion with euphoric pride, and Hawi is once again taken aback by the sheer scale of what he is witnessing. A new community is taking shape – without borders, growing from within the very people themselves, a community of faith, but more than that, of hope. What once was solid was now becoming fluid.

Young boys chase one another, laughing and rolling on the ground, pretending to be fighters. A young girl herds a flock of goats towards a well. A trader staggers in on a pack of mules bearing scent and heady spices from the gold-laden hills to the south. The world, it seems, goes on despite the threat which hangs over it. The new pilgrims wander through the gates unhindered. They walk as though in a deep sleep towards the centre of the town and the marketplace. Some of them drop away, vanishing into the crowd. Faces which have grown familiar over the past weeks now melt away, blending into one complete entity.

The town is in a strangely derelict state, dismantled by war. It seems that building the new world requires the destruction of the old. The buildings that surround the square were ravaged during the siege which culminated in what is now known as the Friday Battle. Everything is scarred and blackened by smoke and fire. A thin cow stands upon the steps of what was the governor's residence, gazing idly at the people passing by. The mid-morning sun that filters through the hole where the roof was illuminates the interior.

The market square is also the executioner's place of work. A swollen body hangs from the gallows, swaying to and fro with the weight of the grey-breasted crows that settle on it. Despite the shouts of the traders and the interminable bustle and the occasional cry of a *darwish* who goes spinning in circles, declaring his devotion – despite all this there is a dark shadow hanging over the town. Hawi grasps the shoulder of a man going by holding two chickens in each hand. 'The house of Sheikh Abbas?' he demands in a hoarse voice.

The man laughs. 'All the sheikhs I know of are in the cemetery.'

Hawi bites his lip. 'The cemetery,' he repeats to himself.

He is alone now. It is as though the town has been knocked back about a hundred years. He turns and walks past the charred ruins, the rubble of battle, trying to reconstruct in his mind how it must have been before.

◆

It was past noon when he entered the low-roofed room below ground where the bodies of the dead were being washed prior to burial. A few tallow candles burned and wisps of smoky incense were issuing from braziers to help stifle the stench.

'Sheikh Abbas? Is he here?'

A pair of anonymous eyes above a knotted cloth turned towards him and then away. Their owner jabbed with an incomprehensible mumble away down the long room, where bodies were laid out on a clay floor kept damp and cool with water. Shadowy figures pushed past him in the gloom that was broken only by a thin beam of sunlight entering through a crack above. Hawi felt a mixture of horror and revulsion. The room was as cold and claustrophobic as a tomb.

An ancient figure of a man was approaching, stiff with age and impatience, or perhaps simply rage? He seemed in a hurry to get his work over with. The bearers moved clumsily, bumping into one another to get out of his way. The old man drew nearer. He raised his head upon finding that his way was barred and snapped something, waving Hawi aside. He pushed his way past, then suddenly he stopped. He turned around slowly and his face began to creak in the direction of a smile. He gestured lamely towards the exit and he and Hawi moved without saying a word in greeting towards the steps. At that moment a commotion arose: some men coming down lost their grip and the cadaver they were carrying slipped to the ground. As they watched, the body, which was swollen with rot, fell sideways. The belly burst open as it hit the floor, filling the room with a foul, swampy gas that caught in the throat. Hands reached forwards in panic and the dead man was dragged, unceremoniously, head thumping against the ground, down the long room, amid an excited babble of voices. Hawi felt a constriction in his throat. He clawed his way to the open air and knelt on the ground, retching. When he looked up, the old man was beside him. Sheikh Abbas opened his arms wide and embraced Hawi.

'Now you come? Now, when the world is cracking at its very centre, you choose to return?' They held each other at arm's length. The old sheikh's eyes were sparkling with tears.

9. The Hicks Expedition, En Route

Water and optimism were running dry. Ellesworth lay on his back staring at the canvas sky. Somewhere in the distance he could hear the sound which had plagued him for weeks now: the groan of the camels. It filled his head day and night, along with the insufferable smell. The heat was intolerable, despite the damp cloths wrapped across his forehead over which he sprinkled a few drops of lavender-water from time to time to revive himself. He felt as if he were floating out on a stream of dead air into a furnace. There was not a breath of breeze in this long flat-walled *wadi* where they were trapped. He lifted the cloth from his face and called out for Spratling. A choking sense of panic rose up within him. He was dying. He felt it with a conviction that seized him like a hand to his throat.

He had dreamed that he was dying. That he was already dead. His body felt heavy as lead, sinking through warm soft mud. He struggled to right himself and managed to tip the cot over on its side. Something warm and wet touched his side. He had tipped over the pisspot. He realised this with some relief, having been convinced for a second that it was blood. 'Spratling,' he gasped. Then there were hands reaching for him and a familiar voice, as warm as his own mother's, saying, 'Come along, sir, right you are.'

'Is it the fever? Spratling old man, am I dying?'

'Steady on, sir.' Spratling, as imperturbable as ever, helped Ellesworth to his feet and coaxed him towards the flaps. 'No air in the wretched tent, sir. We'll get out in the open and you'll feel right as rain.'

'Yes, yes of course, silly of me.' Ellesworth was having trouble speaking; everything seemed fuzzy and far away, as though his ears were full of wax. 'There was a ringing that woke me up, like singing. Is someone singing somewhere, Spratling?'

'Singing, sir?' A dark look crossed the adjutant's stoical features. 'No,' he answered briskly. 'No one singing.'

By now they were out of the tent and the heat did indeed seem less oppressive. He could breathe at least. The sweat began to dry on his back. He straightened up, realising that there were soldiers staring at him. He would have asked for a drink of water, but rations were short and the officers were supposed to be setting an example. The last wells they had come to had been contaminated with rotten entrails: they dared not use them. The ones before that had been filled in and covered over, which cost them hours and even then resulted in a mere trickle, nothing like sufficient for ten thousand men.

Ellesworth dusted off his helmet and put it on his head. Spratling, showing his usual common sense, produced a canteen. Ellesworth refused, feeling the sullen eyes of the Egyptian soldiers upon him. How long, he wondered, would it be before they came to their senses and tried to mutiny? There had already been a series of incidents of insubordination. They had shot two men a week ago for assaulting an officer and that kind of measure was not going to make the problem go away. Straightening his tunic, Ellesworth felt the reassuring bulk of his Adams revolver at his hip. One did indeed feel, as General Hicks put it with uncharacteristic aptness, 'rather like Jesus Christ must have felt among the Jews'. He squinted out across the camp. Another shambles: it would seem they had given up the idea of marching in a square.

Tents, supplies and men, along with the remaining camels, were strewn about in pockets between the clumps of stunted trees and thorn bushes. This was good snake country, he had been told. They loved the tall grass and the shade: if you were the size of a snake you might very well manage to find a decent spot of shade out here.

'I'm off to see if there's any news of those wretched scouts,' he announced. Still dizzy, he picked his way across the uneven terrain. Men were sprawled about on the ground, worn out. Their uniforms were tattered and uncared for: the first sign that discipline was slipping. Ellesworth came across a gathering of ten or so men who were playing a curious game, shuffling stones around a heap of sand. They looked up as he appeared and one of them made some comment which he did not catch. There was a chorus of laughter and another of them took a bayonet and shoved it playfully between his legs so that it stood out of his crotch like an erection. This provoked another round of laughter. Ellesworth chose to pretend that he either did not see or did not understand, as he continued on his way.

He was halfway towards the large baobab tree around which General Hicks had spread his command post when the commotion reached him. He looked around him in confusion. Someone was pointing away towards the string of horses. A shot rang out. Without thinking, Ellesworth dropped down a small incline and fell into a ditch. Dust covered his boots; thorns reached out for his clothes.

More shots came now: a single one, then two in reply. The camp was coming alive around him. Men were shouting, rifles were being loaded. Someone called out for a report and the reply came back, 'Go find out for yourself.' But everything was happening so slowly, as though the stifling air had gelled into a viscous substance through which they waded. No horses were being saddled. No machine-guns or cannon were pulled around.

Crashing past a stunted mimosa, Ellesworth drew his pistol. He was in a small clearing where two men lay dead with their throats slit. The blood pumped out into the sand, crimson and velvety. The sentries' rifles and bandoliers were gone. Then he caught sight of them: two figures moving swiftly through the grass, like shadows beneath the sun, dressed in white rags with cloths round their heads and faces. They dropped out of sight and Ellesworth ran forward. He saw them, with the rifles, slipping lithely into the saddles of mounts which were waiting with a third man. The horses were large: two greys and one black mare. Ellesworth was thinking what fine horses they were. He was thinking that there were three men and that he had only five shots in his revolver. He must get a little closer if he was to be sure of not missing. There was no time to waste, for they would be gone in a second. He crashed forward with a shout, firing too soon. He caught a glimpse of their faces. The rider on the mare swung her round so that her mane shook. She was a long-limbed, muscular horse. The man cantered forward to knock Ellesworth to the ground, then with a single shout all three of them turned and rode off. Stunned, Ellesworth struggled to his feet and loosed off another shot. He cursed his luck.

Then suddenly Spratling was beside him on a horse, handing him the reins to another. Ellesworth saw the glint in the older man's eyes. 'This time we've got the thieving buggers, sir,' Spratling said. They cantered across the broken ground, careful of potholes among the sparse vegetation; then they were climbing up a low incline on the edge of the *wadi*, where the hooves of the raiders were clear. 'There,' pointed Spratling. From the ridge the riders were visible, three wavy plumes of floating dust. They were making good ground. Ellesworth did not look back in the direction of the camp, concealed now from view by the turns they had made; he saw only the open ground ahead and three riders.

'They're getting away,' he yelled.

'Oh no they're not,' replied Spratling.

Ellesworth followed down the lee-side, his horse taking long strides through the loose sand. The land to the north was desolate and open as the bushes fell away – one or two acacias in the distance, but otherwise nothing.

The level ground was firm underfoot and the horses picked up speed, strong and sure. Ellesworth felt certain that the others would be right behind them and that these bandits would lead them to a sizeable haul of the enemy. After all the weeks of sniping and bickering, the daily struggle to gain just a couple of miles, this time they would pay them back. He could not have stopped even if he had wanted to.

They cut through a thin streak of rocky ground between two shattered pillars that seemed to have crumpled away from a face, like sunken cheeks. On this harder ground the trail became less clear and they slowed down to a trot. At the end of the plateau the trail evaporated altogether. An hour went by unnoticed, then another. Then, miraculously, they spotted their quarry again – away to the left, in a shallow dip. They seemed to have stopped moving.

'We've got them now, Spratling,' said Ellesworth breathlessly. They surged forwards. As they came within range, Spratling drew his rifle and let off a couple of wild shots. Ellesworth kicked in his heels while firing his pistol. His head was pounding and he was aware of a distant roar. It surprised him to realise that it came from him: nothing he had ever learned in military training, but a primitive howling yell. The horses were running quick and evenly. He cocked the pistol and this time he saw a spurt of dust kick up near one of the ragged figures. Then, just when they were almost upon them, the three riders leapt into the saddle and like a school of silvery fish they turned with a flash and slipped away at a sharp angle.

'They dropped something, sir.' Spratling pointed at the ground ahead. They drew to a halt. The horses, weak from the long march, were finished – covered in foamy sweat, their legs twitching from the hard ride. Pulling up, Ellesworth dropped from the saddle, handed the reins to Spratling and knelt down. The ground was damp; wet sand stuck to his breeches. A cold fear came over him. He looked up at the weary horses. He looked at the sky and the sinking sun and wondered how many hours they had been riding. He stood up and turned in a circle, gazing at the empty horizon.

'They planned this,' he said to himself. Spratling held up the goatskins, now empty, from which the water had been poured out. The horses were licking the sand, eager for the precious moisture as it vanished.

'Which way was the sun when we started off, Spratling?'

The old corporal looked in the direction of the sinking plate of copper, opened his mouth to say something and then shut it again. 'We've been riding north-east . . . I think.' He turned to look back the way they had come, and saw only the blank hand of the desert. 'Old Ropey' shook his head sadly and sat down suddenly in the dust like a puppet whose strings had been severed. 'Jesus Christ Almighty,' he muttered.

Ellesworth took his arm and helped Spratling to his feet. 'Come along, old man. Better not to waste what's left of the daylight.' They began to retrace their steps. Darkness soon fell and before long they were wandering helplessly off course. Beneath the unfamiliar stars, everything looked different. Their tracks were lost in the skirts of dust that swept across the floor. The sand beneath their feet turned cold and glassy as the night hardened. They curled up beside the tired horses, heads spinning, legs jumping in their sleep. The night sucked them in, like a whirlpool, like a dark dream that had crossed the stars and slipped its fingers insidiously into their heads.

10. North of Kordofan, Wadi al-Milk, October 1883

The house lay at the end of a long cracked pot of a street, smashed into fragments that rested on the stumps of the nameless village. The breath of men, women and children who once lived here blew through the empty doorways, their footprints now overlaid by the tracks of the countless mongrel hounds which had moved in. No one in the Ninth Company, or what remained of it, was particularly interested in examining the entrails of these ruins. They had their tails between their legs. One by one they had been cut off from the garrisons to which they had tried to return. It seemed as though their search was endless. The flag of the khedive was nowhere to be seen; above each town they came to flew the ragged banners of the Mahdi.

Orphaned, as they now appeared to be, they had begun to acquire a new life of their own. They moved listlessly, hoping to drift northwards towards the capital. They stole or took whatever they needed, or rather, what they could find. They were moving in ever-widening circles in order to avoid the enemy, since there was little chance that the Mahdi would be forgiving towards the despised *Bash-Buzuq*. In a bony patch of forest on the edge of some charred fields, they shuffled about, horses nudging one another in the dry heat, impatient to be off.

'Looks very quiet,' murmured Zinzebeir, a frail-looking man with the bones of a bird and long, thin fingers. He was from the Beja people of the Red Sea hills and his hair was long and braided with rancid butter. In the braids he had incorporated the feathers of dead birds. He had a long dagger hanging from his waist and another at his elbow. He seemed to have discarded his uniform in favour of a kind of leopard-skin vest.

'Quiet?' grunted Razig. 'It's full of snakes. I can smell them.'

Alongside him, Faris spat and wiped his mouth with his hand. 'You know, Razig, you are always talking. Nothing but talk. You don't like this, you don't want that.'

Ignoring them both, Zinzebeir turned to Wahab. 'What do you think?' The big *bimbashi* shook his head wordlessly; even he had of late fallen into long, surly silences. Zinzebeir looked down at the ground, his face, normally unreadable, barely capable of concealing his dismay. There were only ten of them left now. Faris and Razig carried on their discussion like two old crows.

'There's been some fighting here, by God,' sighed Faris.

'I'd have to agree with you there, brother. Nothing left here.' He squinted his eyes. 'What's that?'

'Dog,' replied Faris. Then a thought occurred to him: 'We could eat it.'

Wahab groaned, actually closed his eyes. 'I'm tired of eating dog,' he said. He pulled his reins in and turned the horse to begin walking away. The others looked round at one another. There were six of them, not including *Sanjak* Juma, who was still strapped to the rough wooden cot that was dragged behind Abd al-Tome's horse. Wahab had only gone about twenty paces when he stopped, pulling in the reins sharply. He stood stock still, staring at Zinzebeir. The lithe Beja man listened for a moment and then nodded. The air was popping, light pin-pricks of sound like water tapping on thin glass. A fly buzzed Kadaro's face. Everyone was watching their sergeant.

'What is it?' hissed Faris. The others ignored him. Wahab was drifting towards the village now, step by step, a smile on his face. He looked at Zinzebeir and Kadaro detected the faint flicker of a smile there too. The two men were now moving together towards the edge of the burnt fields.

'I still don't hear a damn thing.' Faris shook his head in wonder.

'Not hear, fool, smell.' Razig reached over to tweak the other man's nose. Faris slapped the hand away. Kadaro looked on: in a moment there was going to be a fight. The horses twitched, stepping back and forth nervously.

'Smell?'

Razig spat on the ground through the gap where his front teeth used to be. 'Women! You have been getting that boy to bend over too much. You've forgotten what a woman smells like.'

Faris began to pay attention. 'Women?' he repeated.

Razig made a jerking motion with his hand. At this moment the *bimbashi* seemed to lose patience. With a cry, he kicked his horse into action and began galloping down the street. Faris licked his lips nervously and looked at Razig. 'He's gone mad.'

'The *jinns* have him.'

Then they too, unable to resist, kicked their horses and chased after Wahab. The others followed along behind, with Abd al-Tome bringing up the rear, dragging the wounded *sanjak* on the makeshift litter. Kadaro trotted alongside on the old mare. Ahead of him he could see the others running in a light trail of dust – manes in the wind, tails waving like banners. Like ghosts, or a page of ancient history brought alive through some form of magic, the horses ran at full canter away down that cracked clay street, down the broken seams and torn straps of the village towards the big house at the far end.

◆

It is an old, majestic structure of sun-burnt mud and arches. Once the palace of a wealthy Magrebi leather merchant, it was constructed like a fort. Above the high outer wall an upper storey is visible with shady covered walkways where the soft wind once blew through silken curtains, through windows covered by complex carved lattices of sandalwood. It is a testimony to another age, but it has long since fallen into decay.

In a wave of reckless bravado the men jump the wall of the house without even pausing for breath. A memory that passes through them all like some form of collective madness causes them not to hesitate but to charge straight through as though they are not simply assaulting mud and wattling, but trying to leap over time itself. The dry walls crumble beneath the horses as some go over and others explode through the middle, taking straw and cane along with clumps of mud and goat droppings, birds's nests and eggs – all go flying, bursting into the air along with a surprised cat and several red mice.

The riders circle the pond at the centre of the rectangular yard, now open to the world, firing their rifles into the air. They ride along the verandas, dragging clothes-lines and battered furniture with them. Water-pots explode in their wake, cats leap from their path as though scalded.

By the time Kadaro and Abd al-Tome arrive there is complete chaos: women, half naked, some completely so, are running in every direction. Above the dust and smell of horses is the faint scent of perfume and incense blended intoxicatingly with the sweat of dancing and singing.

'*Istafar Allah al Azim*, what is going on here?' demands al-Tome.

'It's a brothel, you old fool,' yelps Razig, rushing by, one woman already lying across his saddle.

The horses wheel around the long yard, which is by now cluttered with broken beds and pots and the debris of smashed drums and lutes. A flock of pigeons bursts from a hole in the ground. Goats dart here and there. What might have been described as a bold military manoeuvre a few moments ago now resembles a burlesque scene of tricksters and magicians. In the centre of the ring sits Wahab, a blank look upon his face and a pigeon on his shoulder. He dismounts and walks heavy-footed through the chaos to sit upon the ground in the corner and fall asleep with his head in his hands. He dreams only of returning home.

A boy, thinner than a stalk of cane held sideways, and with ears so large that they flap in the wind, steps forwards with a grotesque grimace on his face. He is beating a drum furiously. Behind him come two girls and then a third, wearing thin cotton shifts; they too are playing musical instruments and singing in chorus now. The music is strange and unfamiliar, but al-Tome hardly registers this. An old woman who turns out to be the proprietor of the place hands him a clay bowl containing cloudy *merissa*.

He lifts the bowl to his lips and tastes clay, which urges him to drink more deeply. He drains the bowl in one long draught, tipping his head back, juice dripping down from either side of his mouth.

◆

Night falls upon them with a vengeance, setting off oil lamps and fires so that soon the whole yard is alive with fluid moving shadows flitting from corner to corner.

◆

'For a week now we have tried to drive the *jinn* from her,' explained the old crone to al-Tome. 'But he is *shayn*, very ugly.'

Abd al-Tome pushed his tongue around the corners of his mouth and wished he had some tobacco left. If it had been up to him he would have taken the men and ridden out right at that moment, never mind the dark. But Wahab was sitting where he had been sitting since their arrival, in the corner up against the wall, as bowl after bowl of *merissa* was brought to him. He sat like a statue, swollen and heavy, immobile.

'Who are you, anyway?' the woman asked. And when al-Tome told her she cackled shrilly. '*Bash-Buzuq*?' She chewed on her pipe. 'You don't look dangerous enough to scare a cat.' The sound of laughter reached up through the thin stars towards the night. A smell of *kamanga* wafted from the pipes that were passed around.

'Which girl is possessed by the *jinn*?'

The old woman, her eyes full of smoke, pointed out a young girl, taller than the others, with long legs and an awkward, almost manly, stride. Kadaro stared across the yard.

'What is her name?' he found himself asking.

The old woman took the pipe-stem from her mouth and looked the boy over. 'Noon,' she said, drawing the sign of the letter in the air. 'I had so many children I gave up giving them names and simply gave them letters.' Then a thought seemed to occur to her. 'You want to lie with her?' she asked. 'She is the cleanest of all my girls. Men are afraid of her.' She wheezed away to herself and then stuffed the pipe-stem back in her mouth with a sigh.

Al-Tome and Kadaro sat together watching the events of the evening. 'Makes me wish I had somewhere else to go,' he lamented.

'What is bothering you, old man?'

Abd al-Tome spat drily. 'Women and *jinn* make me nervous.'

Kadaro watched spellbound as the girl began to dance. He noticed the way her hands floated round her head, then down around and behind, stretching out, heels moving with the music in tiny staccato punctuations, like pebbles on still water, barely disturbing the surface. He asked al-Tome to show him again how to write the single letter of her name.

From the litter beside them came the sound of *Sanjak* Juma's groaning. He did this every night; refusing to die although he was by now a mere grey shadow of a man. There was a bad stench around him, raw and putrescent. The blanket stretched between the two uneven poles upon which he was dragged was coated in a layer of blood, grease and excrement. He seemed to be soaking into the blanket, as if before long all that would be left of him was the bones. He grinned moronically, all his teeth having fallen out. His eyes bulged with anger. He no longer spoke.

'The fever has eaten his brain up,' Abd al-Tome said as he tended him. He took care of the *Sanjak* the way a mother would a poorly child. 'It's only the devil keeping him alive. It's our punishment. There's nothing left in there but poison.' Kadaro watched as al-Tome pulled a blanket over Juma and tucked it carefully round his arms. The ropes were loosed for the night, although never removed; for despite their odd affection for their former commander, no man in the unit was prepared to run the risk of this dusty scarecrow wandering round in the dark while they slept. One never knew what such hatred might be capable of.

On the other side of the wall, the old woman removed the pipe from her mouth, dipped her fingers into a bowl of scent and flicked it on to the glowing coals of the incense burner. Clouds of pungent steam rose through the light in iridescent blues and greens.

11. The Hicks Expedition, South of El Obeid

General William Hicks looked up from the final page of the despatch he was writing. The glow of the oil-lamp on his table made his eyes ache. He wondered if he had managed to remain as objective as befitted his position. It was difficult to strike a balance between objective description and impassioned plea, hard to be detached when the entire world seemed to be conspiring against him on every front. He read the last few lines through again:

> *After we have retaken Obeid, and the country is in consequence more settled, it is expected that a small force could conceivably be sent out from there by the shorter route via Shatt to meet an escort coming from Dueim with provisions etc. Water for a small force will in all likelihood be obtainable on opening the wells which have so far been filled in by the Arabs.*

All ifs and buts, and yet retaking El Obeid seemed such a small thing to ask for. That was his first objective and without it he had nothing. The alternative was unthinkable. To suggest in a despatch that he had serious doubts as to whether it was at all feasible would be ill-advised. If the despatch were intercepted, it would give the enemy greater confidence. And if not, then his position would certainly be undermined on its arrival in Cairo.

He put his pen down with a sigh. The thought of failure crossed his mind a thousand times a day. It lingered there constantly. They were surviving thanks to rain pools which were still scattered throughout this unwholesome tract. He had to admire the enemy for their tactics. It seemed that what he needed was constantly just out of reach and consequently his grip on the command of this expedition was brought into question far too frequently for comfort. The local guides were unreliable; one could never be certain as to whose side they were on. How could you proceed through a land when the very men who were guiding you were themselves in the pay of the enemy? Every logistical issue was involved in the hopeless knot which affected this part of the world. The biscuits and ammunition from Dueim which they had been relying on were not forthcoming. His eminence, the governor-general, had then informed him that there was little chance of anything being forwarded to them by that route. Why had the infuriating little man not made this point earlier? Why wait until now?

Hicks was in a state of some despair. His military mind was besieged by the simple irrational details of their predicament. He was hardly able to sleep for longer than half an hour at a time, plagued as he was by an old personal enemy, piles, which had chosen this moment to return with a vengeance – the price, no doubt of long days spent in the saddle. Discipline was getting out of hand. How many incidents of insubordination had they witnessed? The enlisted men were sworn enemies of the khedive and the British. Whose cock-eyed idea had it been to send them out here in the first place?

Even his own officers were failing him. He was particularly disappointed with Farquhar. Colonel Farquhar had not backed him up at the meeting held the previous evening. The man's eyes, Hicks suspected, had never been quite straight to start with, but to turn at this juncture and begin blathering about 'absurd military circumstances' was taking distorted vision a little far. He was an outstanding officer, first class in fact, but on the crucial matter of dropping watchposts behind to safeguard their rear, he had chosen to oppose Hicks. Unfathomable: not only did it undermine Hicks's position, but it also went against every rule in the book. It was absolutely stark staring obvious. It had begun to occur to Hicks that he had been a damn fool to accept this command. He had men who could not be relied upon to hold a post for longer than it took for the main column to vanish around the next bend. He had no supplies, precious little water and officers who despised him for having being chosen over the heads of fellow Egyptians. They were wandering blindly through unfamiliar terrain with guides who one minute claimed to know the land like the back of their hands and swore on their mothers' graves that there was water just over the horizon and the next minute denied they had ever said any such thing.

◆

Abu Doma the guide went missing. He went forwards with twenty-five men to the next station, where they found water. As they were returning, Abu Doma realised that he had left his rifle by the well. Knowing that he would be chastised for letting the weapon fall into enemy hands, he turned back for it. The rest of the men waited, and when he did not show they continued back to the camp. The decision was made to advance the column to the well station. They found Abu Doma sitting under a tree, a flock of birds settled round him like a living shawl, feathers ruffled by the soft breeze. Abu Doma was staring down at his lap.

Both hands had been sliced off at the wrist.

◆

As they advanced, so the land appeared to change. Each morning a new landscape lay before them, waiting for them to unravel its mystery. In a sense it seemed as though they were passing through a region that somehow reflected the state of the soul. Each step was fraught with the terrible fear that one might come face to face with oneself at any moment.

◆

At the staff meeting that afternoon attention was turned back to the business of the square formation. It was impossible to maintain such a rigid formation in the broken ground through which they were moving. The square was torn apart by large clumps of vegetation and changes in the topography, which left them wandering like scattered laundry into the first flat, open stretch. Hicks leaned forward as the officers filed in; resting his elbows on the table he locked his fingers in a steeple over which he surveyed them sternly. 'Gentlemen, the enemy is following along behind us at their own pace. They seem to be unconcerned about our destination. They occupy every camp the very day after we have abandoned the site, sometimes waiting only a matter of hours. Now,' he rested his hands on the table, 'what does that tell us?'

The governor-general stood up and cleared his throat. 'Perhaps, General, this would be a good time to review the matter of the column formation.' Hicks shook his head and said something incomprehensible. Ala'adin Pasha continued: 'From now on we must proceed as carefully as possible. While maintaining a tight rear guard, we must have the flexibility suited to the terrain.' He nodded to his adjutant to translate, before continuing. 'I would like to suggest that we adopt a triangular formation.'

'Triangular?' muttered General Hicks, casting the compass aside as though it were glowing hot.

Ala'adin crouched down and drew the men around him. He began sketching in the sand with his finger. 'Three triangles, each led by us. One by you, General, and one by me, and the third led by the most senior of the officers available.' At that moment a gust of wind blew in from the desert, bringing dust and confusion into the makeshift command post. The general caught the brunt of the blast which went into his eyes and up his nose. He rose to his feet and stumbled round blindly, knocking the table sideways. Hands reached out to steady him but he swatted them away, shouting violently, 'Leave me alone! Back! Get back!' He managed to right himself and stood blinking like an owl, bloodshot and furious.

Taking a deep breath, Ala'adin Pasha began to explain his strategy. 'A triangle containing three smaller triangles within it.' He drew again in the sand. 'The cavalry will cover the flanks here and here with cannon and supplies in the centre. In this way each unit is secure in itself.'

It made sense to everyone present; but the general, his eyes filled with tears and his heart wretched with disgrace, could not bring himself to agree. He slumped down in his chair and gasped for breath, repeating over and over, almost in a whisper, the word, 'Triangles'.

◆

By now the camels were eating the straw of their saddles, for they were no longer allowed to graze outside the security of the square. Fear was eating its way into the hearts of the men. The land itself had begun to encroach upon them. Nobody left the perimeter unless absolutely necessary, for the enemy were adept at concealing themselves within the thorn bushes and crevices and folds in the earth, so that a hundred men could be lying right under your nose on the flattest, most unremarkable rocky plain and you would not see them. Things had reached such a feverish state that it was reputed that some of the enemy actually slipped through the sentry-posts and wandered freely through the camp at night while the men slept. Things would mysteriously disappear: personal possessions, soap, a favoured razor-blade or mirror, a book or journal, a pair of boots, socks, letters from home and even rosary beads. As a consequence, fights broke out between the men, whose nerves were already on edge. Bayonets were drawn and blood was spilt more frequently than one might have wished.

They pushed on towards Shaykan, where they halted to construct better defences, for the night had already begun to fall upon them. By now they were surrounded, and as darkness fell sporadic shots began to sound. People took to crawling from one place to another instead of walking. Shots thudded into the trees, making branches snap off suddenly without warning. All the birds had gone; there was not a bat in sight. From time to time someone would be hit and the crying would begin. No one wanted to risk moving for fear of attracting a sniper. The wounded would cry or scream alone in their misery for hours until they either died or slumped into oblivion. A camel was hit and she went on moaning until someone went over, well past midnight, and quietly slit her throat.

Sleep did not come easily. The hours slipped their smoky coils around the men ever more tightly. The stars were softly eaten up by thin rain-clouds.

By morning, the firing had ceased and an odd kind of peace seemed to have descended on the world. The air was fresh with the damp, dewy smell of dust rising from the light rain. The sun was climbing towards its sentinel post, and the moon, still visible, was a blue smudge on the horizon.

They crossed an open stretch of land where the going was better and began to curve away towards the north-east, with no sign of the enemy. Then the trees burst from the ground again: stunted boughs, hard dry stilts cracking through the earth. They approached a low ridge beyond which was a wide valley with gentle wooded slopes on both sides. The governor-general paused here to look back at his triangle. He was determined to prove to the mule-headed Hicks that his strategy of three smaller triangles flanked by cavalry was practical and workable. They were more flexible, bending with the terrain rather than being shredded by it. It was turning out to be a good day, he decided. Ala'adin Pasha rode on ahead.

The accident happened less than half an hour later, just as they were reaching the top of the ridge. His horse took a bad step and one leg went into a pothole, sinking through a weak layer of mud and grass. The animal went down on its flank, trapping Ala'adin beneath it. Men came rushing up to help.

The governor-general was heart-broken. 'See to her. I'm all right.' He swatted the men aside like flies. 'See to the horse.' The grey mare had been with him for years and he was fond of her. It was more than just luck; the whole incident had a bad feel to it. He had been fooling himself. His optimism evaporated, like a hazy image that vanishes as one draws near.

'It's an old horse sir, getting careless.' The *bimbashi* fed a cartridge into the breech of his rifle. 'The leg is broken.'

'Meat for supper then,' quipped one of the onlookers.

Ala'adin stopped the man who was preparing to shoot the horse. 'Not the gun, man. The noise will draw them to us – use the bayonet.'

'Sir, they already know where we are,' the soldier pointed out with the dull logic of soldiers.

Frustration added itself to Ala'adin's troubles. 'Give me that and hold her head down,' he snapped, reaching out a hand. The mare's big eyes stayed absolutely still, watching Ala'adin approach. He stroked her head gently. 'Never mind, never mind,' he soothed, 'it's better this way.' He could smell her fear. Then he quickly plunged the blade into her neck. Blood spurted out over his hands. He remained on his knees beside her. His hand felt the shudder go through her. Her legs kicked for a time and then she was still. He wiped the blade on a tuft of grass and handed the bayonet back to the soldier. 'Get Medani to tie her to the supply wagon,' he said, wiping his hands on his trousers. Another horse was brought round and the saddle transferred. He mounted and signalled that they were ready to move on.

'At last,' muttered Hicks at the head of the column. 'Even the damn horses are tired of this plague of a country.' He kicked his own mount forwards and the heavy black stallion began plodding, head down, towards the wide bowl of the valley. At the back of Hicks's mind there was a nagging question which seemed to evade him. He plodded on a little further before it struck him: the birds – where were all the birds today?

12. *Wadi al-Milk*

Three days have gone by. The ceremony repeated itself every night. The old woman would sit in a high-backed chair carved from Ethiopian ebony. She herself was from Gondar and when she spoke it was through gaps in her mouth where the missing teeth let the wind blow in a strange fashion which only al-Tome could decipher. An unfamiliar tongue. In one hand she held a pipe stuffed with sweet, intoxicating *kamanga*, in the other hand a bowl of *merissa* which she sipped through a thin silver straw. In the centre of the yard the women bowed and wailed, danced and stamped their feet.

When Kadaro awoke, the morning was cool and the air light. A soft breeze from the south cut through the gaps in the walls. The horses were grazing a short way off, scrabbling in the dust for seeds and stray buds. The wind carried a scent of moisture – somewhere it was raining. On the other side of the ruined wall were the dregs of last night's revelry. The men were scattered around, sleeping in the shade. A strange spell had been cast over them, for no one seemed afraid of being caught by surprise here. Perhaps they no longer cared. *Sanjak* Juma had slept badly. He had howled and screamed all night, calling for his mother and vowing to chase them to the ends of the earth. 'Twaitorth!' he had screamed toothlessly. For the most part, however, he had simply whined like a baby. Now, of course, he was sleeping like one. A palm frond had been thoughtfully placed over him by Abd al-Tome to keep the early-morning sun from disturbing him. Kadaro heard the men discussing whether Juma's mother was a Syrian whore, which everyone knew was untrue anyway because she was Yemeni. They wanted to take matters into their own hands; enough was enough. It would not take more than one swift stab with a bayonet. But Kadaro knew that no one would dare to do it.

87

He stepped through the debris and found himself circling away from the house. Men, women, boys, children, strange people whom he had not noticed the night before were sleeping in odd corners, huddled together in groups. He came across Faris lying face down clutching an empty *merissa* jug.

After a time he found himself behind the house. Here was an enclosed space and beyond that more ruin: corners of half-sunken buildings, fragments of people's homes. There was a stench of excrement, human as well as horse. The wind tore up strips of dust, pages from the ream of the earth, floating by to crumble and vanish. There was a low circular tower made of mud; from the sound of things it was a chicken coop.

Kadaro got down and crawled a little closer, pangs of hunger gnawing at his insides. He peered through a small arch and there was his reward: shining, white and smooth as a pearl. He reached a hand in and extracted the egg. Then, sitting down with his legs folded, he cracked off the top and sucked the contents out like a snake. Smiling to himself now he rolled on to his belly and again peered in. This time he could make out more of the shiny shapes protruding from wisps of straw. He stretched out his arm, to be rewarded this time by a sharp peck on the back of his hand. He cursed his luck and sat nursing his wounded pride, enjoying the sun on his face.

Something made him look up and there was the girl. Dressed in a simple black cotton shift, she stood a short way off, watching him. He jumped up as though stung.

'You're stealing our eggs,' she called. He held a hand up to shade his eyes and began dusting off his tunic. The arms were missing and there were no buttons on it, but he was proud of it none the less.

'I was hungry,' he called out.

She stepped closer. 'They are very special eggs.'

'What?' He was watching her move, the way her legs seemed always poised and balanced like those of a gazelle. He felt his own legs as heavy and stubborn as roots.

'Any man who eats them, remains here as our slave,' she replied, 'for the rest of his life.'

He gave up pretending to tidy his uniform and stood silently, hands by his side, unable to make up his mind whether she was telling the truth or playing a trick. By now she was within arm's reach. There was not much meat on her, though she was taller than him by a head or so. She stood watching him. He had been wrong, he decided: her eyes were two dark pools that contained no light. His voice had fallen now to a whisper. 'I only took one.'

She laughed and he felt the smell of her on his skin, like the feathers of a small bird flying through the fragrant leaves of a tree. Her skin was the colour of limes; it caught the light that way.

'You would have eaten all of them if I had not arrived,' she said, as though nothing in the world could hurt her.

He was staring at the V-shape where her neck met her collar. A tiny fluttering there of a pulse made him think of the way a small bird feels in the palm of your hand. He did not dare meet her gaze, but found his eyes riveted to the flickering pulse. She scared him the way a horse that has broken a leg scared him. They acted strangely, might kick out without warning, not matter how tame by nature. He felt the breeze drying the sweat on his spine through the tattered tunic, felt the sun on the shaven bristles of his skull. He was small and inadequate.

'You smell of horses,' she said.

'I'm a soldier, just like the others,' he replied. 'I mean that I'm as brave as the rest of them, maybe even braver.'

She looked at him curiously. 'What is your name, boy?'

'Kadaro.'

'What kind of a name is that? Where did you get it?'

He licked his dry lips. Where do names come from? Why had he never thought about the matter before? Such an obvious thing, to ask where a name came from, and yet it had never occurred to him, not once in his entire life. He shrugged his shoulders; his hands felt swollen and heavy. 'It's an army name.'

'I am Noon,' she said. But he already knew her name; the eye of the sun floating over the sky. He knew her name because he had repeated it to himself all night long in his sleep, until it was etched into his brain like a tattoo. Noon, who carries the mysteries of words and writing in her soul. She glanced over her shoulder, back towards the house.

For a week now they had forced her to inhale the smoke of burning amulets and herbs. They made her drink strange concoctions, made of God alone knew what, in an effort to banish the impish *jinns* from her body. They tortured her because she was not like them, because she was young and pretty and because sometimes she fell, and when she fell her body began to shake as though *Iblis* himself were possessing her like a husband. Blood came from her mouth and her body lifted from the floor as though she were about to fly. She saw herself as though she were indeed floating somewhere in the air, looking down upon herself biting her tongue, unable to do anything to stop it. She was used to it, but they had never accepted it; wherever she went they had done the same to her, ever since she was a child. But she no longer feared the old women and their potions, for she understood now that whatever it was within her they could never touch it, nor heal it, nor take it away. It was hers. She understood and she endured.

Noon and Kadaro stood there in silence. The kind of silence which he did not know what to do with.

There came a sound: a muffled cough followed by silence; the clucking of chickens; the cooing of pigeons; the rustle of wind stealing through trees. Kadaro held up his hand for silence, but she had already heard. Their eyes met and they moved, together now, towards the crumbled corner of what was once a house.

There were two figures sitting in the shade of what remained of a roof. Sunlight fell through the collapsed roof beams in long triangular sheets. They were in the narrow band of shade, half sitting, propped up against the mud wattle wall, half sprawled on the ground, draped in a layer of dust. Small feathers stuck together with bird droppings covered their skin and bleached their clothes.

Kadaro wondered why he had not noticed the strange smell that came from them, for it was powerful and unfamiliar. He looked more closely. Their faces were red and made raw by the sun. Their eyes were closed and swollen, like the eyes of blind men who can no longer bear to see the world. The skin on their hands and faces was coming away in long flakes, picked off by the gusts of wind that blew round the corner. These figures did not look like anything God ever set on this earth.

'What are they?' she asked, speaking his thoughts.

'*Afareet*, he whispered.

They looked like bird-men who had dropped from the sky. Whatever they were, they looked more dead than alive. Kadaro crept closer, until he was near enough to touch them. No response. Then the one furthest away stirred. His head lolled to one side and back again as flies buzzed around his nostrils. The shelter was alive with ants and flies. The arm of the nearest one was swollen and a rotten smell came from him. The other one was taller, thinner. As Kadaro watched, a shudder passed through the man's body. His head shook as though he were dreaming and he made a sound, the sound they had heard before, which was not a cough, but something like a groan. It was then that Kadaro noticed the pistol. A dull metal gleam lying open in the man's palm, resting in his lap. A revolver like the one Major Hantoub had worn. Kadaro licked his lips and scuttled forwards until his hand was almost within reach of the gun. But he had misjudged the distance and needed to move his right foot nearer. As he shifted his weight, the man came awake. The eyes flickered open and he sat up as though jerked by a rope. The gun hand came up and suddenly Kadaro was staring down the barrel, so close that he could see an ant crawling round the tip. The man's eyes rolled in his head. He growled, made strange sounds that Kadaro could not decipher and fell back into a dead faint. Kadaro rubbed his damp palms on his shorts.

'What is it?' hissed the girl from behind him. Kadaro said nothing, did not move, did not take his eyes from the gun.

'They are going to die,' he thought.

'We must give them water to drink,' said the girl. Kadaro turned to look at her. What was she thinking? The man's fingers were now tightly locked around the pistol; Kadaro would have to prise it out of his grip. He drew himself backwards out of the shelter and led the girl a little way off to a small fig tree.

'Were you afraid?' she asked. He shook his head, watching the dark orbs of her eyes. 'They are almost dead,' she said. 'They couldn't hurt anyone.'

'I knew that,' he nodded, although it still sounded lame.

'Where did they come from?'

'I don't know. They could be foreign agents, spies for the Sultan.'

'Then you must help them.'

Kadaro was not so certain. He glanced back at the clay shelter. He should tell the others. Abd al-Tome would know what to do. 'They are *affranji*,' he heard himself say.

Noon laughed.

'What would they be doing here?' he went on. 'And why should they hide in there, where it is dirty and smelly?'

She answered knowingly. 'To hide their scent, of course.'

'From whom?'

'Anyone. Bandits, dervishes, wild dogs, us.'

There came another startled moan from behind the wall. They stood silently in the leafy shade. Noon made up her mind and began walking in the direction of the high walls of the house.

'Where are you going?' he asked.

'They must have water,' she said over her shoulder, 'or they will die.'

He sat down against the tree, throwing stones until she returned bearing a small water-pot under her arm. Her bare feet kicked up the long hem of her dress as she walked.

'Aren't you afraid?'

She looked him straight in the eye. 'Why should I be afraid?'

Removing a twig he had been chewing from his teeth and pushing it behind his ear, he followed her. 'Why did you say I should help them?'

She turned around to face him, lowering the water-pot. 'Because if you help them they will reward you and you will live in the palace with the Sultan.'

Kadaro threw back his head and laughed, and then he stopped still. He lifted the jug from her and led the way. When they reached the shelter he stopped. 'You'd better stay here,' he said. 'They might try something.'

'No man has ever succeeded with me in that way,' she replied evenly. 'I am protected.' Kadaro considered this for a moment, then motioned for her to wait while he peered around to see if it was safe. Satisfied that there was no danger, Kadaro knelt beside the two men.

'Just a boy,' murmured the thin one, 'just a boy.' Kadaro held the jug for him to drink. The man snatched it, making Kadaro jump backwards in alarm.

Hamilton Ellesworth, now a ragged shadow of his former self, held out the jug and gestured towards Spratling. But the older man was unable to drink until they held his head up and tipped a few sips into his mouth.

'Look at his arm,' the girl whispered.

Kadaro leaned forwards. 'A thorn. He didn't take it out in time. The whole arm is poisoned now.' He noted this with the detachment of someone who has witnessed such things regularly, although in fact he had only seen an infection as bad as this once before and that was in a gazelle, which they ate, except for the infected leg of course. People were usually better at taking the curled thorns out in time.

Kadaro followed Noon towards the house. 'If you tell the others about this they will kill them both,' she said. He looked at her. 'Promise that you will not come here without me?' she said. Finally he nodded his agreement. She laughed and walked off, vanishing through the small door in the wall of the big house. Kadaro followed along, kicking stones.

13. Shaykan,
3 November 1883

The weaver birds burst from the trees at sunrise, like a confusion of thought erupting from an unruly head. They scattered, and then, sweeping back together, they curved upwards and over like a comma: the sign of the letter *Wao*. These are the signs by which we know the miracle of existence. The letters of learning; the language we use to describe the world and which in turn describes us.

Indecipherable, the thunder began to move and the world stopped turning. Upon a raised patch of flat, hard ground a group of riders were assembled. The ponies trembled from the fast ride and jittered back and forth nervously. The riders dismounted and moved easily on foot towards the edge of the hill, to a point where the wind blew through a strangely shaped acacia tree that was bent forwards as though about to fall into the gulf below. The valley was alive with the movement of thousands of small ants: forty thousand to be exact. The *ansar* moved through the bush and the trees, busy concealing themselves in the hillsides and the gentle slopes, vanishing from view as though sucked into the ground.

At the centre of the group of onlookers was a slim man with a light complexion which set him slightly apart from the others. He unwrapped the long white cotton scarf that was bound about his head and face. Dust from the ride had engrained itself in the delicate lines of his face. The sun picked out the piercing dark eyes and the air was filled with the faint scent of myrrh.

Beside him a taller, darker man with the broad shoulders of a fighter and the loose, comfortable movements of a wrestler, stood silently. He had a thin beard of wiry hair. His features were more rugged and his eyes showed more concern and understanding than those of the other. He was restlessly moving, constantly observing. He stared out into the distant plain and raised his arm to point. 'That is their camp, sire.'

Muhammad Ahmad al Mahdi squinted out into the blurry plain. He saw little but sand and a faint scratch of trees. He nodded his head. Wad al Nejumi touched his shoulder. 'A little further to the left,' he corrected. With a faint trace of irritation, the Mahdi thanked his *amir* and turned to the others. 'That is they,' he confirmed. 'And may God show them His compassion.' There were murmurs of agreement.

'Let no man fear death today,' smiled the Mahdi. 'Victory will be ours.' He raised his hands in front of his face. 'The Prophet Muhammad is with us and an army of angels will fight alongside us.' He cupped a hand to his ear with an impish smile. 'Listen and you can hear them singing.'

Abu Anja was there, leader of the trained forces of the *jihadiya*: soldiers saved from the khedive's battalions, captured from the garrisons at El Obeid and Bara. He turned aside to receive a message from one of his lieutenants who came loping athletically up the hillside. The sun climbed towards heaven. The men were in place, the messenger reported. Abu Anja, burly and stoical, turned to pass on the news, but the Expected One had already heard. He stepped past Abu Anja to place his hands squarely on the lieutenant's shoulders. 'Let your men know that God himself will ensure their aim is true. The men who are coming are your former masters, they who would have you as slaves. Tell your men that all believers are equal in the eyes of God.' The sun glowed in his eyes. The whimsical smile was still on his face, so that even Wad al Nejumi, despite his military experience and his physical strength, felt touched by his presence. There was truly a light around this man. He himself had never seen an angel in his life but if ever there was a moment when he might have felt them near, this was it. He glanced round the assembled group.

Firstly, there were the three khalifas, of whom the most trusted was no doubt Abdullahi al Ta'aishi, the nomad whose journey from the western lands to find his chosen master was already legendary. Some said he was the first man to understand the importance of the Mahdi's mission. Then there was Muhammad Sharif of the *Danagla*, and Ali wad Hilu of Kenana, who had known Muhammad Ahmad since the days when he had travelled those regions with his brothers seeking for timber for their boats. Each khalifa was accompanied by an *amir*: respectively Yakub, Adem and Nejumi himself. The Mahdi was the centre of the wheel; he was the fixed point around which they all revolved. He was stamping his feet, however, impatient to know whether all the arrangements had been taken care of. 'Have the orders been given to Abu Girgeh and Abd al Halim?' he demanded.

Nejumi confirmed this: 'They will attack the rear of the column, when the time is right.' The Mahdi nodded briefly and once again scanned the valley to see how things were proceeding. The others looked at one another.

'Victory is ours,' prompted Muhammad Sharif with self-conscious zeal. 'The Angel of Death rides with us.' Muhammad Sharif was much younger than the others, and the one most closely related to Muhammad Ahmad by blood.

'You must remember, Muhammad,' chided the Mahdi, turning back to the group of men, 'that this is a small victory. We shall go on from here.' He looked round at the others, gesturing with his hands. 'On to Egypt and Cairo. On to the holy lands, to Mecca and Medina.' A murmured chorus of '*Inshallah*' echoed from the others. He shook his head lightly as though in wonder at the magnitude of it all. 'I pray that the unbelievers will see that there is no sense in resisting the might of God. Remember,' he added, raising a finger, 'our purpose is not to kill these meddling foreigners, but to restore the will of God on earth. Our task has just begun.'

'*Allahu akbar!*' came from Ali wad Hilu. The others chimed in loudly, with the exception of Nejumi, whose voice was muted. The Mahdi turned in his direction and smiled his benevolent smile. 'The son of Nejumi is thinking of his military strategy. Do not worry your mind; you are a great warrior and you have proved yourself many times. You have seen more of the horror of battle than any of us, and you have your faith. Always remember that you are not alone.'

Wad Nejumi, embarrassed, stepped backwards and bowed his head. 'God is merciful and compassionate,' he heard himself mutter. The Mahdi nodded and led the way towards the horses.

The sun rose higher and the small dust-cloud on the horizon that announced the approach of the enemy drew nearer. The valley below was silent. The men remained concealed, up and down the hillside and even scattered in clumps in the bottom of the valley itself, through which the soldiers must march. Nothing moved.

The Mahdi stepped towards the lip of the hill and drew his sword. He raised it high into the air so that the sun caught its blade and he shouted, the wind carrying his voice, 'There is no god but Allah.' And the reply came back, curling from the valley below. It was the sound of invisible voices chanting like an echo, reeling from down in the earth. It came from the soil that held the roots; from between the cracks in the sun-baked mud. It came on the breeze that hung in rags on the sharp tips of the thorns. And the answer was deep and low and forty-thousand strong: '*Allahu akbar*' – they were ready.

14. Wadi al-Milk,
November 1883

None of the men of the Ninth Company of the khedive's irregular cavalry noticed the absence of their young stablehand. The horses were not dying or complaining, they were being fed and watered regularly. And no one was particularly interested in horses these days; they were more concerned with women and with the intoxicating brew, *merissa*, of which there seemed to be an unlimited supply in the dark, cool rooms below the house. During the day they sat around in the sunshine in various states of undress or lay on their backs in the shade and stared at the sky. From time to time an argument would break out, but no one had the energy to fight, so they would call each other names for a time and promise to take care of business later. Not even the women held their attention as they had in the beginning, except perhaps for Faris, who rarely came out of the upstairs room which he had commandeered for himself. He was seen once a day as a rule standing at the wide window, stretching his arms and yawning, before beckoning to one of the girls to come up to him. The girls were growing tired of Faris, but luckily, with nineteen of them, there was plenty to keep him occupied. Most of the men preferred sleeping. Wahab sat in the sun cleaning his rifle and repairing his saddle, slotting all the shells he could find into his bandolier and then oiling that. Nobody thought about horses, for where should they go from here? And no one paid much attention to the whereabouts of the boy except for Abd al-Tome, who had grown fond of the place and spent his time either wandering up and down looking for things to repair or else haggling with the old crone. 'I am very careful about keeping my accounts straight,' she kept saying, pulling the smooth, carved-bone pipe-stem from between her red gums and smacking her lips together. 'I'll send this bill to the khedive himself.'

Abd al-Tome repaired the windows that were in danger of falling on to people's heads. He went all the way around the upper veranda replacing damaged balusters. The pasha's house was beginning to receive some of the attention it had been starved of for so many years.

One day as he was on the roof trying to patch up some holes with straw, woven *dom* palm and mud, he spied Kadaro emerging from the wall of one of the crumbled structures behind the house. With him was the strange girl, Noon, whom the old woman regarded as a curse on herself for having given a nasty venereal affliction to a passing Turkish colonel the year before she was born.

'What are they up to now?' Abd al-Tome asked himself.

That evening while the others were eating, he followed them through the stooped door in the rear wall. 'Kadaro,' he called, bringing the boy up with a start. The girl stood silently beside him. 'What have you got there?' Kadaro and Noon remained silent. Abd al-Tome made to step forwards but the girl moved to block his path. The old man looked back and forth between them. He began to laugh, a throaty chuckle. 'What is it?' he asked. 'Have you found a puppy dog?' he winked, 'or are you learning how to make them?'

Neither of them replied. 'Let me see,' Abd al-Tome said quietly.

Kadaro, holding the tray, gave a sigh. He shrugged. Noon stepped back a pace and lifted the revolver. A strange look came into the old man's eyes, which were light and hard like polished amber. 'Where did you get it from?'

Kadaro felt his stomach churning. The old man's eyes never turned towards him, but stayed pinned to the girl, whose slim wrist also showed no signs of wavering. 'What did I tell you, boy?' he whispered. 'May the Lord protect us from women, for they are surely the strangest creatures He ever put into this world.'

The three of them stood there. Abd al-Tome shifted his feet. His legs were getting stiff. 'If you are going to shoot me then get on with it,' he said after a time. He looked over at Kadaro. 'Are you just going to stand there?'

Kadaro hesitated, torn between the old man and the girl. 'Two *affranji sirdar*s,' he blurted out.

'*Affranji* officers, you're sure? Not Turks?'

Kadaro ignored the glint in the girl's eyes and nodded quickly.

'Where did they come from?' The old soldier scratched the grey bristles on his scalp. He indicated the gun: 'They gave you that?'

'I took it,' insisted the girl.

'Where are you going to take them, these prisoners of yours?'

'To Khartoum,' said the boy. Abd al-Tome laughed and turned away. He padded off in his bow-legged fashion through the darkness towards the house, calling over his shoulder, 'Just take care with that gun, whatever your *sirdar*s promise you, you'll need it.'

The following day around mid-morning Zinzebeir came riding into the yard in great haste. He had spied a dust-cloud moving fast enough for cavalry, coming this way.

'They might be ours,' sneered Faris, who did not want his idyll shattered just yet.

Wahab, however, got to his feet. 'Then you tell us when you find out,' he said. 'I'm not waiting.'

The others were somewhat divided and a short discussion ensued. 'What about the girls?' asked Razig. A couple of the others, numbed and sedated by their stay, mumbled their agreement.

'We take as many of them as want to come,' Wahab conceded. They moved quickly now, throwing their things together, collecting rifles and ammunition pouches.

'What about you, boy?' asked Wahab, climbing into his saddle. Kadaro shook his head. The *bimbashi* shrugged. 'It's your life.'

They filed past him, the horses looking thinner and more dusty than he had ever seen them. The girls, who were saddled on the spare mounts in pairs, were crying for some reason. Zinzebeir raised his rifle in salute. Faris and Razig were in the middle of a dispute. Abd al-Tome appeared, leading the horse that dragged the litter containing the remains of *Sanjak* Juma. 'You're almost taller than me, these days,' the old man said to Kadaro. He looked down at the reins in his hands for a moment, then looked up at the horizon and shrugged.

And so it was decided, Kadaro thought. For the first time Abd al-Tome looked very much like a child. He recalled the time when he had first joined the *Bash-Buzuq*. His mother had sold him to the army, although he did not know the circumstances. He recalled only a warm, comforting smell which came to him on humid nights in the rainy season and this was the closest to sorrow or loss he ever came to feel. It was al-Tome who had taken him in, looked after him as though he were his own son. It was al-Tome who made sure he got enough food, who protected him from the wandering fingers of those who sought to use him for their pleasure. Abd al-Tome talked to him as a person, not as a child. He read to him from the Koran and talked to him about that mystery of mysteries, religion, and when he talked, it all seemed to make sense.

'Why, even the Prophet Muhammad himself had no idea what his mission would be.'

'He heard the words of the angel Gibreel.'

'Yes, and when these wondrous words began to come into his mind, when he, an illiterate man, began to spout poetry of such beauty and wisdom, how do you think he felt? He was in torment.'

'How long must I wait?'

'Until you are sure that the voice you are listening to is the right one.'

◆

The house was empty now. The wind blew through the big rooms. Dust settled on the floors, in the corners and on the old woman who sat by herself in her big chair, waiting. Out by the chicken shed Noon waited for him, among the broken clay and the dead birds. She waited and he went to her like a dream. They had the only beast left behind: an old mule they had found wandering in the thorny scrub behind the house. The younger of the two 'generals' was awake. Together they managed to get the old one, whose legs were too weak to support him, up on to the mule and they strapped his wrists there to keep him from falling. Then Kadaro turned and led the way out of the nameless village. None of them looked back once.

15. The Battle of Shaykan,
3–5 November 1883

As they were dragging the dead horse over the lip of the valley, Medani spotted a clump of ashen branches and instantly thought, 'Firewood'. He hopped down from the cart and urged the old mule to stop, handing the reins to the boy sitting beside him. Then he walked alongside, throwing branches up on to the cart. After a while he called the boy to come down and help him. They lodged a branch behind one of the wheels to act as a brake. 'Keep that cart moving,' called a passing *bimbashi*, but Medani did not care about keeping the formation – that was someone else's task.

'Yes, yes,' he nodded back. 'They can say what they like,' he muttered to himself, 'but I know who is blamed when the tea is not ready because the wood is too wet and smoky.'

He was actually kneeling on the ground, pulling a thick trunk free from under a low mesquite bush, when the firing started: a colossal roar, like the collapse of a mountain. His heart turned to stone. 'May God demolish their homes.' He was about to stand up when a stray bullet whistled through the leaves above his head and thudded firmly into a tree. He threw himself to the ground and as he did so, he saw the boy scramble back into the cart to get a better view. He was about to call out, to tell the fool to sit down, when the boy pitched backwards to land on a pile of sacks in the back of the cart. The bullet must have struck him square in the chest. No sound came from him.

Medani lay still, his face pressed into the earth. Bullets were flying in every direction and men were rushing around shouting. He heard the dull, uncertain stutter of one of the machine-guns starting up. He crawled forwards with his head close to the ground until he could peer into the valley. Both sides and the bottom of the valley were filled with the smoke of rifles; the firing was coming from every possible angle. He wriggled backwards into the hollow where he had been lying, clasped his hands over his head, closed his eyes and began to pray.

◆

Up ahead, Sherwood Louth's pack-mule began to stampede. As it kicked and snorted he was thrown off its back. It vanished into the bush, leaving him down on one knee with turmoil all around him. Everywhere he looked he saw men falling – whether wounded or killed outright he could not tell. Beside him lay a camel with its head, inexplicably, split open. He heard screaming, and for a while he did not realise that it was himself, screaming at the top of his voice. He saw the enemy too. Amazing how simple they looked: old men, tall thin men, young boys, with the same rusty swords and hopelessly outdated rifles, barefoot, clad in thin, patched garments. He saw the soldiers forming into lines, trying to arrange their pattern of fire to the best effect. A bare-headed officer beside them was shouting orders, until he too fell in the confusion of smoke and bodies.

The enemy were all around them. They simply erupted out of the ground. The dead camel smelt of warm piss. Its sides were worn raw where the ropes and saddles had dug in. People were jumping over Sherwood. He saw a wounded man with blood pouring from his head, and another, with disbelief on his face, trying to pull a spear from his chest. Something heavy fell on Sherwood's back and panic gripped him. He wriggled and kicked his legs, punching and rolling until he was free. Afterwards he discovered what had pinned him down: a dead boy. By now his hearing was almost gone, his ears rang with the constant exploding of rifles. The soldiers were firing as fast as they could reload their Remmingtons, but the *ansar* came on more quickly than the soldiers could cut them down.

As he crawled, trying to claw his way into the earth, clutching handfuls of it with his fists, Sherwood's hand came to rest on a rifle dropped by a soldier. The barrel was warm, like a discarded limb. His hand closed around it momentarily and then he quickly pushed it away. A wounded man dropped to the ground in front of him, blood spurting from a hole in his chest. Each time he tried to breathe another pulse of blood would emerge. His head lolled sideways and his eyes, as he went down, caught Sherwood and held him transfixed.

◆

The front triangle received the brunt of the first wave of the riflemen's fire. They had been almost atop the small wooded knoll that marked the end of the valley bottom when the firing began. General Hicks saw the ground in front of him rise up in a paroxysm of scrub and dust: a wave of men, where a moment ago there had been silent earth. He swung his horse round. A soldier, seizing his chance, rushed at him and tried to pull him from the saddle in an effort to secure his own escape. Hicks drew his sabre and cut the soldier down in a flurry of swift blows. He shouted orders for the Nordenfeldts to be swung round towards the flanks. A group of *ansar* burst from the trees, making for him. 'Like peacocks,' he thought, 'with their colourful patches.'

Further back, on the right flank, Ala'adin Pasha was struggling to dismount while his horse wheeled in terrified circles. He struggled to bring it under control; the reins had been cut, sliced by a boy who ducked under the horse's head, evading his sabre blows. One foot was free, but the other was caught. Panic began to take hold of him, but he yelled and kicked and managed to extricate himself. Dropping to the ground, he drew his pistol in time to see an old greybeard of a man appear out of the ground and run at him with a long spear. Almost absently he raised the barrel and pulled the trigger. The man vanished from view. All around him were the shouts and screams of men dying, calling for help.

He called to the *bimbashi* to rally the men, draw the camels into a barricade. He needed to know how Hicks was managing up ahead but, in all the confusion of men and horses, it was hard to see much further than a few yards. They were in a small clearing, a break within the trees surrounded by grass and bush. They needed to rally and pull back up the slope out of the valley. Hicks and his men were in the depression at the bottom of the valley. It was a perfect trap.

Miraculously, a lull came in the fighting. The shooting from the hillsides slowed to a trickle. The men were beginning to rally, appearing out of the trees, crawling on their bellies, running as if the devil himself were behind them. Falling on their faces, they clung to one another; knelt back to back, firing, loading, dragging the carcasses of dead mules and horses around them for protection. Then silence, like a miracle, descended upon them. Nobody dared move lest he should break the spell and call hell down upon them once again. Someone was weeping in soft, halting sobs. The air was thick with the buzz of flies. The smell of excrement and blood and death hung sweetly rotting over them. It rose from the dust and the grass. They clung together, shoulder to shoulder. Their eyes searched for movement, but there was none. As suddenly as it had come, the inferno had disappeared.

◆

Dusk drew near and the light began to fade. Ala'adin moved among the men. Pale eyes lifted to meet his and then quickly flicked away. There were whispers in the tree-tops. Wings rustled in the long grass. He stooped here and there to lend a hand of reassurance. Whatever animosity there had been between the soldiers and the officers was now gone. The dead animals were covered in flies which buzzed insanely; hawks circled in great gliding whirls. Darkness fell. The little food available was now passed around. A case of ammunition was shared out. They were serenaded by the whining, snivelling sound of wild dogs which peered red-eyed and eager from the shadows. Some dared to come in, squabbling and tearing at the carcasses. All night they stayed, whining impatiently. From time to time someone would lose his nerve and let off a few shots at the unfamiliar stars that winked in among the trees.

All night, voices called softly from the hillsides, urging them to give in to the will of God. A young boy sang the verses of the opening *sura* of the Koran with such beauty that it made the beleaguered soldiers weep.

Dawn came and with it the firing. Whatever embers of hope they might have raked into their imagination in the lonely darkness were immediately extinguished. They were surrounded. They could move neither forwards nor backwards. It was odd, Ala'adin thought to himself. 'They seem to be in no particular hurry. They have no fear of us whatsoever.'

Late in the afternoon there was a commotion in the trees ahead. A flock of horses and camels came rushing into the open. Through the confusion Ala'adin glimpsed General Hicks, still mounted on his horse, waving his sabre with one hand and firing his pistol. He was driving the animals like a shield ahead of his weary men. They were trying to break through.

'Up,' Ala'adin shouted, getting to his feet. 'We must help them.' The men rose and together began to move forwards. 'General,' Ala'adin waved his hand and shouted. For a second he thought Hicks had looked his way and smiled, but then a group of *ansar* burst from the trees like a swarm of bees. Like a man trying to swim upstream, Ala'adin struggled forwards. The general seemed almost within reach. His pistol was empty. Ala'adin saw him throw it to the ground and begin hacking at a man who with great agility was ducking under the head of his horse, from side to side, as though it were a game. Then the horse went down and Hicks descended into the sea of arms and faces, to vanish. A camel rushed by and Ala'adin just had time to jump aside to avoid being knocked down. The firing had increased now to such a din that although he was shouting like a madman no sound emerged.

And in that silence, Ala'adin found himself suddenly alone. He wheeled round to see a boy no older than twelve rise up out of the ground and drive a short, stubby sword between his ribs. He watched the roughly tempered blade disappear and he felt the brief searing pain and then a numbness. The short sword was wrenched from the boy's hand as the governor-general reeled backwards. Recovering himself, the boy rushed forward and knocked him to the ground. Ala'adin lay there. The rough iron hilt was bound with palm fibre, not even leather. He was intrigued by its shape and texture. A hair fluttered in the air. This is the way men have died for centuries, he thought. He could hear the air escaping from his perforated lung like the roar of a distant sea. The world was silent, but for that roar which was like a seashell held to his ear. Puffs of gunsmoke still erupted from the hillside; a pretty sight, like a field of cotton waving in the sun.

The boy stood for a moment, and then the doubt washed from his face and he stepped forward jubilantly. Placing one bare foot on the dead man's tunic he pulled his weapon free and raised it high. He threw back his head and howled, 'Victory is ours!'

◆

When the shooting stopped, Medani the cook was lying on his belly beneath a thick clump of bushes where he had spent the night. Thorns gouged his flesh but he felt no pain. Ants crawled in a long line up his legs and bit him until he was swollen all over, but still he did not utter a sound. His face was covered with earth from where he had dug himself into the ground. A riderless horse clattered by with a severed leg hanging from a stirrup. He wanted to wait until it was night, but he was afraid of being discovered. Agitatedly he removed the tunic he had worn and threw it back into the bushes. He crawled forward until he reached the body of a dead man; turning the body over, he found ants crawling from the eye sockets.

'May God watch over you and guide you, you son of a dog,' he spat through his teeth. His fingers shook as he removed the blood-stained shift and pulled it over his head. It smelt of sweat and another man's life; it was his now. Then he stumbled barefoot towards the valley where a scene of carnage awaited him. There were bodies piled on top of one another. He had not realised what was going on, not exactly, not in terms of the human cost of all that gunpowder and noise. He stumbled along, looking for a familiar face, something he could recognise amid this strange harvest. He wiped his face on his sleeve. A horse which had lost the use of its legs rolled from side to side trying to rise, before slumping back to the ground.

He watched as a group of *ansar* pulled a bedraggled figure from beneath a pile of dead men. The Englishman was crying and shaking like a baby. He was covered from head to foot in blood, but he himself seemed unharmed. They pushed him and shouted questions at him, but he appeared numb, as though in a trance. They pulled the bag from his shoulder and searched it, and finding only books, they threw them aside, trying on his hat instead. Finally they tied his hands together and led him away.

Medani moved on, and soon came across a group of men who were kneeling around a medicine-chest. He saw a man dip his finger into a jar of ointment and raise it towards his mouth, obviously thinking that it was some kind of food. Instinctively, Medani reached out a hand to stop him. The faces turned towards him. 'It's poison,' he explained wearily. The jar was flung back into the chest and the man wiped his finger carefully on his tunic.

A hand reached out to grasp Medani's shoulder as he made to leave. 'Wait,' the boy smiled. Medani turned to look into his face. He was young and reminded Medani of a nephew whom he had not seen for years. 'How did you know what it was?'

Medani shrugged and looked around for an answer. He pointed back the way he had come and said, 'I have seen it before, I was spying on them.' Another man stepped closer.

'Who is your *amir*?' The medicine-chest was forgotten as the group turned their attention to the bewildered old man. 'Where did you say you were from?' He could smell their hot blood. He turned from one unfamiliar face to another, becoming more confused. 'I fell.' Medani put a hand to his head and let his gaze drop to the ground.

Now the first man reached out a hand to calm him, saying, 'Don't worry, old man,' but Medani pulled backwards and the *jubba* was torn, revealing his military undershirt. They pressed forward now as a surge of fever went through them. 'Hang him.' 'Son of a dog is one of the Turks' infidels.'

'No, as God is my witness,' wept Medani. 'Brothers!' he implored them. Hands reached out for him. Suddenly, a tall figure appeared.

'What is this?'

Medani looked up to see Wad al Nejumi standing before him. The crowd was quick to put their case. The *amir* raised a hand for silence. He stepped forward. 'Old man, are you an unbeliever?' Medani shook his head. 'There is no God but Allah. Muhammad is his prophet,' he mumbled.

'He is a traitor,' someone growled.

'I'm not a soldier,' stammered Medani. 'I'm just a cook.'

Nejumi nodded. 'Come with me, old man, there has been enough blood today.' And with that he turned and led the way.

16. The White Nile,
December 1883

'He will die within three days,' the girl said, and she was right. The poison in his arm devoured him. His lips dried up like leather and burst. His eyes turned black as obsidian. The other *affranji* sat in the dust, too exhausted to know what was happening. Kadaro scraped a hole in the sand and they built a mound of sharp rocks over the dead man.

The three of them made slow ground. The only mule they had was sorely lame. She limped along as they took turns on her back. The wind brushed the hem of the girl's dress and gently erased their footprints as they went.

◆

Kadaro was explaining what he knew about the Turks. 'They always reward a man for hard work; they are fair.'

Noon rejected his theory with a jerk of her chin. 'You know nothing about them,' she said. 'You are a soldier, boy. A soldier does what he is told because that is his duty. If he gets a bone thrown his way he is eternally grateful.'

Kadaro was once more alarmed by this slip of a girl. How did she have all those things stored in that small head of hers, he wondered? She knew more than Abd al-Tome, and he was older than the desert. He turned to look back the way they had come. Across the flat, soft ground, broken only by the occasional smudge of small acacia trees, he could see the figure of the *affranji*. He was staggering, walking with his head up towards the sun, weaving like a bird. This was not going to get them far. The girl, meanwhile, was strolling ahead as though walking through a marketplace. He sighed and tugged the halter once again.

'Wait,' he called out. She turned to look at him and then carried on walking. With a curse he slapped the side of the mare and hurried to catch up with her.

'Why don't you wait when I call?'

'Because it takes too long.'

'I'm in charge here,' he said, slapping a hand to his chest. 'You can't just walk off, you might get lost.'

'I'm not in your army,' she replied. 'If I want to walk, I can walk.'

'That's not right,' was all Kadaro could say, shaking his head, wondering to himself why, every time he opened his mouth to this girl, he felt as though he were being soundly whipped. 'That's just not right,' he added.

'You could get lost just as easily.'

'I know the land.'

'You haven't been here before. You told me so.'

'No.' He could not grasp the spell she had put on him. Everything she said was so hard to wrestle with. One minute he wanted to kill her and the next . . . 'I know the land,' he said at last. 'I've travelled. I know how it . . . is.'

She held a hand up to shield her face from the dusty breeze. 'All right,' she consented. 'Which way do we go?'

Kadaro swallowed. His throat was dry and his feet were tired. He squinted to the south. 'Those trees there. I think they thicken towards the east. We follow them.'

They both turned to look back. The younger *jinn* was dancing in a circle, singing – a strange, unrhythmic wailing, like a dying calf. Kadaro spat on the ground and shook his head. 'His mind has come apart.'

◆

They watched the dust-cloud approaching. It grew from a small blur on the horizon, sweeping up with the wind to fill the sky with a dense ochre hue. The wind tugged insistently at their clothes, and the smell of the dust – ancient and ponderous, light as the centuries, dark as the tomb – was already upon them. They lay down; there was nowhere to go. The storm went on into night. Kadaro made them cover their heads with whatever they could find; blankets and scarves. They lay like the dead, being slowly buried.

◆

The *haboob* passed. Kadaro's eyes flickered open. The sun had dropped and the world, released from the intensity of midday, was calmer. Something had woken him up. He glanced round him. The girl was sleeping on her side, a small dark rag of cloth on the sand. The younger *jinn* was also asleep, out of the shade on his face, arms and legs splayed like a dead man. Kadaro sat up against the bole of the tree. The trees were bigger here, thicker. Their dry, sharp branches rattled like the legs of long insects scratching against each other. He could smell the river.

In the last weeks, Kadaro had guided them cautiously through the barren landscape, turning up water where it was impossible to imagine water could be found, finding food in the form of *fago* roots in the ground or dry pods of *dom* fruit which they chewed. For the first time, he seemed to understand the land. He began to see things which he had never noticed before: small, subtle changes in the colour of the dust and the swell of the plains. The countless miles of bone-dry sand and rock began to speak to him. He could not explain it, nor did he understand why it should happen now. He smelt the trees, half a day's march away; stretches of hard, cracked mud where the water would lie when the rains came; tiny yellow seeds where grass would appear. He could spot the tracks of gazelle and kudu, and see the tiny pellets which indicated red mice, also edible. The land began to expand before him.

The route took them east, and then a diversion sent them first in a northerly direction and then south, back the way they had come, before swinging east again. It made little sense, but the roads were patrolled by vigilant bands of men busy recruiting and dispersing the news. They slept in the open or in the shelter of ruined villages. They met few people, and those whom they did meet were as frightened as they were of contact. They moved in wide circles, as if taking part in some ancient dance ritual for which there is no name.

◆

Kadaro brushed the flies away from his face and squinted at the distant sway of yellow mimosa flowers. He was on a flat stretch of ground; to the east was a slight ridge, and as he climbed this he saw a row of canes, dried out, their stalks yellow and desiccated. Once someone had lived here, a farmer and his family perhaps. He paused to examine a strange, large-leafed plant from whose branches hung puffy green pods. He reached out to touch one and pressing it extracted a white fluid that seeped on to his fingers. He wiped them carefully on his breeches.

Something caught his eye, a movement, and he dropped to his knees still clutching the green puffy balls to his chest. Below him was the sparkling river. There was someone down by the water, in the shallows: the girl, Noon. She was bathing, her naked body a flawless beacon of light. The water came to her knees and he saw the flash of sunlight reflected from her skin as she poured water over her body. She seemed to encompass every colour of the rainbow: reds, blues and greens. Her skin was like a ray of light splintered apart. He felt his thoughts growing muddy while his body stirred and his loins grew stiff. She was the most beautiful thing he had ever set eyes on. He shifted his weight and the movement caused a weaver bird to burst from the canes. She turned and looked in his direction. Kadaro's heart was in his mouth. His chest hurt so much that he could hardly breathe. She was standing there, gleaming in the sunlight, and he knew in that instant that he would never be able to step forwards into the light. He ducked down and began to run.

◆

How long he walked, Kadaro did not know. He lost himself in the simple knowledge that was the river. He felt safe here and soon began to forget. It was in this manner that he came across the boat. It was a small boat. Two men stood unloading it in the shallows. A short,

112

stocky one and a taller one of just over average height, with strong shoulders and big hands. Kadaro could see his face as he climbed up from the river: it was a face worn by sand and wind. His complexion was dark and smooth with a few wisps of hair on his chin; his nose had been broken, bent almost flat on one side. Kadaro wiped his hand across his mouth and, feeling towards his belly, cursed himself for not having brought the pistol with him. The smaller of the two men was trying to drag the boat up on to the bank but was caught in an undercurrent and was now toiling. The bow was swinging into the stream as the man stumbled up to his thighs in water, the legs of his *sirwal* tucked up rather ineffectually now as he was forced further and further out. Kadaro bit his lip; it would be bad luck indeed to watch the boat go drifting away downstream. With the boat they could reach the capital within two days. He prepared to go down and help the floundering man, since his companion, unaware of the predicament, was still moving up the slope towards the trees with a dead gazelle on his back. The boat made another swing and the small man seemed to lose his footing suddenly, going in up to his waist.

Kadaro was on his feet and running. He raced down the incline, forgetting everything but the boat. He splashed into the water. Hurling himself forwards he grasped the side of the hull. The small man looked at him. 'What in the name of the Prophet are you doing?' By now the boat was under his control and the boy's help was superfluous. The fellow ploughed his way back into the shores while Kadaro, doing his best to look useful, pushed against the hull. When the boat was up on the sand, the man turned his attention to the newcomer. 'What snake-hole did you pop up from?'

Kadaro shook the water from his arms and head. 'I was walking and I saw you. You seemed to be in trouble.' The man spat on the ground and resting his hands on his considerable waist said, 'I've been handling boats since before your mother was born.'

From up the hill came a shout; the tall man was on his way down.

'Who is he?' he asked, looking back and forth between the two of them for an answer.

The stocky man shrugged his shoulders. 'He says he was walking.'

'Walking?' echoed the other.

'Down there,' indicated Kadaro.

'Walking where?' the tall man looked to his friend and again received only a shrug in reply. They all looked up the river, where nothing but a single crane was visible, winging its way gracefully over the wind-trimmed waves. The two men turned back to examine the boy. The heavier one reached out a hand to touch the tattered edges of Kadaro's tunic. 'He's a soldier.'

'I was,' Kadaro explained. 'I left them ...' It seemed that his explanations were of little value. The two men were looking around, scrutinising the surrounding land, the trees that rose from the low slope and the blank, silvery mud that ran along the water's edge.

'Maybe he's not alone,' said the tall one, voicing both men's thoughts.

The smaller one cursed. 'We've got no time for soldiers.'

The tall one cast a glance in Kadaro's direction. 'Are there others with you?'

The other man cursed this stupidity. 'You think he would tell us that a hundred of them were hiding in those trees?'

'Dead,' replied Kadaro. 'They were killed. I am alone.'

The tall one shifted his weight from one foot to the other. 'Don't you have family?'

Kadaro shook his head. 'Dead.'

A look of sympathy filled the shorter one's face. He scratched his ear, suddenly at a loss. 'All of them?' he asked.

Kadaro nodded.

'How did you get here?'

'I walked.'

The two men weighed up the situation in silence and the taller one stepped over to the boat. 'We've got no time for soldiers,' he repeated. Then he pulled out ropes and an ancient but well-preserved rifle. He handed a sack to Kadaro. 'Here, you carry this. There's enough food for an extra belly. But I warn you,' he shook his hand in warning, 'Khamis is a hawk when it comes to young boys.' The two men laughed together as they walked off up the shallow slope.

His belly full, Kadaro sat staring at the roaring fire. His thoughts turned to the others who were out there in the darkness with no food and this knowledge was not without its satisfaction. The two men paid him little attention. They had gathered wood and built a fire and begun carving up the gazelle into strips to roast. From time to time they looked over and threw him a piece. They were drinking from a goatskin which he guessed contained something stronger than water. Their voices were getting louder and their questions more offensive. 'So you soldiers like to fry the kidneys of women and small children?' said the short one with an unpleasant leer. Fat greased his mouth.

The other man snorted. 'That's not the *Bash-Buzuq*, that's the slave soldiers – the *jihadiya*.'

The heavy one shrugged and looked towards Kadaro with a cold gleam in his eye. 'I don't like soldiers.' His eyes were growing narrower, Kadaro noticed, as the night progressed.

'I used to look after the horses,' ventured Kadaro. The men fell silent to consider the implications of this fact. They chewed away, looking over from time to time. 'Did you see much fighting?' asked the tall one.

Kadaro nodded and jerked a thumb over his shoulder.

'We were attacked by the *ansar*.' He shook his head in dismay. 'They cut us to pieces.'

'Ha ha.' The stocky one, Khamis, laughed out loud. 'They cut them to pieces.' He nodded to his partner. 'I told you they would,' he crowed. 'I told you so.'

The other man was less impressed. 'Don't show our guest how foolish you are, Khamis. There's no difference between them, whether it's the sultan's boy-soldiers,' a wave in the direction of Kadaro, 'or those people of the Mahdi. You give any man the power to rule a land and it goes to his head.' He tapped his skull with a bone. 'They start thinking not only that they are in touch with God, but that they are God.'

Khamis stabbed the ground between his crossed legs with a stick. 'At least the Mahdi is one of our people.'

The tall one with the bent nose looked up. 'What is your name, boy?'

'Kadaro.'

'What kind of a name is that?' The men chuckled away. 'One of our people!' The tall one began to fill a pipe with tobacco. He reached into the fire and took a twig to light it. He puffed away contentedly for a time. 'I won't have anything to do with any of them. All I want is the freedom to come and go as I please. That's all a man needs; the freedom to go where he wants and do what he wishes.'

They sat in silence for a time. A piece of meat sputtered and shrivelled slowly on the fire. No one had the appetite to reach for it.

'What do you hunt?' asked Kadaro.

The two men looked at him, and then at one another. The taller one indicated the bundle of hides. 'Gazelle, kudu, snake. We go south for things like leopard, but only if there is a demand.'

The stocky one grinned and wriggled his toes. 'People like them for slippers.'

The tall one sighed wearily. 'Sometimes I get tired of all your talk,' he muttered. 'You remind me of an old woman in a marketplace.' On the ground beside his stretched-out legs was an ancient ornamented pistol. A dagger-sheath protruded from his sleeve above the elbow. Kadaro sat back against the tree and thought about his plans. By now, though, after the long day and the unaccustomed meat, he was feeling distinctly drowsy in the warmth from the fire, which spat and hissed, crackling like a conversation. His head began to feel very heavy and his thoughts began to repeat themselves.

Suddenly he was awake. The fire had gone out. Only a thin plume of damp smoke curling up through the spindly trees remained. The tall hunter was on his knees, the long brass barrel of the revolver aimed out at the surrounding shadow of trees. Kadaro began to move. The gun swung in his direction. The man held a finger to his lips and indicated that the boy should stay where he was. There was someone moving through the trees, drawing nearer; slowly, as though with caution. Everything was silent and still. The fire chose this moment to flare up suddenly as a piece of wood caught the flame. The burst of light outlined them all in the small clearing. 'Put it out!' someone hissed. Kadaro caught sight of the tall hunter's eyes. The stocky man cursed and moved over to pour a handful of sand on the fire. At the same time Hamilton Ellesworth stepped into the clearing. He was obviously not certain what was on going on, but he was carrying a pistol, which he waved carelessly about. A shot went off. Khamis, with a snarl, threw himself in the direction of Ellesworth, his knife drawn. A cloud of smoke filled the clearing. Kadaro lay on the

116

ground, his eyes closed and his hands over his ears. When he looked up the *affranji* was standing over him, pointing at him with his gun. Kadaro unfolded himself slowly, squirmed around on the ground. Dust and broken twigs slid down his neck. He worried for a moment about scorpions. He was going to die. He waved his hands in front of him. 'No, sir! Good boy Kadaro!' he gasped. 'Good boy, sir. Kadaro fetch boat.' He saw a flicker of a doubt in the *affranji*'s eyes. He turned around and began scrabbling frantically in the dust. 'Boat! Boat!' He drew in the sand. Ellesworth faltered. The barrel dropped. He bent down to examine the diagram. He said something which Kadaro did not grasp and gave a nod of his head. Kadaro fell backwards and lay there, gasping for air. He watched Ellesworth walk away. The girl, strangely silent, followed obediently behind.

The two hunters lay sprawled in the clearing. The stocky one had collapsed face down over the fire. His clothes were smouldering and wisps of smoke curled out from under him. The tall one lay spread-eagled, mouth and eyes open to the moths and ants. Kadaro stood up slowly, his legs cramped and shaking.

◆

In the distance he could hear the river shedding its skin, and the hiss and coil murmured a relentless rhythm in his head: *Shimal . . . Shimal.* The north awaited them.

PART 3

The Hour

17. The Gezira Plains, South of Khartoum, 1 September 1884

As far as the eye could see, the plain was dotted with shabby white tents and half-finished shelters. The dust of ten thousand hooves, of horses and camels, of mule-drawn gun-carriages and kitchen wagons and funeral processions and children and wives and orphans and slaves mingled in an endless progression of bereavement. When, Wad al Nejumi wondered to himself with a sigh, would it begin to resemble an army and not a gypsy camp? His day was a constant series of signals and acknowledgements. Messengers appeared breathlessly at his side, gasping out their despatches as though their lives and the fate of the world depended on them, as on occasion it might – but not today. The swagger of swollen-headed lieutenants was all too frequent for his humour. How many of them could he rely on when the cannons began to pound?

Wad al Nejumi had sent out a plea to every sheikh who had pledged allegiance to the Mahdi, to send him their best *amir*s and as many soldiers as they could muster. For five months now they had been assembling here on the soft belly of the plains south of the capital. Were they enough? He wandered restlessly about the camp, trying to take stock of what they had and where. He was trailed in his perpetual roving by an entourage of secretaries and attendants; scribes busily scribbling notes, taking down orders and despatches, intercepting newcomers. The men were not trained soldiers, they were *ansar*, followers; they knew nothing of discipline. They had a tendency to push their way forwards like a herd of goats, insisting on throwing their arms around him, or kissing him on both cheeks. Women thrust babies into his arms, so that they might be blessed. Al Nejumi was always too polite to refuse them and so he stood helplessly with a lost look on his face, resembling to all the world a simpleton who had been kicked in the head by a mule.

He roamed through the crowds, which were trying to make sense, just as he was, of how large and powerful they had become. They carted cannon trolleys this way and that. Young boys perched on the barrels like monkeys, throwing live shells from one to another like so many shiny watermelons. He had never seen such spirit. And yet it was his job to harness this energy and direct it. They had constructed mud ramparts connecting their outer defence posts along the northern perimeter, facing the besieged city. They brought together as many of the captured enemy soldiers as they could; being trained in the use of the cannon, to help with their maintenance and with the training of those who were to man the weapons when the time came.

Everywhere he went, Nejumi kept his eye open for anyone who could be of use. In the back of his mind there was a constant image of the terrible retribution which was surely being planned by the Turkish sultans and their infidel mercenaries. They would be back; no matter how long it took, they would return. And if it was true that Khartoum needed simply to be squeezed like a melon-seed for it to crack, then all well and good, but first they would have to press the outlying forts: at Omdurman across the river to the west, and at Halfaya to the north. And it was vital that they cut the telegraph line to Cairo. Nejumi was a strategist. He had the loyalty of the *ansar* and he knew which of his *amir*s to send in first. But even so, if rumours of an approaching enemy force were true, then there would be a long fight ahead of them. He could not desist at this stage. The sooner Khartoum fell, the safer they would be.

The northern lands were still in enemy hands and there was news of steamers trying to break their way through the river blockade with food supplies for the besieged town. The people of Khartoum were beginning to starve, according to reports which now arrived daily. News came by messengers in all guises: spies whose faces were familiar; soldiers who had simply dropped their rifles and run; old women who staggered half-insane into the camp. Nejumi would sit silently, listening to their reports. Each scrap of information was chewed carefully over in his mind before its value was decided. Each morsel had a particular place into which it seemed to fit. In truth, he trusted no one, since the very nature of such informers was unreliable. Nothing could be taken for granted. Even a small garrison could hold out long enough for reinforcements to arrive. No matter how weak they were, their guns were accurate and their men well trained.

But there was something more awaiting him on the other side of those walls of mud and straw, something that was nothing less than a legend, an *afreet* of the most cunning and dangerous kind. Nejumi knew that he was up against more than a worn-out, hungry, isolated garrison of soldiers. He was up against Gordon Pasha. The very mention of the name confounded him. He knew nothing of the man himself, saw only the traces of his strategy in the deployment of his forces. He knew him by rumour alone; as a fervent, hard and unpredictable man whose motives were a mystery.

From time to time Gordon would send out one of his beloved steamers, odd-looking with their armour devices and wooden buttresses along the gunwales as shields. His faithful slaves in their Turkish uniforms slid nervously upstream, letting off a few spare shots: rifle fire and the occasional small cannon round. He scared a few horses and usually drew more fire than he let loose, but he was marking his territory. It was a game. They circled each other like dogs, waiting for the time.

And time was a delicate coil. The longer Nejumi waited, the weaker the thin slave-soldiers behind the walls became. But one hour too long and the fragile wings would snap. Nejumi's task was simple: to find the natural keyhole in the defences, and turn it at precisely the right moment.

The supreme commander climbed on top of one of the captured Krupp cannon and watched a group of men practising a charge with spears and shields. They looked like a pack of unruly dogs yapping at each other's heels. His observations were disturbed by the arrival of a flock of commanders, chasing after favours as usual. He dropped to the ground and they followed.

'Sidi, have we decided the order of the attack?' they asked. 'How should we proceed, and which unit shall take the lead?'

Nejumi allowed himself a moment of indulgence. 'Why, mine of course,' he replied, stroking the thin wisps of his pointed beard. 'We will lead the attack. It is my responsibility, so it is only fitting that my unit should bear the brunt.'

Since the victory at Shaykan, Nejumi had realised that his role was

123

a difficult one. So much energy; so much power. He was afraid, afraid that all could be lost through a single oversight. The respect he saw in the eyes of those who now gazed upon him was comforting. For the moment at least, these men would follow him anywhere.

He turned now to address them. 'I want each of you to ensure that his men will be able to move swiftly and efficiently when the time for attack comes. It is of the utmost importance that we remain as one unit, with one mind,' he tapped his skull, 'not all marching in ten different directions at once.' There was a slight ripple of laughter.

'But everyone knows that the infidel Gordon has only a handful of loyal men by his side.'

Nejumi rounded on the man who had spoken and straightened up. He was in fact a tall man, though his loose-fitting clothing and easy physical grace concealed this most of the time. 'I know you mean well,' he said, so softly that his voice was barely audible over the cacophony of noise that surrounded them. 'An attacking army can fail because of one weak point, no matter how powerful the tip is; if the sides are weak it will collapse.' He looked round the assembled faces. 'The war does not end here,' he announced, raising his voice somewhat as he launched into his stride, 'as I'm sure you all know. The enemy are in Suakin and we will move there and onwards through the world, until we arrive in the holy lands and until every city from here to the Indian Ocean and beyond is once more restored to the ways of righteousness as revealed by the Prophet, may peace be upon him.'

The sermon over, he took a breath and turned to more practical matters. He pointed out towards the west. 'We hold this line, between the two rivers; from Mahi Bey's tree to Jirayf. I want shelters built for the women and children. I want to know about the trenches, all of them. Send your artists forwards and let them draw. I want detailed plans of the fortifications; how many men stand guard by day and also by night? How many gates; how heavily sealed? I want to be able to hold this line until the time comes. No one must get in or out of the town unless with our permission, understood?'

'How will we know when it is time?'

'God will make it known to us,' smiled Nejumi, with only a hint of mischief. He then turned and left without so much as a word.

A messenger appeared by his side and handed over a scroll. The scribe nearest grasped it and read aloud. The Mahdi was moving northwards on the western bank of the White Nile and would remain on that side, probably heading for Abu Saud where they would make camp. Nejumi told the runner to take back his confirmation. He strolled on through the crowd. A boy walking a goat went by, holding its hind legs and guiding it forwards like a cart. An old man who could hardly walk, assisted by his son, cheered and raised his spear jubilantly at the sight of his commander: 'Death to the infidels, victory is ours.' And Nejumi saw the face of the boy and trusted the doubt which he saw there more than a thousand salutes and assurances of victory. 'Take care of your father,' he said as he went on his way.

A group of men were examining one of the Nordenfeldt machine-guns with the assistance of a tall Shilluk man from the slave cadres captured at El Obeid. They stripped the weapon in the sand with dextrous skill and rebuilt it. The soldier was explaining how to load and fire. The first time he had seen Arabs listening to a former slave, Nejumi thought to himself. Yet another of the miracles of war. When they noticed the presence of the commander they began shuffling and moving aside, hands behind their backs; Nejumi stepped forwards and clapped the tall soldier on the back. 'Listen carefully to every detail this man gives you. Our victory depends on it,' he said to them.

◆

On the plain, dust mingled with the harsh sunlight. Camels moaned, tugging at their halters. Everything had suffered on the long journey here and now was the time to mend what could be repaired: tents, broken saddles, spears, slippers and rifles. Ncjumi found a group of children playing out the battle which still lay ahead of them all. They were arguing as to who should pretend to be Gordon, for the very name had come to symbolise all that is evil in the world. People told stories of the time when Gordon was sent out to patrol the land – how he would cross the desert at high speed almost like the shadow of a bird, to descend with the wrath of some white *jinn*. How he was hard and mean and came from a special tribe which the Turks employed to strike fear into their slaves. There was no doubt in Nejumi's mind that Gordon was only the closest link in a chain which stretched far away to the ends of the earth, to a power which was barely imaginable. Their fates were interwoven and it was at times like this that he wished the whole thing were over and done with. He wanted to know what lay at the other end of that chain.

The only person he could think of who could make any sense of what was happening was an odd fellow whom he had met some months ago now in the house of Sheikh Abbas in El Obeid: a scholar, who rumour had it was once a hair's breadth from being strung up as an apostate. He had studied all the ancient books and had travelled abroad for many years. But despite this he was a simple fellow who made no attempt to impress you with tedious narratives of journeys undertaken, exotic places visited and kings dined with. He had spoken in an unassuming fashion that nevertheless made a strange kind of sense. 'Whatever our opinion is,' Nejumi had said, 'not one of us at this moment in time can say that we would wish any harm to Muhammad Ahmad. The Mahdi is our talisman. He holds the entire country by a single thread. Without him, none of this would be possible.'

'But what of all the lives which are to be lost, of the blood which has been spilled and which is still to be spilled?'

'Such things do not concern us,' Nejumi replied. 'Every man has the right to be free. I believe that. Whatever his fate at birth. He can be rich or poor, but he has the right to be free. No man has the right to control another man and treat him as though he were a beast. This is the way the Turk has been treating all of us. And who will hold these people together when the devil is gone? Will the Mahdi still hold them in the palm of his hand?'

A familiar figure now came into view and Nejumi stopped to consider the sight of old Medani chasing after a small boy who was dodging under the wheels of the wagon, weaving a path between jugs and sacks and pots and pans. The boy wheeled and slid aside as the old man swung a switch at him.

'Hey, old man,' called Nejumi. 'Don't you recognise your commanding officer when you see him?'

The old cook, dusting himself down slowly, straightened up, gave a throw-away gesture and turned back to his wagon. Three men were busy laying out bricks in the sun to construct the new shelters. They looked on in awe at the way the old cook treated their *amir*. Nejumi, ignoring them, pulled his sword out from his waist and placed it to one side before sitting down on a sack of flour. 'Don't you have any of those biscuits left?' he asked with a sigh.

'Don't you have an army to lead?' retorted Medani, dropping a small sack in front of him. Nejumi smiled and stuck his hand in the sack. He chewed away contentedly for a time. 'I hear that Gordon eats chicken every night.'

'Hah,' laughed the cook, 'I think the ears of the noble *Amir al Umara* are growing a little deaf with age.' He pointed with a knife. 'Those are my kitchens he is eating in and I'll be very much obliged when you manage to get them back for me.'

The onlookers went slowly back to work, assured now that the old cook was not going to be hung or decapitated on the spot. Beside the fires that burned in the makeshift canteen carcasses were sliced and thrown into pots, vegetables were being cut up. Nejumi dusted the crumbs off his *jubba*. 'Tell me, old man, what is he like, this Gordon Pasha?'

Medani pulled a face and scratched his chin. He played with the end of his knife, testing it with his finger. 'He puts chickens to sleep, wanders round the yard every day swinging them under his arm to put them to sleep.' He adjusted the cap on his head. 'In fact on the whole the infidels are very like chickens in nature: always running around in a great hurry, pecking here and there. But,' he paused to consider the point, 'they pick up every last piece of grain.' The old cook nodded towards the dust and chaos of the camp. 'We fight like a flock of goats. Look at them, they run here and they run there, but they never listen to a word you tell them.'

Nejumi snorted. 'Maybe you'd like to exchange places for a few weeks, old man? It's lucky for you that I like your cooking. Abdullah al Nur or any of the other commanders would have sliced your head off for that kind of talk.'

Medani shrugged. He was eternally grateful to this man for having saved his life at Shaykan, and besides, he liked him. 'The Turks,' he explained, 'treated me well. And besides, an old head like mine is worth very little these days. It is the young ones who fight this war for you and God help us if we win because they will be too full of themselves and the world will end up just like before; run by fools who speak for the pleasure of hearing their own voices.' He began pushing dough out into thin sheets. 'The wise men will be those who keep their mouths shut; those that don't will be dead.' He glanced up at Nejumi, who looked away. 'Take care of yourself, son of Nejumi.'

Nejumi stood up and adjusted his clothing. He lifted his sword in its leather scabbard and looked out at the crowded, sun-beaten plain. 'Let us take this Khartoum first.'

Medani tapped his forehead. 'Khartoum is in the mind. It is not Khartoum which is the problem, but what lies beyond. The soldiers behind those walls are scared. They have nothing to eat but mules and the bones of skinny dogs. Soon they will be eating the gum from the trees, if not each other. If you take Khartoum then you must be ready to go onwards, for they will not let you be in peace after that. You don't know the country of the *affranji*. It is full of high mountains and rain that hits the skin like stone. We know nothing of them. God alone knows what brought them here.' He wagged a cautionary finger. 'You ask yourself, how many of these men will go on beyond Khartoum, up through the country to stand before the gates of Cairo demanding entry?'

'It is the will of God, old man. Didn't you know that?'

'I pray to my god and you pray to yours, isn't it like that?' the old cook continued. 'The rest is vanity.' He waved the knife menacingly. 'Now go back and fight your war, I have a kitchen to run.'

18. Sirdar Gordon Pasha,
The Palace, Khartoum

Upon catching sight of himself in the large, blotchy mirror that adorned the long hallway outside the waiting-room of the chief-of-staff, on a clear, cool morning in late August, with the breath of rains long past still dying on the innocent hyacinth scent that drifted in from the gardens beyond the yard (where the butcher boys scattered the feathers of pigeons like ancient kings distributing lotus petals), Captain Hamilton Ellesworth, putting a hand to his face, wondered whether the scars still showed in his eyes.

In the six months since his return to the relative haven of the besieged capital, he had tried to make sense of his experience. The other officers were keen to know what had happened to him in all those months he had been missing. All they drew from him was a blank look and a shake of the head as though to prove that it was indeed empty of knowledge.

On that terrible night when he ran ashore just to the south of the western fort, the soldiers had been about to arrest him along with the others. 'Don't you know who I am?' he had demanded over and over, marching in circles on the beach, shouting into their bewildered faces. None of the people he had known was left and it took some time before they located an old watchman who said he recognised him. 'What news of General Hicks?' was his next question to the sandy-haired young adjutant who had been sent to escort him to the barracks.

'Hicks, sir?' the soldier echoed blankly, as though reminded of a ghost.

Ellesworth stumbled through the town like a man from another age. It seemed to him that it was not he who had changed, but the world which he had left behind. The men walked with slow, dragging footsteps as though a curse had settled in the swampy air. He asked

129

about Spratling and eventually learnt that Spratling had died months ago. He then accused his guides of having murdered his adjutant. They threw the boy in prison; the girl simply vanished. Where, they all kept asking, had he been? What kind of a question was that? He had been trying to get back here, wasn't that enough?

'You have been missing for almost a year, sir. Everyone assumed you were killed in action.'

It occurred to him that perhaps they would have preferred him dead.

They gave him a bed in the infirmary and a beady-eyed man with one eyebrow locked in a permanently cocked position came to see him once a day. He would stare at Ellesworth for a long time without saying anything, or else he would sit and sing homecoming songs in Serbo-Croat to himself while holding Ellesworth's wrist. On occasion he was joined by an officer who stood and rocked on his heels and tut-tutted. 'Shows what can become of a civilised mind when it is forcibly exposed for long periods to the savage mentality.' The two surgeons would walk away deep in conversation. The rest of the ward was filled with drooling idiots, who talked to themselves and bounced imaginary children on their knees, or crawled on the floor barking like dogs. Some had head wounds with great swathes of bandages holding their skulls together, others suffered in different ways, screaming all night in pain. None of it bothered Ellesworth, for he, like each of them, was in his own world.

They sent an intelligence officer to him to try and ascertain all that he could. Whenever he set eyes on this guileless young fellow, Ellesworth would inevitably burst into tears. Perhaps it was because he was reminded of another young man from a lifetime ago. He had nothing of significance to say regarding the enemy's position and strength, and he could detect their suspicion. They believed that he had run away to hide his head in the sand and save his own skin. He lay awake night after night wishing to God he had perished alongside Hicks and the rest of the poor bastards.

The adjutant, a local man, entered the waiting-room, snapped his skinny heels together, saluted and told him that he was to go straight up. At that moment a fight broke out in the yard and everyone ran to watch. Ellesworth walked off alone and climbed the steps to the upper level of the *serail*.

The tops of the palm trees rustled in the breeze and through the open doorway and the window on the far side, he could see the river. The wide room was a scene of chaos. It took him a couple of moments to locate the *sirdar* stretched out on the long divan on the right-hand side of the room, one boot resting on the floor beside the sheathed sabre with its halyard and plumage and the other one draped over the padded arm like the long, slim form of a snake on a branch. From the window and the riverbank below Ellesworth could hear the chatter of birds and men.

Unsure as to what his next move should be, he crossed the room to the large teak desk. It was strewn with papers and half-empty cigarette tins. His eye was caught by something and he stooped to retrieve a sheet of paper which had drifted on the breeze to the floor. It was a diagram of a human heart, portrayed with the accuracy one might expect of a lecturer at a medical college. The heart contained a bullet and there were scrawled notes in pencil alongside describing how the projectile should be removed. Another sheet, also on the floor, showed a caricature of Gladstone, seated on a thunder box, out of which shouts for help were issuing. Ellesworth felt the corner of his mouth curling in distaste. There were other cartoons describing press hounds; an obscene one of Queen Victoria; various sketches of the area showing the enemy's placements and strength. A lot of question marks were dotted here and there.

On another scrap was a carefully penned piece starting with a quotation taken from the Bible: '*Cursed is the man that trusteth in man and maketh flesh his arm and whose heart departeth from the Lord (Jeremiah xvii.5), who seeks by any arrangement of forces or by exterior help to be relieved from the position we are in!!! With what heart can a man accept this, for with what heart can he make arrangements if he does not trust in their success!*'

A movement behind him made Ellesworth wheel round, hurriedly dropping the paper back on to the desk. A small red mouse was watching him from the top of the divan. It paused, quite confident of its surroundings, sniffed the air and then moved, with no particular hurry, along the spine. Ellesworth watched its progress, transfixed.

The mouse now drew up alongside the *sirdar* and dropped lightly on to his chest. It nibbled for a moment at the red tunic and then moved up, still sniffing, until it reached the *sirdar*'s face. Ellesworth waved his hand, hissed through his teeth. He picked up a piece of paper, screwed it into a ball and was preparing to launch it at the irreverent rodent, but hesitated. The mouse looked momentarily in his direction and then carried on nuzzling at the general's whiskers. Not wishing to wake the man, Ellesworth decided that the best way out of this predicament was the door. He was just about to move when, as though lifted from a spell, the sleeping man awoke.

The blue eyes flickered open and Ellesworth found himself face to face with the other most famous man in the country. General Charles George 'Chinese' Gordon yawned and stretched his arms above his head; then, noticing the mouse, he lifted it gently from his neck and placed it carefully on the back of the divan again. He sat up and rubbed his neck. 'Is it that time already, Stewart?'

'Sir? . . . no,' Ellesworth began, not quite sure where he should begin. 'I mean . . . I . . . it . . .' He clicked his heels resolutely and announced loudly, 'Captain Ellesworth reporting, sir.'

Gordon's eyes flickered in his direction, meeting his gaze for a fleeting moment, freezing him there, before wandering away. The general nodded now as though he understood. 'Oh, yes, . . . of course, Captain . . .' He paused again and for a long moment there was silence. The two men looked at one another wordlessly as though a thought had interposed itself between them before passing onwards to wherever such thoughts might go. 'Ellesworth.' He rolled the name around. 'What's your first name?'

'Hamilton.'

'Not much better,' decided the general. 'Let's stick with Ellesworth.' He rose to his feet, revealing that he was taller than Ellesworth. He had a crop of uneven straw-coloured hair and his face was lined and dusty. But it was the eyes which dominated the face, clear and unnaturally steady. Eyes lit up with the vision of a far-off city whose streets were silent, inhabited only by the smell of lost rains and the echo of footprints on cobblestones. The prospect of returning to London terrified him.

He crossed the room, stretching the sleep from his stiff shoulders.

Scrabbling among the debris on his desk, he found a tin of cigarettes that was half full. Without offering them to Ellesworth, who would have declined, he lit one.

'How did you get here, Ellesworth?'

'By boat, sir.' Ellesworth faltered momentarily. 'In the company of some locals I came across.'

'Initiative,' nodded Gordon. 'That's good.' He was still rooting through the papers on the desk as though he had mislaid something. 'I often wonder what it would be like to have been born a simple fisherman in these latitudes.'

'Fairly tedious, I would imagine, sir,' suggested Ellesworth, not realising until he had spoken that he had said the wrong thing.

'You've seen them at first hand Ellesworth,' continued Gordon Pasha. 'You must have learnt a good deal about them, the Arabs I mean. That's why I wanted to see you.' This last he added as though he had just made it up, which of course he had. He stretched his mouth into a smile. His eye went back to his desk and then after a moment he dismissed the matter of the mislaid paper with an irritated shake of the head. A feeling of uncertainty returned to Ellesworth and his eye lit on the thin sheaf of papers which he had placed upon the desk on his arrival in the room; his report had by now been sucked into the whirlpool of the table-top. It was inadequate, he realised suddenly. It contained nothing but long, rambling accounts of sunsets and walks in the moonlight. A shudder went through him as he recalled the number of inane conversations he had recorded between himself and Spratling, walking through the desert. What possible relevance could such trivia have? He was embarrassed. 'I – ' he stumbled, 'am composing a report at the present time . . . A full report which I will deliver as soon as possible.' His stammering brought the good Pasha's mind back to the mental state of the officer who stood before him. He would not press the matter of the report; with an idle wave of the hand he lit his third cigarette.

'I saw lights,' Ellesworth blurted out, suddenly feeling the need to offer something. He was reminded by the sketches on Gordon's desk of the town's defences.

The blue eyes shot in his direction and the straw-coloured eyebrows flew up. 'Lights?' The general was intrigued. 'Lights', he repeated, scrabbling for pen and paper. 'Torches? Flares, guns, camp fires, blazing cities, fireflies? What kind of lights, Captain?' The blue eyes were as penetrating as azure beams of light in a sunlit ocean corridor. The room began to spin and Ellesworth, sweating, shuffled over to a chair and indicated his need to sit down. The general nodded impatiently; Ellesworth collapsed into the seat.

'I was in a great hurry to get here, of course. Time seemed to be of the essence.'

'Time', observed Gordon, 'is the one thing we have plenty of. We have no food, no decent troops, no decent method of communicating with those damned intelligence officers at Halfa and their Mr Kitchener, and we are surrounded on all sides. Waiting, my dear captain, is our business.' An odd smile flitted across his face. 'In fact, one might say that it is our sacred duty to wait. We are just like them, you see, at the mercy of the Almighty's intricate plan.'

He made a clicking sound with his tongue and stubbed out his cigarette. 'Now, Ellesworth, where exactly were these lights?' He was sketching rivers and lines of fortifications from memory, adding little blotches of ink here and there for trees.

'I just remember light floating by in the dark, as though, well almost as though we were drifting out into the sky, out among the stars.' Gordon set down his pencil. To Ellesworth, the voice which was his seemed to be coming from far away, sounding hollow and filled with echo. He was dimly aware that the man opposite him was rising from his desk and striking a match. Sulphurous fumes filled the air and then the thick, earthy smell of dark tobacco. Ellesworth felt a sinking sensation in his belly, as though his life were slipping from his reach. His throat was dry. 'It was a long time ago,' he said, apologetically.

A curious look came over the other man's features. 'How long?'

'Six months.'

For a long while the general did not move. The light in his youthful face changed as though clouds were racing by. At length he moved to the window. 'You have been away a long time, Captain,' he said. Ellesworth could think of no reply.

They faced one another as though each of them were wondering the same thing, and Ellesworth found his mind tumbling back through the previous months, back to the moment almost a year ago when he had taken off in pursuit of the dervishes, and he realised that something inside him had changed. He realised too that Gordon was staring at him oddly and then he felt the tears that were rolling down his face. He lifted a hand as though to stem the flow, but more tears came. He was shaking and gasping for air. His chest felt constricted and painful.

The general came closer to Ellesworth. 'Captain,' he exhaled, blowing blue smoke into the air, 'I am sending a steamer down to Halfa. Lieutenant-Colonel Stewart will be in charge. I am recommending that you accompany him.'

'I thought all hands were needed here, sir,' Ellesworth whimpered.

But Gordon was now staring through the open window, down at the messy bank and the rows of fields that stretched away along the sides of the river where the weaver birds wheeled in dizzy curves. The *Abbas* was moored there, listing naturally to one side the way an old man leans his elbow on a table. Men wandered up and down the gangplank bearing cases and trunks. Absently, Gordon reached for his telescope and aimed it across the water towards the Northern Fort. Ellesworth had heard that the general spent most of the night up on the roof of the seraglio observing the enemy camp to the south and any possible movement of troops.

Without removing the telescope from his eyes as he scanned the horizon, Gordon said, 'They think they are up against a bunch of half-witted heathens, Captain. Savages and all that. They under-estimate as always the resources of these people.' He set down the telescope and turned. 'Have you ever read their holy book, the Koran, Captain?'

Ellesworth was slightly taken aback and unsure of the motive of such a question. 'I . . . well, I glanced at it once, sir. Very flowery, I thought.'

'Flowery?' Perplexity made the general look boyish. He reached for a volume that lay upon his desk: a copy of Sale's translation of the Koran. 'One has to understand this to understand that Mahomet was free of sin; indeed, they acknowledge that he erred. No Musselman will say that Jesus sinned. They are prepared to stand and fall by their own deeds. Mahomet holds no mediatorial office for them.' He dropped the book and stared piercingly at Ellesworth. 'The God of

the Muslims is our God, Ellesworth. What I would give for a battalion
of men as devoted as the Mahdi's.'

'Sir?'

'Do you believe in fate, Captain?'

Ellesworth did not reply. Gordon, seated again at his desk, looked
up when no answer was forthcoming.

'Lucky for you, don't you think, that you did not make it back to
General Hicks's side?' The eyes were cold and the smile was thin. The
good general was probing his man. 'Your skull would be in among
that pyramid of dead bones they built at Shaykan.'

'I should have died with honour,' mumbled Ellesworth. 'My duty
as an officer of the queen's army.'

Gordon rolled his eyes upwards. 'The queen's army,' he sighed.
'This has very little to do with the queen, wouldn't you say? This is a
dirty back-room squabble between like-minded brothers into which
we ... adventurers have been dragged.' He waved a hand to swat a
fly. 'That is how we will go down in history, Ellesworth: adventurers,
brigands, mercenaries ... bandits.'

The tone of the conversation was beginning to irritate Hamilton
Ellesworth. This man seemed to him insidious, devious – he could not
find quite the word. Gordon smiled perceptively. 'A man of reason, I
believe, a man of science. Plutarch's *The Parallel Lives*, Captain; have
you ever read it?' The answer was a shake of the head. 'Well, I believe
it is worth a thousand volumes of the Staff Officers' Handbook,
which you have no doubt read and memorised dutifully.' He lifted a
pencil and began sketching on a corner of a sheet of paper containing
logistics. 'It calls for self-sacrifice and that is what we need a little
more of around here. As far as self-sacrifice is concerned, the Muslims
are far ahead of the Roman Catholics and the Protestants.' He looked
up as a tall officer with sad eyes entered the room. Saluting in a
perfunctory manner, he threw himself down on the divan. The general
smiled. 'Ah, Stewart, what news?'

Stewart sighed. 'The *Towfikia* steamed down to the Mogran this
morning and then in the direction of Halfaya. They spotted two
runaway slaves on the beach who signalled to them. They pulled in to
take them up whereupon they were fired on. One man killed and two
wounded.'

Gordon sucked in his teeth, sounding a note of regret. 'They are getting their nerve up again,' he noted, carrying on with his sketching. 'Captain Ellesworth was just telling me of his exploits, Stewart. You know each other of course.'

Stewart looked weary. 'Captain Ellesworth was under my command when he was sent here two years ago.'

Gordon's eyes rolled as if he had been struck in the forehead. 'Of course,' he nodded, shooting Ellesworth a sly smile. 'You too are an intelligence man.' He spoke the words as if they were a pronouncement of guilt. Ellesworth had the impression that the *sirdar* regarded the Intelligence Corps as being lower than the low. Gordon struck a match. 'Ellesworth will be travelling downstream with you, Stewart, when you go.'

There was an awkwardness, an air of culpability. It occurred to Ellesworth that the two men had already discussed him. Stewart got to his feet and came over to shake Ellesworth by the hand, a firm, solid grip. 'Welcome aboard, Ellesworth. Delighted to have you along.' Ellesworth felt the creeping claws of paranoia reaching for him again.

'How are the preparations for departure coming along?'

Stewart wheeled towards Gordon. 'Seems that word has got around, every man and his dog has been pestering us for a spot.'

'Damn. Well, don't let us keep you. I'm sure you have a thousand things to see to.'

Stewart saluted briskly and was gone. Gordon followed as far as the doorway and called down over the veranda, 'Achmet. Tea, if you please.'

Ellesworth had been planning to make his excuses, but now realised he would be forced to remain seated and accept a cup of tea. Gordon smiled. 'Be good to get home, eh, Ellesworth?'

'I hadn't thought, sir.' He shifted in his seat.

'Old blighty. Back to cosy firesides and dark winter evenings, society dinners and all that rot.' Gordon sounded a bitter note.

'I had thought my place to be here, sir, the situation being so critical.'

A dry laugh escaped Gordon at this. 'Critical?' he repeated. 'Tell that to Gladstone and the rest of those pompous creatures in

137

Whitehall. The crucial moment went by them as they were drawing their rugs across their laps and sipping Madeira. "Khartoum?" "Steady on, old chap, you'll give yourself indigestion." "Who was it now? Oh yes, Gordon. Never did like the chap." "Quite, quite, but we ought to at least make some effort, don't you think?" "Now let's not be hasty. We ought to wait and see how the land lies." "Always thought he was a little off-beam. By the way, how's the wife?" etc., etc., *ad nauseam.*'

Ellesworth sat through this little performance open-mouthed. It had all the inventiveness and madness of some bizarre side-show at a country fair. The general moved this way and that, eyes rolling, hands flicking out spasmodically from his sides. Into the room came a flock of characters from a world away, irreverently massacred.

Silently, the shaven-headed Ahmad appeared, deposited the brass tray with the tea and slid noiselessly back through the door. The stoical look on the man's face made Ellesworth think of the absurdity of the situation in which this burlesque was being played out. The moment passed and Gordon slumped into an armchair; a deep silence descended on the room. When Gordon's voice returned it was restored to the calm, low tones of before. 'The critical moment,' he was saying, 'has passed us by, marked only by an embarrassed silence.' He gazed whimsically down at his boots. 'We are the silent point that marks the centre of man's morality.' He assumed the air of a man waging a single-handed fight against the powers of darkness which sought to wash him out with the tides of the century. 'Slatin has converted. I trusted that man like a son, and he has betrayed his own conscience. But I understand him better than he knows, for we are all so alone here.' The startled blue eyes flickered towards Ellesworth. 'But I will never forgive him. I have always known that this moment would come. Somewhere deep down inside my consciousness I have known that I would one day face the question of conviction of faith in a place as primordial as this, where the elements and mankind are at their wretched, most primitive worst . . . and utterly alone. This is how we come into the world and this is how we must take our leave.'

In the ebbing afternoon light, the river breeze turned softly through the corners of the room, caressing the smooth arms of the chairs as though preparing them for the pyre which was to come. Steam rose from the glasses of tea which sat untouched on the small table; Ellesworth thought again of making his excuses. He wanted to go back to the barracks to lie down and still this turmoil which spun in his head like a whirlpool, sucking him downwards.

General Charles George Gordon stood at the window. A shadow crossed the room and he made a startled sound. 'Look!' he cried. Ellesworth got shakily to his feet and moved towards the window. The general was pointing at the sky. 'Aren't they marvellous?' And Ellesworth watched as a cloud of bright soft puffs of eloquence swarmed overhead, trailing behind them the long mournful cry which cranes make. The flock winged their way effortlessly across the smudge of murky water, heading north, and vanished into a point in the aching sky. 'They are flying towards that fool Kitchener and his men who cannot understand a word I say and whose despatches are indecipherable.' Ellesworth watched the man with a fascination which made it impossible to tear his eyes away. The blue light of the sky filled those haunted eyes.

'So close,' Gordon whispered to himself. 'Just across that strip of dirty water. He's there.' He stepped away from the window, leaving Ellesworth alone. Down below on the muddy quayside, men were still ferrying fuel and supplies on to the low steamer. Smoke curled from the thin, dark funnel and copper drops spilled from the paddles. Firewood was packed in neat stacks. Men were talking to one another in loud, clear voices; somewhere someone was singing. End-pieces of conversations drifted up like snatches torn from a page of a book he would never be able to read.

'They would like to come and save me. I am more important than the battalion, than the country. A culture of celebrity has grown up around us. Words have lost their meaning and are used by the hacks of daily ragsheets to build their stuffed gods, like guys to be thrown upon the bonfire when the time comes. We live in a new age of idolatry. One feels a certain sympathy for Mohamet, who refused to allow a single portrait of himself to be painted. The Musselmen regard Christianity as a simplification. An ignorance owing to a lack of the complete facts as they were revealed by the final prophet. The complete facts including of course the language of the Arabs.' His tone rose and fell as his mind moved restlessly across tracts of information, like a man struggling, thought Ellesworth, to make sense of a world whose image had shattered in his hands.

'What they will not tolerate, however, is the worship of idols. Is that not an interesting paradox? The followers of the Mahdi are fighting to restore the true faith and we in our ignorance seek to defy them, when it is also true that we have lost our understanding of faith. Where do we go from here, Ellesworth?'

He moved around the room sipping lukewarm tea from his glass. There was no keeping pace with the progress of his thoughts.

'I really do believe that the Lord created animals for a purpose, putting us humans above them to remind us of that purpose. The Lord created himself in the image of man; the difference between us and Him being our sin. Our future happiness resides in being able to realise the fullness of His Godhead and our finite intelligence.' The *sirdar* shook his head. 'A depressing thought.' Nevertheless an inspiring one, obviously, since he set down his glass and sat down at the desk to begin scribbling his thoughts into a ledger which he retrieved from beneath a pile of papers and a revolver.

Ellesworth sat patiently, the tea untouched in his hand, unable to bring himself to move. Then Gordon stood up abruptly, throwing his pen down and reaching for his red *tarboosh* which he balanced on his head. He smiled and patted Ellesworth on the shoulder as he passed by. 'Liaise with Stewart about the departure. Now I must go and see to my chickens. One learns so much from them.'

Ellesworth sat staring at the shadows made on the wall by the tops of the palm trees swaying gently in the breeze.

19. Omdurman, The Mahdi's Camp, October 1884

The entire land was on the move. The caravan of followers and pilgrims stretched out over the landscape in a single curling line of humanity. Men, women and children, bearing their possessions wrapped in cloth, dragging mules and camels behind them, wandered north in search of hope. The precise whereabouts of the Mahdi himself were, as usual, shrouded in mystery. He came and went with the ease of a fluid spirit passing across the baked stone that lies beneath this desert like a shining diamond, giving renewed resonance to the words of the acclaimed warrior Abdel Rahman Wad al Nejumi: 'He is the soul and they the body. If God had not sent him then we would have to call on our poets to invent him.'

A small figure hurried through the hastily erected barriers of thorns, tents and flimsy shelters with his usual air of imperturbable distraction. The forces were collected in a camp on the western edge of the small village of Omdurman; this in turn reached down to touch the western bank of the river which arched northwards towards the distant sea. Hawi had slept badly and this morning was feeling his age. His limbs were stiff and his head ached as though he were becoming ill with fever. He prayed silently that this would not be so. With the coming together of so many people, sickness had spread from one party to another, paying no heed to loyalty or limitations.

He had been summoned by the Khalifa Abdullahi himself on this occasion. It was not the first time, and he feared it would not be the last. Since his days at El Obeid he had discovered that his reputation preceded him everywhere he went. The very same notoriety which in some quarters invited suspicion and ostracism had an enticing effect in others. The khalifa had insisted on meeting him and talking about his ideas. At first he suspected that this was simply a passing whim; but he found himself increasingly called upon to adjudicate or advise on one matter or another. This was no simple feat: the list of advisers and wise men was endless. What was more, the demands carried a price, for being in close confidence with one of the most powerful men in the Mahdi's camp meant that the wrong word could be very dangerous. He trod the line as carefully as he could, but it required every ounce of tact he could summon.

In the distance, cannons could be heard. Some said it was the artillery teams training, others that it was a tactic designed to frighten the enemy into running down the river to Egypt. They were near today and it seemed likely that it was part of the offensive against the fort at Omdurman where a small force was still holding out. That morning three men had been executed at dawn for spying. They lay upon the ground, in the sunlight, their heads covered with a black gauzy net of buzzing flies. Hawi hurried by, covering his mouth and nose with his scarf.

The khalifa's enclosure was circled by two concentric fences of thorny branches. Beyond the guards armed with spears and rifles were several tents housing servants, advisers and wives. With each passing day, new shelters appeared. The bodyguard, who were never alternated but lived right on their master's doorstep, recognised him and let him through. Hawi removed his slippers at the door of the large white tent which had once housed General Hicks, and stepped inside. The floor was covered with a fine wide carpet that must have weighed the equivalent of ten men. As his eyes crossed the room he found the pockmarked, stony features of the khalifa. They exchanged greetings curtly and Hawi felt, once again, the hands of constriction reaching for his throat. Over the past year or so he had discovered within himself a capacity for keeping his reactions carefully under check; actions that would once have caused him to lie awake at night wrestling with his conscience now aroused little feeling. He told himself it was a sign that he was growing in age, that the ferocity of youth was a flame which dwindled with the coming of wisdom.

The tent contained a small number of notables, who all stood to greet him. Abdullahi returned to his place and, as was his habit, asked Hawi to sit beside him. He sat, pushing aside worries about this favouritism, which he feared would one day have a price attached to it. To his left was a thin man whose face seemed to be made all of bones, angular and wooden in expression. He apparently understood little of what was being said, and it later became clear that he was deaf. He was a spiritual healer of some kind sent by Makk Adem of the *Taqali* kingdom in the Nuba mountains. From time to time he would mutter the same verse of the Koran as though this were the answer to everything. In fact it became clear to Hawi that everyone in attendance was in some way or another an authority on matters of the spirit. The khalifa beamed broadly and called for breakfast to be served. Bowls of food were shepherded in: roasted meat and hills of rice as well as *assida* and *gorassa*, baskets of boiled eggs, onions and beans, fried aubergine and *bamia*. The others rolled up their sleeves and set to work, while Hawi sat and chewed idly on a few dates. There were tense nods and grunts as they ate. Never, thought Hawi, had so many superstitious people been brought together at one time. The story that Abdullahi's father was himself a renowned seer and visionary of great repute among the *Ta'aisha* was a cause for some controversy, since there was a thin line between superstition and paganism.

The khalifa was busy trying to engage his guests in chat, displaying his considerable social talents. 'Abdel Latif is a well known man of vision. He has assisted over many difficult years in predicting the best time for planting crops and also for a number of hunting raids, isn't that so?' There was some polite laughter, as those who had been raided were probably present amongst this motley collection of spell-casters and readers of coffee-dregs. The khalifa reached for a chicken leg and pointed. 'Over here we have our brother Idris, the most celebrated Idris I might say, who has spent many years under the tutelage of the *Kadirriya* school in Baghdad.' Idris was a small, pale man with the shaved eyebrows and eyes of a salamander. On his head was balanced the largest *tarboosh* anyone had ever seen. Beside him was a muscular, dark man whose hair was buttered into long, tangled locks of a most outrageous kind. He wore a waistcoat of leopard-skin and carried a satchel made of worn, shiny leather out of which a small, white-faced monkey would poke its head from time to time to receive some morsel of food, which it would then gnaw furiously with short, sharp teeth. The khalifa overlooked this man, having obviously forgotten who he was or where he came from. The silence only increased the mystery, but someone later told Hawi that he was a man of incredible powers from the marshes in the south. He could transform himself into a hawk, could walk upon water and had been known to bring the dead back to life. He contributed little to the discussion, since someone had forgotten to provide him with a translator and he could speak very little Arabic.

But the khalifa, in his element as the showman in these conditions, had now reached Hawi in his round of introductions. 'Some of you might remember him from the time fifteen years ago when he gained notoriety for his radical views on reforming our great religion. I believe his thoughts almost cost him his life at one stage.' A chuckle of laughter circulated, leaving Hawi with a tightly forced smile on his face. The khalifa regarded the heap of rice in front of him. 'He did not agree with certain aspects of our *sharia* law, I believe.' He looked round the assembled faces. 'And yet who can say that our tough but effective laws have not held the peace for thirteen hundred years since the time of our great prophet Muhammad, may the blessings of the Lord be upon him.' He proceeded to deliver a long and badly formulated lecture on the merits of corporal punishment and the general history of religion, which brought tears of boredom to the captive audience. 'But, in the end, as a sign of the generosity of the noble cause to which we are committed, Hawi is here because he represents a wealth of knowledge and he argues with great appetite.' A big paw clapped Hawi on the shoulder. One could not help being charmed by the khalifa's sense of humour. It was also clear that, being an astute man, he had decided that it was important to pander to peripheral elements of the campaign and had done so by inviting all their wise men to a council. Almost as if to underline this point, the sufi salamander raised his chin and asked in the impeccable language of the ancients, 'Sire, what, might I ask, is the purpose of bringing us all together for this fine meeting?'

Abdullahi tossed the chicken bone to the floor and looked round the faces assembled before him. He leaned forwards and everyone stopped chewing. 'As you are no doubt aware, we are on the verge of clearing the Turkish dogs out of this land once and for all. Let the world know that we will not be slaves to unbelievers who wish to rule us from across the seas. We will not dance to the pagan tunes of distant horns. The divine mission of our gracious Mahdi ensures our victory, may God bless him and all who walk with him.'

There was a muttered consensus on this point. The Khalifa Abdullahi raised a stubby finger and pointed it at the canvas above their heads. 'Let no man say he is more loyal to the Mahdi than myself. He is the guide. He is the spirit of our movement, but it falls to my humble self to deal with the practical matter of ensuring our military success. The Mahdi has said there need be no mourning for those who fall in battle and we all know that this is true, for they proceed to the greatest glory ever achievable by a man. They ascend with honour to the gardens of paradise. We must rejoice in their passing.' He managed to work himself into such a fervour that he quite lost his direction.

A plump sheikh on the far side of the Persian carpet took this moment to promote himself by raising a finger. 'Sire,' he said, interrupting the expectant silence. 'There is no one here who would doubt this matter of the martyrdom of the *ansar*, but the question remains of how we can help, with our humble wisdom and knowledge.' He was trying to make light of all this with a broad smile and a sideways rolling of the head which threatened to dislodge the clumsily wound *imma*. 'None of us would dispute the light which our noble Mahdi has spread across the land and indeed the world, but the guidance which is sent to our Mahdi from the Prophet, may peace be with Him,' his face became serious now as he was beginning to tread on delicate ground and was moving dangerously close to actually saying what he thought, 'is in all ways complete and divine.' He spread his hands out wide, opting once again for the safest course. 'What can we mere mortals add to this?'

The khalifa was chewing a handful of peanuts and took his time, much to the sheikh's discomfort, before answering. 'What you say is true,' he nodded finally, drawing a sigh of relief from the plump figure across the room. 'But our enemy is a cunning beast and we must be on our guard. Each of you is in his own way an expert on matters of a particular region. You are gifted with the special wisdom of your peoples who are now united under the banners of the Mahdi, may God bless him.' Abdullahi paused, thoughtfully gazing down at his hands. 'My father too was like you,' he said, and then lifting his eyes, his face broadened into a smile and he stretched out his arms. 'Come to me with your visions, your dreams and premonitions. Good or bad. This is a special time and the whole world is alight with the mission at hand. We must be alert for any sign whatsoever.'

And Hawi reflected that his initial thinking had been correct: the khalifa, beneath his jovial manner and his apparent recklessness, was a cautious man and a shrewd strategist. He had invited these men here knowing that they were close to the individuals who ruled the various factions in the Mahdi's forces. Nothing was more crucial at this time than their solidarity. They must all be made to feel that their part in the fight was vital and that they were respected. The only exception to this was himself; he had no sway over the wielding of power.

The rest of the meeting consisted of repeated pledges of loyalty with each man doing his best to outdo the others present. They all wanted to be at the head of the assault on Khartoum which was being planned at that moment by the formidable Nejumi.

When the meeting was over and the guests were making their exit, the khalifa signalled for Hawi to stay behind. Once they were alone, Abdullahi began to talk about a speech the Mahdi had made to a group of soldiers camped at Shatt some months previously. 'A fine speaker,' he was saying, 'whose words are whispered through his soul by the angels and the Prophet himself. But on a parade-ground in front of a thousand men, his words, though true, do not carry the weight they should. The men cannot hear the fine details that illuminate the thread.' He spat. 'They are ignorant sons of farmers for the most part. Herders like myself.' He laughed and thumped his chest. Hawi knew that he was witnessing yet another of the khalifa's acts. 'They need only to hear words of encouragement, something simple.'

'But surely it is encouragement for them to see the beloved Mahdi?' Hawi pointed out deftly.

The khalifa nodded, the small eyes moving round carefully, one minute staring at some spot on the sheepskin upon which he sat and the next fixing al Hawi in the way that a hawk fixes his prey. 'You are the only one of these wise men whom I would trust with my life,' he said quietly. 'You know why?'

Hawi shook his head slowly.

The khalifa gave a deep belly-laugh. He rested a hand on Hawi's arm. 'I will tell you what you do when you think there is a snake about.' His eyes glittered like wet stones. 'You keep the herd on the open ground, away from the grass, so that you can see it.' He paused, falling silent to study Hawi carefully. 'Many have said that you should have ended your days at the end of that rope. You still have many enemies, my friend.' He winked conspiratorially. 'That is why I know I can trust you.'

Hawi decided that boldness was called for. 'A man who gets through life without making enemies can hardly be said to have had any impact on the world. Muhammad himself, may the peace of God preserve him and keep him, made many enemies.'

The khalifa frowned. 'Do you say these things because you believe them, or simply to hear the sound of your own voice?' He shook his head. 'Never mind that now. Tell me, did you visit the prisoners as I asked you?'

Hawi nodded. 'I did, sire.'

'And?'

'They are in a poor condition. Their spirits are broken.'

The khalifa clicked his tongue impatiently. 'They have not seen the light of God yet.'

'They cannot see beyond their hardship,' explained Hawi, who had been shocked to see the state in which the prisoners were being kept. They were dirty and unwashed. They took no interest in their appearance. He was most concerned with the fate of the *affranji*, as the khalifa had asked him to pay special attention to the Europeans.

'Why do you suppose they persist in denying the true faith?'

Hawi thought for a moment. He had the odd sense that in some way Abdullahi admired his stubbornness. For all the accusations of brutality and merciless cruelty, Hawi had the idea that there resided in this man a respect for learning. On good days Hawi drew solace from this, from the idea that something truly worthwhile might emerge from this chaos and destruction. On bad days he saw differently.

'I think, sire, that they are afraid, as all men are afraid when faced with a truth whose fact is so awesome and undeniable that it requires

147

the abandonment of everything. It requires strength and courage to admit that one has lived one's life on a lie, or at the very least, a misunderstanding.'

The khalifa was amused by this. He slapped his thigh and chuckled. 'You are indeed a man of many talents. You speak with the silvery tongue. Wisdom drips like honey from your words.' A good day, reflected Hawi. But then came the riposte. The burly man's eyes narrowed. 'I fear, however, that you seek to deflect me from the true path of your thoughts, for it is obvious even to a simple herder like myself that what they live in is not despair, but hope; hope that somehow they will be released by the forces of the infidel who even at this moment are seeking to summon up an army to avenge their dead. This is no secret.'

The khalifa dismissed Hawi but asked him to return that afternoon. 'I want to see these wretched creatures myself. You will go with me.'

Going anywhere with the khalifa was never a simple matter. The personal entourage of bodyguards and scribes and secretaries trailed along behind as they made their way through the swell of soldiers and camp followers, past the half-finished shanties and the piles of belongings and children and beasts. There was laughter and shouting. A crowd of small boys attached themselves to the party – running alongside, jumping into the air, cheering. Mothers dragged small children out of the way. Scrawny dogs scampered beneath shelters of reed mats and palm leaves.

The prisoners were kept by a large mimosa tree which overhung a shallow embankment. A breeze from the river rustled the leaves above their heads. The prisoners sat or lay on the ground, their hands and feet shackled with strong chains and manacles.

The guards came to their feet as the procession approached and moved swiftly among the prisoners, prodding them with rifles and spears.

'On your feet, infidels,' chuckled the khalifa. 'Your master is before you.' He strode about, hands clasped behind his back like a statesman inspecting his troops.

The prisoners were mostly priests, religious people who had travelled here to preach Christianity. They had been picked up along the way in the remote towns where they had settled. A thin, bowed figure crept forwards. The khalifa ignored him at first and then, turning, he beckoned him. The figure, his back bent like a crab, came scuttling forward. His eyes, bulging from their sockets, darted left and right; he could hardly stand still.

'Abdel Kader,' the khalifa greeted the man drily by his adopted name. 'No doubt missing your governor's quarters in Darfur?'

'Sire,' replied the man, bowing his head, 'I beg of you one more chance to serve. I can write to Gordon and convince him to surrender.'

The khalifa scratched his belly. 'You still consider us simple-minded fools. You have tried once and he refused to reply; that is his affair and yours. You will not accept that we know what we are talking about when we speak of God.'

'Sire,' stammered the frail Austrian. 'I have sworn my allegiance to God. You know this.'

'God knows all things and sees all things.' The pockmarked face shuddered as Abdullahi leaned closer. 'He can see into your heart when you lie,' he whispered.

Bowing even deeper, Rudolph Slatin withdrew a pace. A guard came forward and spoke: one of the prisoners had requested to see him. Abdullahi beamed in Hawi's direction. 'You see, Hawi, how the fleas jump when I step on to their blanket?' He motioned and the prisoner in question was brought forward. His *jubba* was torn and stained. He could hardly stand.

'What is your name?' asked the khalifa. The man was swaying backwards and forwards like a stick of cane in the wind, mumbling something, his eyes on the ground. The khalifa leaned forwards and snapped, 'What does he say?'

Hawi stepped closer; the stench of the man made his stomach turn. He listened to the harsh rasping: 'Sh . . . Sh . . . er . . . w . . .' Hawi stepped back and Slatin was called forward again. 'This man wants to say something,' the khalifa said, as the swaying man collapsed into a heap on the ground. 'Tell me what it is.'

Hawi leaned forward to hear as Slatin crouched down beside the figure and tried to coax some life out of him. Hawi had heard the language of the French spoken in Cairo.

'Perhaps with some water?' Slatin looked up hopefully. The Khalifa Abdullahi nodded his consent and one of the guards soon returned with a jug. They helped tip some of its contents over the man's mouth. Some of it must have gone down, since he soon began spluttering and coughing.

Abdullahi spat on the ground. 'I don't trust any of these people,' he announced disdainfully.

Hawi nodded his tacit agreement. The man was now retching and clawing the ground. He managed to soil the foot of one of the guards, who then began kicking him savagely. Hawi reached out a hand to restrain him. 'He will die if you continue,' he said simply.

The man, with a look at the khalifa, stepped sharply back, saying, 'Apologies, sire.'

Slatin was bent over the fallen man. 'Speak now, man, for your life depends on it.' He then rose and crossed to the khalifa. 'Sire,' he said, 'this man would indeed like to say something.' A look of boredom lifted from Abdullahi Muhammad Adem's face and he stepped forwards. Slatin helped the fallen man to his feet and together they hobbled closer to the khalifa.

'What does he say?'

Slatin translated. 'He says that he is the envoy of the queen of the *Inglisi*, Queen Victoria, and that the queen would be very willing to bow down before the might of the Mahdi. He would be willing to carry a message to her from the Mahdi,' Slatin sighed, obviously finding it hard going, 'and he feels that she would listen to reason.'

The khalifa was amused. 'This dog knows the queen of England?' he roared. 'He would speak on her behalf?' He stepped closer and pulled the man up by the scruff of his neck until their faces were touching. 'God sees into the hearts of those who profess belief but do not feel it.' He turned to the guard and told him to give the man two hundred lashes of the *courbaj*. 'See if he changes his story.'

Hawi found himself moving. 'Sire,' he gasped, hardly aware that he was speaking. 'Sire, this man will not last two hundred lashes.' He spoke low and urgently, trying not to draw attention to the nature of their conversation. 'If he is lying, then he will find his fate, but if you give him a chance to recover, then he will see that compassion is the greatest strength of the faithful.'

With a look of perplexity, Abdullahi stood for a long moment staring at Hawi. 'You are a strange bird,' he pronounced finally. He snapped his fingers at the guard. 'Give them all a good meal and fresh clothes,' he announced loudly. 'Guard yourself well,' he whispered in Hawi's ear. 'If you ever cross me again in public, I will have your head.' And with that he walked out of the enclosure.

Hawi stood rooted to the spot, realising only now that his legs were shaking. He looked down at the wretched figure of Sherwood Louth, who was unaware that his fate had been changed by this man, and he muttered to himself, 'God help us all.'

20. Khartoum, The White Nile Defences, 25/26 January 1885

A lone white owl swoops down over the river. The stars are droplets of molten glass squeezed from a handful of dirty night – a million demented fragments. Far away, the elephants are sleeping and the rain has stopped. The swollen river begins quietly to subside, and as it does so the moon picks out a path that glitters and winks, illuminating a way through trenches now filled up with mud that beckons like warm flesh.

The haunted soldiers sleep now. Their bellies are swollen like drums and ache from the gum pellets, sack-cloth and ashes on which they have been feeding – washed down with handfuls of earth and palm bark and cockroaches; bars of carbolic soap; old wood; thorn berries; leaves of any description. They even chewed the leather bindings of their beds. They sleep on, dead to the world, dead to their hunger, dead too to the sound of bare feet creeping through the defences. Across the river silt they come now: singly, in pairs, in large disorderly groups, pushing and shoving to be at the front, breathing heavily from the exertion of uttering a thousand prayers. With lucky *hijab* charms clutched between their teeth and guns covered in the inky scrawl of holy scripture. With swords and spears; ancient ostrich rifles; shields made of rhinoceros hide. Bearing banners, scars and patches, they come silently; and they look around them as they go for a glimpse of an angel circling overhead or a rider on a white horse floating on the horizon. They hear only the cry of the owl which tells them they are not alone as they slither and slide, sinking even now up to their ankles, to their knees in the clay-like mud that splutters and coughs like some huge, slumbering ancient beast. Men are prone to vanish without warning. Others fall aside, screaming in pain as the caltrop teeth bite into their feet, slicing through leather soles and flesh, crippling horses and men alike, without distinction. They are not flesh, but spirit; not bone, but belief. And so, like an unbroken thought they come; in an endless stream that trails back southwards, following the riddle of the river to its very source.

Fathers call to their sons on this dark night, fearful of the sacrifice which the task ahead of them might demand. When the Hour comes the thunderbolts will increase and the rain will destroy all dwellings except for the most humble tents. And the sun will rise in the west and earthquakes will rock the world. This is how we shall know the Hour. People will act like locusts, devouring the weak, until the Hour comes.

The buzz of wings grows louder and harder. A machine-gun stammers in the distance as the first blows are exchanged. Spears are driven through midriffs and tunics, dissecting viscera and filling the air with cloying blood. Sword-blades sing, slicing through arteries as sweetly as if through sugarcane. Livers are ruptured, lungs perforated, nerves severed. This is how life vanishes – swallowing itself, folding itself up in the swollen palm of the damp, glistening plain.

The horses come on, ragged flags and tassels fluttering, grinding their teeth at the bit. With muscles straining and eyes bulging they charge onwards. The howls of their riders are not for this world, but in anticipation of the next. They are here to cleanse the world. They are the ungrateful orphans poised to cut the bonds imposed by this unholy adoption.

What was a planned military strategy becomes a horde of screaming men and boys running rabid through the streets, eyes wide and hands outstretched, striking anything that moves. They are possessed by the spirits of the dead and departed, and of those who shall die tonight: the souls of all the sons and daughters, mothers and wives who have died or been carried away by the terror of the sultan, of the khedive, of the *sirdar*. There, the magnificent serail now lies before you; come running. The gates are open. The guards have fled. There is a light burning beneath the cracked grey bell of the dawn and they know who must be hovering like a firefly around that glow, and so they cross the lawn like thieves, tip-toeing into the cave of the *jinn*. They pass the place where the chickens, whose empty cages now stand open, once lived; past the place where the tread of peacocks can still be discerned if one listens carefully; past the long, pale scythes of cactus and the paper-thin bougainvillaea, the guava and the *neem* trees, whose leaves tremble and blow; past the pods of carob fruits and through the twisted whorls of unripe tamarind, until they reach the foot of the stone staircase which leads up to the first-floor veranda, and here, here they pause to glance at the faces of their companions.

They look at one another and they see farmers and herdsmen and traders and simple people. This is who we are, they think. This is what we have done. We have come from places far beyond the imaginings of such fine palaces; places rarely seen and never heard. We have come to stake our claim.

But in that instant a voice comes from above. It is a voice they know. It comes from beyond the walls constructed to keep them out, beyond the gardens and the guards. It comes from within and it is the same voice which gave them every stillborn child, every sickly goat, every drop of fever, every stony year, every lost son or brother fallen in battle, every league walked; this is the voice which defines and confines them. And so they rise as one to smash the reflection in that warped glass, knowing that they have no choice; that choice was taken from them before they were born, before they were named. They take the stairs in one headlong rush. There in the smoky glow of oil-lamps and tobacco, a lizard is perched halfway up the wall, motionless.

The figure in white is standing, calm and somewhat bemused, as they clamber over one another to reach the door. It is as though he has been expecting them for months, which indeed he has. He too recognises this moment for it is also his. He raises a hand awkwardly, absurdly even – whether in command or in greeting it is not clear. He asks them, demands of them, their leader. But his words are muffled. Dust fills his mouth and their ears. He makes as if to turn away, with what appears to be a gesture of weariness. They watch him, their weapons hanging limply by their sides. This is the man whom they have feared for so long? This is the evil coil lurking at the heart of the beast? They watch with amazement as he strolls away from them down the veranda. The world is silent. The palms no longer sway in the soft breeze. Then one man steps forwards, recalling the anger which brought them here; two others join him. They rush together and thrust their spears forwards. They drag the groaning, dying man across the stones in a frenzy of anger and disgust and they roll him down the stairs to fall in a heap at the feet of the others, who are waiting.

Dark wings pass through the trees and stillness descends on them as they peer in wonder at this odd rag of a man who has been hurting them for so long. And through the holes made by the spears entering his body, life now escapes with a hiss.

Away across the river, in that very instant, a shiver goes through Muhammad Ahmad al Mahdi where he sits awaiting news, and the smile that so many have seen gracing his face disappears. He blinks his eyes as though in a dream, and catching a glimpse of a white owl flitting by through the trees he knows, as the shadow crosses his heart, that it is over.

21. Khartoum,
26 January 1885

In the dusk, hooded figures are busy throwing bodies on a pyre. Their eyes are dull with fatigue. They ache from the heat and the stench. The fire grows and the wood crackles, timbers from houses fallen down, carts tipped on their sides. The town is dotted with such fires, for those who died defending it were infidels and are not to be buried facing Mecca. The men do not look up as a thin, dark figure leading an ebony horse moves slowly by. Without his entourage and his flags one would have difficulty recognising the *Amir al Umara*. But his orders have been heard and the town is being methodically cleared, house by house, street by street. Women are rounded up in one place and wealth in another. Any food is delivered to the military barracks.

◆

Nejumi's face was drawn and weary, though things had gone astoundingly well. They had been helped by recent floods which had washed away the fortifications on the south-western flank of the town. Once inside, they had met little resistance. After months of preparing for the worst it was something of an anticlimax: in many places the troops defending the city had even started sewing patches on to their clothes in readiness for surrender. But this was not his town, and for him the victory had a hollow ring. It was as though the town contained an evil which contaminated all who entered her.

As he walked, giving orders here and there, a large flock of soldiers taken prisoner filed by. They were in a pitiful condition, their calves swollen from eating gum from the trees. It was ironic how much food they had discovered hidden in the walls or holes in the ground. Food concealed by merchants and traders, stored away in the homes of public servants as if they had no idea how serious their predicament was. 'What kind of society is it that lives in plenty while those defending it are starving in the streets?' he wondered.

A messenger arrived at his side, having looked for him throughout the town. Nejumi made him wait while he questioned a gang of young *ansar* leading a prisoner in chains. 'Where are you taking him?' The boys looked nonplussed, as though the question had never occurred to them. 'What did you do?' Nejumi asked the man, who stood with his head bowed and his hands tied behind his back. 'I'm a carpenter,' said the man simply. Nejumi addressed the boys: 'All craftsmen and anyone of any use to us at all is to be taken out of the town to the camp. Take this man there and get him some food if he is hungry.'

The messenger stepped forward and Nejumi nodded for him to read the despatch. The Mahdi would wait for his word before crossing the river. He was eager to visit the grave where his mother was buried. He would enter the town in style when everything was under control. Nejumi gave his agreement and sent the messenger on his way.

Moving in the direction of the river, he paused for a moment to examine some fine houses. The war, he reminded himself, was not over yet. The relief expedition from Cairo was less than a week away. They must learn to fire the cannon accurately in order to hold the town.

A large man with a moustache was standing in the street shouting to a group of men. Nejumi greeted him and asked for a report. There was little trouble in this sector, the sturdy figure announced. A sack of jewels and gold had been found down a well, and several stashes of food. He laughed. The funny thing was, he said, that the men had found a cupboard full of bread and would eat it only with a little thin oil, aspiring to the asceticism of their beloved Mahdi. He had not witnessed greed, even among men who, he knew for a fact, had robbed their own grandmothers.

'He is the soul,' repeated Nejumi, dully, 'and they the body.' The big man beamed and clapped the supreme commander heartily on the back before realising his mistake and muttering apologies. Nejumi walked on, murmuring to himself, 'You live long and you see much.'

Presently he reached the open gateway of the governor-general's former residence. He had often imagined what this moment would be like, seen himself charging towards the serail with sword lifted above his head and a thousand screaming horsemen behind him, cotton billowing in the wind. He smiled to himself. This simple entrance in the company of just his own horse was far more fitting.

The garden was a sight to behold. Leaving the horse to nibble the grass, Nejumi began clambering up the branches of a sturdy guava tree whose fruit swayed amongst the yellow-green leaves. Like a mischievous child he answered their call, balancing with his legs and jumping for branches until he was high up in the dizzy sway of dancing pods. The exertion made him laugh. He sat down to catch his breath, clinging to a branch overhead. His hands were sore from the rippled wood. He bit into the first fruit and a sour taste filled his mouth. Congratulating himself on his luck, he chewed contentedly for a while. Then he began stuffing the fruits into the corners of his garments and was about to make his descent when a voice called up: 'I must have heard it wrong, but I thought the *amir* had made it clear that any man caught looting risked death.'

Nejumi dropped to the ground beside Medani and handed him a couple of guava. 'You are not wrong, old man, but in this particular case I see fit to clear myself of blame.'

The old cook gave a wide yawn. 'I hear the fiery gates of *Jehenum* opening.'

'*Jehenum*,' snorted Nejumi, 'is always with us.' He nodded towards the remains of the building before them. 'You came perhaps to see your old home?'

Medani waved a hand for silence. 'Not so loud,' he said, looking over his shoulder. Some men were carrying sacks out of the palace stores. Everything that could be lifted was being moved. Two men were carrying a long divan down the stairs. Nejumi called out, stepping away from the trees. 'Where are you taking that?' The men looked at him and then at one another as if to ask, taking what? Nejumi indicated with his hand. 'We don't need that kind of thing. Don't waste your time with it. Look for anything useful: maps, papers and so forth, not furniture.' The two men started back up the steps.

Carefully avoiding a pool of congealed blood, Nejumi ascended the steps. A gentle breeze came through the tall trees and brushed along the veranda. He walked the length of the house and then passed through the wide double-doors. This, then, was where their fate had been discussed, where everything had been decided. Papers stirred in the breeze.

Everything had been ripped to pieces: the paintings on the walls slashed, the table turned upside down, lamps broken. A small mouse crept through the debris, pausing here and there to sniff for clues as to which direction it should take. Lifting it up carefully, Nejumi crossed the room to the window that opened on to the river. Medani had followed him silently and now stood by the door, surveying the destruction. He shook his head. The last time he had seen this room the world had been turning in a different direction. 'May God guide us,' he muttered to himself.

'They never even knew we were out there,' Nejumi murmured.

Something down below in the dark green trees caught his eye. He turned and dashed through the room, dropping the alarmed mouse in his haste. Coming down the stairs, he took the arched corridor which led to the river. A group of ten or so men stood beside a shapeless lump of meat lying in the mud. Two of them had been kicking it, turning it over with each blow, while the others looked on. Nejumi strode into the middle of the group.

'Whose idea was this?' he demanded. The hardened faces stared sullenly back. 'You mean you do this without an idea why?' Still no response. Nejumi tried to speak calmly, to keep his voice even, but his hand lay on the hilt of his sword and they knew that he was ready to use it. 'The difference,' he said, 'between a man and a dog, is that a dog thinks that he has no responsibility for what he does or does not do. A man knows differently.' The men remained silent. He looked round the group with loathing. 'Get back to wherever you are supposed to be. If I ever see one of you again, I will kill you.' The men vanished through the trees without a word.

Medani came forward from the wall of the scrail, where he had been standing to watch. 'It is a bad business,' he said mournfully. 'It will bring evil upon us.'

Nejumi looked down at the remains of the body at his feet. 'The Mahdi told me to bring him alive.'

'He was not a bad man,' the old cook muttered, looking away.

'This is war, old man.' Nejumi spat on the ground and flexed his shoulders. 'Now come on and help me bury him quickly.'

Together they carried the corpse some way through the trees to a cool, open place. They dug, breaking the ground with Nejumi's sword and using their hands and fingers until they had clawed a deep hole in the earth. They threw the battered corpse into the hole and covered it well.

'Not a word of this, old man, not to a soul.'

They walked back round and through the garden. The cook looked back at the veranda, where he had walked so many times. 'And what of this place?' he asked. 'What will happen to it?'

Nejumi shrugged. 'We must burn it to the ground.' He climbed on to his horse. 'This is their place, old man, the desert is ours.'

◆

The town fades into ruin and oblivion. Across the river the Mahdi plants his flags in the sand. It is Year One. The world has been renamed.

22. Omdurman,
22 June 1885

The Hour has come, as it surely must, for all of us. The mice are eating through the mud to reach the wisps of straw that are hidden in the walls.

He cries out in the watery light. His eyes are on the shadows that sway in the smoky wraiths of the oil-lamps. The mice will gnaw through his bones. The worms will crawl through the sockets of his eyes.

Give me a sign, a real sign; something I can touch.

'Where is Abdullahi? Where is my brother?'

The men gathered round the bed are startled to hear him speak. They huddle amongst themselves. Like a great ominous leviathan resurfacing from the depths, silence momentarily swells to fill the room. He persists. The men elect to do nothing. They sit; to them the silence is comforting, even warm.

Again a tremor runs through the thin form that lies draped with a thin sheet on a low bed of loose strings. The men who are watching over him become uneasy; they mutter and fret. He stretches out a hand and grasps the first, the nearest hand to his. 'Abdullahi,' he groans, and because it seems to comfort him, the man whose hand it is says nothing.

A faint smile flickers weakly across the drawn face, whose skin is suddenly loose and dry as old paper. He has aged in six months more than most men do in thirty years. To the man holding the frail hand, it is as though he might take to the air and fly at any moment. The pulse is like that of a little bird held in his palm.

'When I was a little boy . . .' the voice tails off. The men, three of them in all, want to stop him; to tell him that he needs all the rest he can get, that he should not tire himself with useless talk. But not one of them speaks.

161

'When I was a little boy in Labab—' a long sigh and then, 'they wanted me to work on the boats. They wanted me to cut the wood with an axe, to plane it down. To use hammers and blades.' The voice starts and stops. The words are little more than a croak. The men lean forwards, their eyes fixed intently on one another so that they may be alerted the instant one of them manages to decipher the message concealed in the anecdote. 'I told them, I said ... my hands are not like yours. They laughed at me and told me, "Little brother, soon your hands will be rough and strong like ours." I said no, these hands were not meant for such work; these hands had some other purpose.' The laughter returns in a croaking whisper. 'I knew,' and a nod of the thin, pointed chin, determined and self-assured; a momentary flash of the old self. 'Even then I knew,' he continues. 'I refused to eat for two days.' The dry lips move, but no sound emerges. He tries to wet his lips. 'After that they said I need not work on the boats.'

Silence again.

The men are helpless witnesses. They say nothing. Darkness creeps through the spider cracks that run in crazy patterns up the walls.

He lapses into sleep and the night drags itself slowly onwards, towards the morning that will not come. Outside, the city which now bears his name, where his flags flutter in the river breeze, holds its breath. Even in sleep, his mind will not let him rest. A sign, no more; anything at all.

The absence of angels. The mice grind their tiny teeth against the walls, burrowing their way through.

There is a commotion at the door and the three wise men stand to attention, feeling like culprits. The small room is suddenly crowded. They shuffle amongst themselves, wordlessly searching for space. Wise men, men of learning, of wisdom, of centuries of dust, elbow their way through the door like errand-boys sent to the marketplace to fetch bread. At their head are the three: the khalifas – the flags of the red, the green and the black. The silence they bring with them is a terrible gravity. It is the silence of those who fear being left behind; the silence of burden.

Without warning he comes to once again. The spiders are weaving their webs. 'Baba?' he asks, mistaking Abdullahi for his father.

162

Abdullahi is in tears. His world is falling. He leans down and murmurs, 'It is I.'

'My brother?' The spindly fingers reach up in the darkness, feverishly, and clutch at the cloth of a sleeve. 'You and I, brother. You and I . . .'

'Sire, we are all here. Ali wad Hilu and Muhammad Sharif. All of us are with you.' The voice trembles with emotion and the rough, pockmarked features shudder uncontrollably. The slender thread that held the world together is about to part between those big hands, callused by rope and leather. Abdullahi has the hands of a herdsman and the feet of a wanderer, of a nomad; they know only the open land. In this room his body is like a curse, cumbersome and unbearable. He longs for lightness, ease. His limbs seem to swell, so that even the slightest movement feels awkward and clumsy; the only influence of grace on his life lies fading before his eyes.

'I have no brothers, only companions,' whispers the voice.

Abdullahi beckons over his shoulder. 'Water,' he urges. 'Fetch him a drink.'

'When I was a child,' says the dying man, 'my grandmother used to say to me when I came home with a bird from one of my traps, she used to say, "If you let the bird go, God will give you a drink of cool water when you arrive in heaven."' The voice tapers off and returns. His fingers grip Abdullahi's hand. 'In order to gain something, you have to let something go. That is why I have been chosen now.'

Now Abdullahi is forced to speak. Smoke from the brazier catches in his throat, making him cough harshly. Among the coals and the incense they have cast pages torn from the holy book. The room is filled with the ashen plumes of dead words, now blurred and confused. 'We need to know,' he weeps, tears dropping on to the big hands in great splashes. 'Who will it be?' He feels the others behind him, pressing against his back, their breath in his ear and their eyes on his neck. 'Tell us, sire, who will be your *wakil*? Who will replace you? Who will be *Khalifat al Siddig*?'

He is murmuring now, delirious with fever, moving his head from side to side as if to shake a demon off his chest. His forehead is cold as a stone at the bottom of the river. They lean closer.

'You and me, brother, together we will ride to Mecca and Medina.

163

We will pray side by side. They will fall before the mighty sword of righteousness.' And he begins to laugh; a long, haunting sound that makes his body shake and turns the blood of the witnesses cold. The laughter tapers away and then the eyes open and everyone in the room draws back in fright.

'Izra'il? . . . No . . . not yet, not so soon.' Then with a whimper, 'Mama . . .?' And he falls back and lies still.

It is over.

◆

A moment went by that seemed to last an eternity. No one dared to speak until one of the notables – a short, thrifty fellow with ears that swept backwards like an owl – stepped to the centre of the room and raising his palms upwards began to recite the opening words of prayer. The others joined in, lips moving, eyes rooted to the bed.

'Whom did he name?' asked Muhammad Sharif after a time. Abdullahi said nothing, did not even turn to look at him. The others were shuffling their feet and talking in low whispers. Eyes darted round the dimly lit room, trying to calculate where the partitions would fall: who would be in and who out.

Finally, it was the voice of the notable with the pointy ears who decided it. 'I heard him say something with reference to you, Khalifa Abdullahi.' And this was enough, for no one had really doubted it. 'He loved you like a brother,' came another voice.

And Abdullahi felt the field beginning to assemble itself around him. He listened as they began to praise him and urged him to go on with the struggle. 'God must have a reason for doing this,' the voices whispered. 'It is up to you, Abdullahi, to discover what that reason is.'

Abdullahi raised his hand and the voices gave way for him. 'I heard him tell,' he began, 'of a dream in which the Prophet came to him and told him that he was needed urgently in the next world and that he must leave off his duties here.' And the words flowed clearly and without hesitation, coming from somewhere within. 'And the Prophet, may God bless Him and keep Him, said that just as Muhammad

Ahmad was the successor of the apostle of God, so would Abdullahi al Ta'aishi be the *wakil* of the Expected One.'

And so it was. The only sign of dissent lay unspoken in Muhammad Sharif's eyes.

They buried him where he lay. They built a wall of brick around him to keep the darkness in and the spiders out.

PART 4

The New Caliphate

23. Omdurman,
1886

Since Khalifa Abdullahi had taken a liking to him, Hawi had found himself increasingly called upon to play a part in matters of the new state. The reason for this persistence remained obscure. It was a year since the Mahdi had died. The magnificent white, oval dome of his tomb rose majestically over the town, lending an air of assent and authority to the proceedings. The mystery of his sudden death remained unanswered.

The Khalifa Abdullahi, Hawi had learned at first hand, was an impulsive fellow, who preferred to trust his instincts rather than his head. Since the death of his beloved master, his life might have been in turmoil, on the inside, but on the outside he was stern and unforgiving, demanding respect in a different way to the Mahdi. In the days following the fateful hour, Abdullahi made everyone take a solemn oath of allegiance. Many advised against it, fearing that it was too soon after the death of the man who had inspired and blessed the whole land with his presence. Some said it was better to carry on for a time, without announcing the Mahdi's death, for such news might well destabilise everything, coming only six months after the fall of Khartoum. The objections were overruled; Abdullahi decided that it was a matter of the utmost urgency to send news of the death and the name of the Mahdi's successor to every outpost in the land.

It was at this time that Hawi was chosen to supervise work at the printing press. Abdullahi explained why: 'You have a strange mind, my friend,' the burly man purred, placing his big paw on Hawi's shoulder. 'You can read, can't you?'

'Surely I am not qualified for this.'

'Oh, always you have an objection!' wailed the khalifa. The round, puffy eyes were watery and restless. It was a hot day and beads of sweat were pouring down his shaven scalp. He looked like an *afreet* emerging from a river of steam. 'If I am to speak what comes into my head, I need a man who can understand me.' He shook his head, scraped his forehead dry with his finger. 'Sometimes I might go too far. You will tell me what you think, but you will not judge me, as some of the others would. They don't know what it is like to take a chance, never having done anything out of the ordinary. You are the only scholar mad enough for the job.'

As his first task in this new capacity, Hawi was to help Abdullahi write a letter to his people in Darfur, explaining the succession. 'All the divine secrets have been gathered in the letter Bá. And God has placed that noble mark on a man, the Mahdi said. A brother came to me and pointed at my right cheek. Others gathered round and discovered the letter there.'

No matter how many times Hawi was summoned to the khalifa's house, he never escaped a stirring in the pit of his stomach which told him that not only was his life in possible danger, but something much more central, more intangible was at risk. He found the clumsy man not without charm. His gregariousness was appealing. He was unpredictable and very shrewd and in his own way a very honest man. The rooms of the house, the largest in the central compound of the town, were often transformed from one week to the next as some new idea caught him. It seemed wonderfully apt that a man hailing from the nomadic wanderers of the western deserts should be so obsessed by furniture and fixtures, tables, chairs, saddles, rugs. He was constantly changing his mind and ordering carpenters to start chopping and cutting him something new. When on occasion a visitor from a distant land appeared, he would be called upon to give his opinion of the workmanship. How, he wondered, did local work compare to that seen in the palaces of the north and the far east?

Faces in the khalifa's house were also subject to constant change. The servants who answered the door and showed Hawi in were rarely the same on two consecutive visits. Often there were children running about in the yard outside the two-storey building, but Hawi never recognised them as being the same. He had no idea how many women belonged to the household and the place was always overrun by a stream of relatives, close and distant, who had made their way from Darfur.

170

It was plain to Hawi that his standing amongst the established cohorts of the *ulama* made him a safe and trustworthy confidante for the khalifa. He was virtually isolated. The others would not have anything do with him; they shunned him like a pariah. He had not been hung for apostasy all those years ago, but as far as the wise men and councils of advisors were concerned, he might just as well have been.

◆

Prophetic dreams, such as that which had inspired the letter to Darfur, began to occur with increasing frequency. Hawi found himself summoned at all hours of the day and night to come and note down what had taken place. Inevitably the details would change as Hawi set up his scrolls and prepared his quills and ink, while the khalifa paced backwards and forwards behind him, calling to the servants to get out of bed and fetch him warm milk with honey. When the process of writing began, they would proceed with the utmost care, finding the exact word needed, for it was vital that none of these revelations or forecasts should offend anyone.

Afterwards Hawi would be sent directly to the printing house to rouse the typesetters from their beds. The smoky oil-lamps would be lit while inky-fingered boys greased the cogs and began to creak the heavy handle round until the yellow flyers came shooting out from between the presses to begin winging their way to every corner of the country. The khalifa had had a dream and everyone was going to share it.

'I am the successor, obviously. No one was closer to him than I.' The burly figure stalked the rooms of his divan, his face creased into a smile. 'Why, he compared me to Abu Bakr, the companion of the Prophet Muhammad. Did you know that?'

'No, sire,' Hawi murmured, though of course he had heard this said on numerous occasions. But in the past year things had not been easy for the son of the Ta'aisha. There had been plenty of trouble, both internally and along the frail borders of the new state. The strong man sat down beside Hawi beneath the shelter. The tops of tall palms were waving in a gusty wind, heavy with thin yellow dust.

171

'I know there is dissension,' the khalifa was grumbling. 'Some of our brothers are dissatisfied. Especially Muhammad Sharif.'

'It's only natural that he should be the one,' Hawi pointed out. 'He was of the Mahdi's family.'

Abdullahi slapped his hands on his knees. 'He is too young to understand.'

'You think he is conspiring against you?'

Abdullahi seized Hawi by the arm and leaned close to him. The wind was getting stronger and the yard of the house was deserted, and all the windows shuttered. 'It was meant to be this way.' Abdullahi's voice began to falter. 'God . . . planned it for us this way. He intended for us to go through this time of pain.' His fingers dug into Hawi's forearm. 'Does that make sense to you, as a scholar? Could there be a sign in all of this?'

Hawi was wondering why they could not go inside to discuss it. 'I really am no expert,' he coughed.

The khalifa stood up with a grunt of impatience. 'If not you, then who?' he demanded gruffly. 'Those doddery old fools of the *ulama*?' He waved the notion aside with a swipe of his paw. 'No.' He shook his head. 'We have no use for their simple-minded thinking. They look at me and they see a primitive herdsman. Most of them were against us from the beginning.' He looked at the open window of the divan, filled with light and sky. 'No,' he murmured softly, 'this is a time for change. This is our time.'

24. Omdurman, 1887

In contrast to his duties as a scribe and his post at the printing house Hawi's seat on the council of seers was sheer relief. He was not called upon to do anything most of the time, other than participate, to sit in his place and listen to whatever ideas came up. The council had expanded with time, since everyone wanted their people to be represented. There were visionaries; soothsayers; diviners; romantics; astrologers; weather predictors and analysts of alphabets; numerologists; rainmakers and peddlars of lucky charms. They called themselves The Council of Vision. Their first meeting had been in the khalifa's tent nearly two years ago now, in the hot summer before the fall of Khartoum.

Meetings were held inside the central compound, in the open yard outside the offices of the khalifa's administration. All around them were the simple brick buildings where the clerics and the judges sat by day. Apart from the judges, it was surprising how many of the civilian posts were held by the very same people who had occupied them during the days of the Turkish occupation. These functionaries carried the weight of authority more than any army ever could. At night, with the light from the stars and a small fire, the members of the council whispered to one another out of respect for the silent, dark walls that surrounded them.

'Brothers, brothers!' Sheikh Baladi clapped his hands, calling for attention. The collection of mystics and scholars (never could a more volatile group have been assembled in wisdom or in need) began to settle down. Sheikh Baladi was a small, rather pompous fellow who tried to disguise mediocrity with heavy doses of zealotry. He took himself very seriously and tended to regard any unruliness as a personal slight, simply because he had been nominated as chairman. He raised his hands up high in the warm play of sparks and embers.

'Brothers, we have been presented with an interesting case which has confounded the minds of the best scientific and medical scholars in the land.' Hawi looked round the faces of his fellows. Was he the only one, he thought to himself, who was irritated by the way in which the ostentatious sheikh exaggerated the importance of this council's duties? The only reason they existed, as anyone with an ounce of common sense knew, was a result of a decision made years ago on the spur of the moment in an attempt to appease the regional chiefs and their superstitions. The khalifa himself was somewhat embarrassed that he had ever had anything to do with them and most of the time pretended they did not exist. They were an advisory body with no real power. They met, Hawi had long since concluded, for the sake of their own vanity.

'This girl was born and raised in a house of whores and drunks. She had no formative training and no instruction in religious matters whatsoever.' Sheikh Baladi signalled to a guard by the entrance to the yard. The members of the council were talking amongst themselves. 'She is said to be possessed by a *jinn* of great tenacity and evil.' The guard led a small, slim figure clad in black rags across the yard. 'I am sure that with our collective understanding of such matters we can cure this girl of whatever it is that ails her.'

The girl was asked to tell her story, which she did simply and straightforwardly. Hawi found himself leaning forward to catch every word. She looked frail and light as a bird. She recalled the suffering she had endured in the early days and recounted a long journey, how she had left her home. She told of a young boy from the dreaded forces of the khedive's *Bash-Buzuq*. Her extraordinary tale spun like leaves on the surface of a river. She began to talk of how she loved sailing in boats, listening to the wind and feeling the rush of the water beneath them.

She told of her arrival at Khartoum all those months ago. When they landed the boy was chained up and taken away and she was left alone in the street. The gates of the barracks closed in her face behind the Englishman who had wanted to love her. Upon seeing the high stone walls and the guns, he had become ashamed of her. He turned slowly away from her, shaking his head when the guard asked if she were to be admitted. And as the big doors swung together she saw him through the narrowing gap turn in the bright light, his head bowed, walking away through the dust, his clothes in tatters, towards a group of officers who waited in the shade of a veranda on the far side of the parade-yard. They looked stern and rather stupid in their stiff uniforms. The high doors crashed closed on the life she had begun to imagine for herself.

She drifted through the town, lightly, hardly touching the surface of the ground. She had nothing. She slept in the streets, beneath trees in the park, by the river where the birds nested in the palms. She begged for food in the marketplace. People took pity on her.

Before the liberation she had been handed to an unpleasant *bimbashi* in the army who had locked her in a room in a small house full of women who were being kept to entertain the troops. The house itself was simple enough, ranged around a decorative paved yard with a small palm tree and a hole in the ground filled with water and little golden fish that swam around sparkling in the light. It was pleasant enough, but every week the door would be opened and they would be allowed into a garden by the river lit by flares and decorated with coloured paper lanterns, and there would be fireworks and a wretched collection of tone-deaf musicians would go through the motions with their brass instruments and violins, and the women would stand around under the trees and wait for the officers to become intoxicated enough to press themselves upon them. Most of the decent men had left a long time ago; those who remained were the desperate ones, who had nowhere else to turn, who had come here because they had no choice. Men who were wanted under other names for terrible crimes in distant cities. Fraudulent clerics, paedophiles, murderers and rapists, evil-hearted men with the rope-burn of the noose on their necks or the black strips of treachery pinned over their hearts by firing-squad commanders; all of them had their secrets. Some of the girls were shrewd prostitutes who had learnt their trade in the notorious brothels of Salamat al Pasha. Others, like her, came from further afield. Some were even younger than she: wide-eyed and terrified of what lay in store. Many had lost track of their families along the road, or had been caught stealing a handful of maize or some dates in the marketplace. Either way they ended up in the women's place, which they were assured was better than ending up in prison.

She promised herself that she would escape at the first opportunity. Where exactly she would escape to she did not know, but one way or another she would do it. Anything, she decided to herself, lying beneath the grunting, sweaty form of an artillery lieutenant who smelled of onions and dead fish, would be an improvement on this.

Such things, however, never proceed along the shortest route, otherwise where would we all be? And so it was that on a particularly strange afternoon when the smell of stagnant ditch-water filled the small room where she lived, she was called upon by a *sanjak* from the infantry to perform a particularly degrading act with Iskander, his one-eyed mongrel hound. The dog was entirely innocent in the matter and probably felt as put out by the idea as the girl, who made up her mind that this was the limit. Before the bewildered hound knew where he was, the girl had lifted a brazier of coals and incense and scattered them on the bed, which caught fire instantly. The room was filled with smoke and screams as the *sanjak* flapped his hands and tried to put out the flames which had attached themselves to him. Noon stood on the far side of the room, where the breeze which was sucked through the window kept the smoke away from her, and watched as the man reeled and fell, the skin floating from his body as he burned.

The screams alerted the rest of the house, but Noon told them to stay back and they, not wishing to interfere in the officer's pleasures, did nothing but stand outside, ears to the door, wrinkling their noses at the strange smell, until finally Noon opened the door and exited. Why, the girls asked, had the man not been able to get up off the burning bed? They looked at Noon and she shrugged. What did she know about it? She had been struck stiff with fear, unable to move. The rest of the story never emerged, despite the arrival of the soldiers, heavy footed as always, knocking things over in their clumsy haste, banging this way and that as they charged cursing round the small yard. She was taken away. Some said she should be tried as a witch, but the authorities thought this a little too difficult to enter into the records of the khedive's army, so she was taken to a hospital which was in fact a prison for women who had either lost their minds, or else were no longer beautiful or young. Here they told her of the child she was carrying about which she already knew.

And in that terrible place she was taken under the wing of Father

Venturi, a benign man with eyes that drooped from the corners of his face and were held up by a sad smile. He told her that he would save her. He told her about Christ and he showed her a fine leatherbound book with hand-painted illustrations that were over two hundred years old (he held up his fingers to emphasise this time-span). The etchings showed religious scenes. The baby born under a bright star (like the Mahdi and his comet, she thought). The three wise men (like the three khalifas). The man on the cross. She had little interest in religion, but she realised that it was all-important for the priest, and she liked the pictures of the fat white babies with wings, blowing trumpets.

Father Venturi took her to the church along with some of the other women, accompanied by several soldiers to ensure that they did not run away or act indecently. The church was cool and dark and the stone walls felt comforting. It smelt of wood-varnish and dust that had infiltrated the corners and the high roof-beams. He taught her to pray. She held her hands together and knelt down when he told her to do so. They all ate a simple meal of bread and pressed guava juice and a hard yellow cheese which Father Venturi himself had prepared. Noon liked these outings, for the sad-eyed priest was the only one of the *affranji* who was kind enough to take the time to talk to her.

One day when she had one of her fits, she woke to find herself lying in a room lit by candles – a hundred or more. She could not recall being brought in there and she wondered if they thought she was dead. Sitting beside her, now fast asleep, was the priest. She could remember his smell; she climbed down from the table and sniffed him. After this, Father Venturi, who had an interest in medicine, pressed the medical orderly to let him have Noon over at the church every day to perform menial tasks such as sweeping and tending the small terraced garden, in the hope that this would give him an opportunity to assemble a comprehensive medical analysis of her condition.

Gradually he fell in love with her. Noon, of course, was aware of his growing interest and wondered how long it would be before he made his intentions clear. But Father Venturi was a slow mover and he was wrestling with his conscience. He had long since toyed with the plan of abandoning the church and fleeing to the Red Sea coast to live a frugal existence in the clear air that blows in over the waves.

177

Eventually, unable to take the decisive step and equally unable to bear the torment any longer, he hung himself from one of the sturdy beams.

On the day that he died, Noon woke up to see the moon peering through the sharp blades of a palm tree. They slept on the veranda of the infirmary on whatever bedding was available, for the infirmary was filled to bursting-point with invalids of all kinds. The soldiers who lived beneath the stairs at the back of the house had resorted to eating old rope and dog tails and boiling the leather from their guns and the bark from palm trees, and they were dying by the dozen of malnutrition. They lay coughing all night, vomiting bile. The mental patients, meanwhile, wandered the grounds freely, guided by their own secret light.

The soldiers in the barracks were thin and hungry too, their faces as shadowy as mongrel dogs. They dragged people away on a regular basis. Those taken never returned, and some said this was because they were served as food in the barracks at night, that there was a pile of human skulls underneath the big table where the men sat to eat.

When the *ansar* came everyone was sleeping. They said they had come to liberate them all. And when Noon climbed on to the wall to look out over the town, she saw the pyres of smoke coming from the direction of the church and she knew that what was God was no more and that just as the sun turned through the sky so did the earth turn also; that what was good became bad and what was once bad became good; and that she might just as easily have been the queen of a distant land wealthy beyond imagination as a crazy whore with nothing but the clothes on her back.

They collected all the women together and led them out of town. The wives of merchants, the beggars and thieves, the ones like her, the mad and the sane – they took them out to the camp of the famed warrior Wad al Nejumi, who looked like any other Arab bandit to her. They were given food and a place to sleep. They were told that they were free now, and those who had no men to take care of them would be allotted to a household where they would live. No single women without husbands or brothers to fend for them were to be allowed to roam the streets or live alone. These were the rules of the Mahdi for the new society in which the law of *sharia* was absolute.

The first husband they gave her was a good man, a simple fellow who had done some great service and had now been provided with a large house. Everyone was busy all the time. He had ten servants who took care of everything. He was a little old, but he was rich and he made no demands. She was for a brief time happy, until one day the *jinn* came for her again. She fell to the floor and began to shake. She bit her tongue until blood ran from her mouth. The women in the house began screaming and tearing at their hair. When her husband came home, he took a grave view of the affair. She tried to explain that it was something in her head and it came only very rarely and she never hurt anyone. But he was not convinced. The older women whispered that it looked as though the *jinn* took her like a man, and this was enough for him. He divorced her on the spot.

◆

The story concluded, Sheikh Baladi got to his feet and began trying to think of something to say. 'Since that day, brothers, this girl has been living in the streets like a common beast. Now what can we do to save her?' There were various half-hearted motions and an ensuing discussion. Most of those present had found the story good entertainment, but as for finding a solution for this creature, there was none.

Hawi, too, had been intrigued by the story. He felt an odd kind of sympathy with the poor creature, who was considered dangerous because her body behaved unpredictably. The world was ruled by convention. The reason why they had followed the Mahdi was because it had suited them to follow him. People were no longer convinced by revelations. They did what they felt would assure their well-being, or improve it. The girl, he had noticed, was no longer afraid. The audience had been shocked when they heard of the burning room, but this tiny slip of a girl had not hesitated in her description. He smiled to himself as he stepped through the door of his home. The two of them were not so different. She affronted people by falling on the floor and kicking her legs, while in his case it was his mind, the way he thought, which caused alarm and offence.

25. The Far North,
Nubia, September 1888

The battle may have been over, but the war went on. A small pack of weary horsemen moved almost unnoticed through the town. Hardly a head was turned in their direction as they made their way slowly towards the road leading south, for they were barely distinguishable from any of the thousands of *ansar* who had overwhelmed the small town. No one remembered having seen them arrive two days ago, dusty and irritable after their long journey from the capital.

At the centre of the party, which numbered no more than sixteen men in total, were the three commissioners. A closer examination would show that their *jubbas* were tailored from the finest cloth; they rode large horses and sat astride the finest saddles. From there they noted with disapproval the state of almost anarchy which seemed to reign among the *ansar* who occupied the town. None of them looked back at the small collection of shelters that were scattered across the shallow bowl of the plane, off towards the stubble of forest that marked the river to the west, where the *Amir* Nejumi had planted his tent.

◆

Inside the command tent, Wad al Nejumi was deep in conversation with Halim, his most trusted friend. They sat close together so that their voices could not be heard from outside.

'Supposing,' posed Halim, 'no food is sent.'

Nejumi held out his hands helplessly. 'What can we do? If there is nothing, we must take what we need.'

'But the villages are empty. The stores are filled with dust and mice. The rains have been poor and the river is lower than anyone can remember having seen it.'

180

Since his return from Omdurman a few weeks ago, Nejumi had been turning this way and that looking for a solution to this mess. 'We have to keep moving, food or no food.'

'North?' queried Halim. 'But we have hardly enough men.'

'Then we must find more. Go through the villages. Send out recruiting agents. Take anyone who can carry a spear or a knife.' He stretched out on the rug upon which he slept, suddenly exhausted. 'We are alone in this matter. We can expect no help. I will not give them the satisfaction of seeing me fail.' He gave a hollow laugh, which contained little humour. 'We have guns and shells and cannon, more than any general could ask for, but we have few men to fire them and those that we have are starving.' He glanced over at Halim again. 'How many are we losing each day?'

The other man tilted his head to one side, not wishing to make matters worse. The men were vanishing into the night at a worrying rate. Ten men at a time, sometimes as individuals, sometimes in groups. Knowing what his aide's silence meant, Nejumi lay back and put his hands behind his head with a sigh. 'Increase the nightly patrols. We cannot allow them simply to wash away like dirt in a river. God knows we are all tired of war.' Three years was a long time, he was thinking. When Khartoum fell to them, he had known that the spirit would go out of the fighting men. Khartoum had been something to aim for. It was all becoming far more vague, now. Where were they actually going? What were they going to do when they got there? And he was supposed to be the leader; why was he asking such questions?

Lack of supplies was not the only problem. There had been other incidents which had shaken the support of the *ansar*. He was thinking of the Batahin, whom he had managed to recruit on his way back from the capital. They would have killed him on the spot, if not for some of the men who had fought with him at Khartoum.

'You know us,' they had said. 'You know that we fight and we are not afraid to die.'

'I know,' was all Nejumi could say.

'Then why does the Khalifa Abdullahi treat us this way?' The town was in mourning. 'They have slaughtered our brothers, our fathers, our sons, for what? For saying that we are tired of this war, that our people need rest, that we have mourned enough. In return, he slaughters us like sheep.' The khalifa had sent word to them that he needed their men to fight.

As he looked around the group of men who stood before him he had felt shame for what he had become. These were simple men. They worked the land. They had sent their men to fight for the Mahdi and many had fallen. Now they said, enough was enough. They said the khalifa was not the Mahdi. In return he accused them of treachery and executed sixty-five of their brothers in one day in Omdurman. The executioners swung their heavy swords until their arms were too tired to lift the blade any more. Until they were covered in blood from head to toe and the ground was littered with a harvest of severed heads and strange limbs. They swung from the gallows in threes and fours in a macabre spectacle to which the whole town had been invited.

'Not one of them begged for mercy, not one of them cried out,' said an old man who stuck his face into Nejumi's. 'That is not the way of the Batahin.'

'Your brothers did not die in vain,' said Nejumi, feeling an emptiness in the place where his words came from. He stepped backwards and raised his voice. 'You men know who I am. You know my word. I would not send any man out where I would not go. I would not send a man into battle, if I was not prepared to stand alongside him.' He looked around the assembled faces. 'You know this in your hearts. Then know this also, I shall ride north to take Halfa and from there on into Egypt.' He lifted both arms up above his head. The sun beat down. They stood there sullenly, unconvinced. 'I shall follow the river to its end, because that is what the Mahdi himself asked me to do before he passed on. We are going to take the word of God with us to convert those unhappy people who live without belief; a belief that has been stolen from them by the corrupt ways of the Turks.' He let his hands drop to his sides. 'I'm not a man for speeches, you know me by my actions. But I am a fair man and . . .' he held their gaze evenly, 'I need your help.'

Nejumi now got to his feet and pushed up the flap of the tent. 'I think we should move into the town. I'm tired of being a nomad.' The camp was looking dilapidated and disorderly. 'They laughed at me,

Halim,' he said, without turning. 'All of them, sitting beside that pompous half-witted dog.' He turned now as something else occurred to him. 'Did you hear the story of the hair, Halim?'

A perplexed look crossed the other man's face. Nejumi laughed lightly and sat down on the rug again. 'It seems there was a hair which someone brought to our khalifa, saying this was a hair which had graced the head of Muhammad Ahmad al Mahdi, and he held his hand out like this.' Nejumi extended his hand. Halim sat open-mouthed, not knowing what would come next. 'Then,' Nejumi snapped his hand shut, 'our noble *Khalifat al Siddig* snatched away the hair from the unfortunate man's hand and . . . swallowed it.'

A frown appeared on Halim's face. 'He ate it? The hair?'

Nejumi nodded.

'Why?'

Wad al Nejumi grew tired of the telling. His voice dropped a notch. 'He said the light of the Mahdi had entered his body along with the hair and it now grew there like a tallow candle.' He sighed, and for a moment neither of them disturbed the distant sound of small weaver birds on the roof of the tent.

'They laughed at me and they sent me out to die. As if I haven't already proved my worth.' Anger and frustration spilled out of the taciturn man.

'The Baggara are all like that,' offered Halim philosophically. 'They come from the desert and know nothing. Now they think they bought the whole country in the market because their brother is sitting on the Mahdi's horse.'

'Perhaps,' Nejumi laughed.

He recounted the visit by the recently departed commissioners. The oldest of the three, a solemn-looking man with the uncertain eyes of one who is uncomfortable with the truth, had started the enquiry. 'We hear that you are camping to the north of the mosque, and the army of Musaid Quaydum is to the south.'

Nejumi replied briefly, as though it were of little consequence. 'It is more convenient that way,' he said.

The man continued talking as though there had been no interruption. 'Abdullahi al Ta'aishi is worried that this matter will weaken us

183

in the eyes of our enemies. There must be no sign of conflict in our side.'

'We are here simply to ensure that the cooperation between all sides is smooth,' chimed the second commissioner. 'Victory is all that matters.'

'If victory is all that matters,' Nejumi snapped back, 'then send me food and men to fight instead of giving everything to al Zaki's army in Abyssinia.' The three commissioners shuffled their feet. Nejumi continued, stepping close to the oldest one. 'How does anyone expect me to be able to keep this army together when I have no visible support from him?'

The commissioners answered him with blank looks.

Night was falling. Nejumi and Halim stepped outside to pray before seating themselves on the reed mats.

'Of course, they had brought me nothing,' Nejumi said, concluding his account. The memory of his humiliation at Khalifa Adbullahi's hands still burned inside him. 'Look here,' the burly khalifa had appealed to his guests on that occasion, 'Abu Ghannu captured Shakka. Abu Anga gave the Ethiopians a good beating, and Osman Digna is on his way to Suakin, but you, oh great *Amir al Umara*, you sit in Dongola for two years and do nothing.'

After a silence, Halim said, 'Tell me about Muhammad al Fahl.'

'There was nothing to be done,' said Nejumi, 'my hands were tied.'

'He was not a bad man.'

'He was a stupid man. He deserved to be beheaded just for saying those things in front of other people. He should not have spoken such thoughts aloud. Not even in his sleep.'

Halim looked down at the ground. 'No one is to be trusted, then.'

Nejumi seemed to detect a change in his friend's voice. He looked across in the gloom. 'There will be more executions like that. As time goes by our attention will be turned away from our enemies out there and towards those inside our homes. Towards those we call brothers, family and friends.'

'But you would not have done it if news had not spread so fast.'

With a sigh, Nejumi let his eyes scan the horizon.

Here and there the orange-blue tips of windy flames danced across the night plains. 'My only mistake was in not killing him straight away.'

He knew that Halim found it difficult to believe what he was hearing. But what Halim did not understand was that things had changed. They had gone beyond the days when they could speak of wrong and right. These days, what mattered was obedience. Obedience was right and disobedience was wrong. The difference between them was the difference between life and death.

The conflict between the armies of Nejumi and Qaydum became more bitter with each passing day. Enemy boats cruised up and down the river just to the north, and patrols were sent out to gauge their strength. One such patrol sent only one man back. He stumbled into camp and found himself before Nejumi.

'All of them are dead,' he wept, not recognising the *amir*.

Nejumi looked at him for a moment, before turning away. 'And why are you still alive?' he asked simply.

The cavalry patrols sent out to monitor the camp were increased. Food was being stolen at an alarming rate. 'They are starving. They have no choice but to steal to feed their families.' The river fell and the harvest failed. This was the year of the great famine.

Yunus al Dikaym, whose reputation for hard-hearted cruelty preceded him from Abyssinia, where he had retaken Gallabat from the Ethiopians, arrived from Omdurman to take charge of affairs in al Urdi. In a great gathering in the mosque square after the noon prayers he read his orders to the assembled army.

He was to take care of matters. Musaid Qaydum and Wad al Nejumi were to be to Yunus as a corpse in the hands of him who washes it. Privately, however, he was as partial as everyone else these days. He confessed to Nejumi his dislike for Qaydum: 'He is a little slave boy from the ignorant Baggara whose importance is related to his proximity to the khalifa's ass. Take no heed of him. You, Nejumi, are among the first followers of the Mahdi and certainly you are one of the greatest military men we have.' The grisly features smiled in a distant kind of way. He had a hide like a rhinoceros, but he was safe, so long as he was on your side. 'How many victories we owe you,' he was saying.

It seemed that Yunus's personal preference had saved Nejumi from

185

an unpleasant fate. He had a glimpse of how it could have been in the constant baiting of the hated Qaydum. When Yunus sent him running round the square bearing a spear to illustrate how a charge was performed Nejumi almost felt sorry for his adversary.

◆

Halim came to Nejumi, looking frail and exhausted.

'They will soon be too weak to march,' he explained. 'We must take Halfa. He who dies, dies. At least the living will be saved.'

Nejumi sighed. The moment he had feared had now arrived. He went to Yunus al Dikaym and told him of his decision. 'If any man can succeed, it is you,' said the laughing Yunus.

It took three months before the orders came allowing the army to leave.

One night the camp was woken up by the sound of the big drum. Lifting their swords and spears, the men ran towards the stand at the centre of the town and looked around for their leader. The drummer stepped forwards and it was Nejumi himself. As they watched he raised his hands and began to recite: 'God most High has said, The people said to him, "Your enemies have assembled against you; be afraid! But they feared not, only their faith increased." And so it must be with you.' They stood bewitched by the moonlight and the silver shining figure of their lord before them, his words coming to their sleep-befuddled, frightened minds as though in a dream.

'The devil frightens only those who follow him, and you have no enemies to fear, but me. Fear only me if you will be faithful, and follow me as only those who have fought beside me can.' And with that he stepped from the light and vanished, leaving the men to turn to one another and ask what the meaning of this could be.

Nejumi took his men the following morning and crossed from the town to the west bank to begin the march northwards. Camels, horses, goats, women and children swirled across the river like a flock of believers heading into the desert sun. Their leader was not a prophet, but a man, plain and simple, just like them, and his fate was theirs. The army of Wad al Nejumi numbered no more than five thousand fighting men and eight thousand camp followers.

26. Tushki, The Nubian Desert, July 1889

Waking to find his head wrapped in cloth, he wondered for a moment whether he had died and been buried already. The cloth was dusty and smelled of the world and it seemed strange to him that a man could be dead and yet still feel the sensations of the physical world. This was not how he had imagined it would be. Perhaps he had not after all been deemed faithful in his thoughts and God in his wisdom had condemned him to one of the seven levels of purgatory closest to the world, so that his suffering might continue until the Day of Judgement.

Voices came to him now, not far off; the voices of men, women and even children. Reluctantly he sat up and pulled off the makeshift shelter, erected only the night before from a few stripped palm branches and an old head-scarf, which had collapsed on to his head during the course of the night. He looked around the early-morning camp. This was the most pitiful excuse for an army God had ever put on earth, that much was certain. Children wandered wailing round the dazed-looking adults sprawled upon the ground. Every face wore the thin grey look of fatigue. They had not eaten a proper meal for days now. They had slaughtered as many of the pack animals as they dared to. They had eaten camels and even horses and someone said mules too, though he had declined that particular night. Beside him a soldier whose name he no longer remembered was grinding date-stones between two flat rocks. They would make a kind of flour out of this to mix with water and cook like flat bread.

How far they had come! Cutting down through the Belly of Stones, beyond Sarras and Ma'tuqa. Now they were north of Halfa itself. North of the Egyptian front line, moving towards Assuan and after that, Binban. It all seemed something like a dream; as though it were not really happening at all. The guards on duty at the frontier fort at

187

Halfa had waved to them, simply watching them walk by, off into the desert; this was not an invasion, but an excursion, conducted with the permission of the very people they had come here to conquer.

At Metemma they came across the upturned, rusty metal hulks of the steamers abandoned by the retreating British Relief Force three years ago, in whose tracks they were now following. The dismantled craft, discovered quite by accident, lay in the shallows, on the sand, like mysterious tributes to a modern god of machinery.

As they headed further north, towards the border post at Wadi Halfa, they kept away from the river. They were moving now only in the hope that they would come across something better further along. Even the dates on the trees were unripe, but they ate them anyway. The soldiers carried their children in their arms as they walked for hours following the moon.

◆

Ma'tuqa had been a disappointment. Up until then they had been pinning much of their hope on their brothers to the north joining them and rising up in the name of faith against their oppressors. But the Egyptians, it seemed, were not particularly interested in matters of religion and had no sense of their own oppression. 'They have a different sensibility to us,' as it was drily noted by Halim. Nejumi and Halim had marched into the town of Balluja with a light party of their best men in order to tell the people of Egypt of their great mission. But even as he spoke, Nejumi noticed women and children from the camp, moving through the crowd begging for food.

They had taken up a position in the centre of the small town and sounded the *ombeya* to call the people. Nejumi addressed the crowd from his horse, his arms held up wide.

'People of Balluja,' he began, 'know that we have come to you in friendship and brotherhood, for you, like us, are believers in the faith.' He spoke clearly and powerfully, as usual. 'People, let me tell you that the Turks and the *affranji* have fled from the might of the Mahdi's sword. We have come to you now to tell you that the time has come for you to join in this glorious movement. Let us go together. Our people have been brothers since the beginning of time.

Let us go to Cairo and on to Jerusalem and the holy lands on our mission of liberation. The world has lost its respect for Islam, for our simple way of life, for too long. Your rulers have been corrupted by the ideas of the *affranji* infidels.'

As he spoke, Nejumi slowly became aware of a distance between him and the crowd. They looked upon him not as a liberator, but as something far less important, more amusing even. He became conscious of his appearance and began to wish that he had dressed in something more impressive than this dusty *jubba*, the belt of which he had not loosened in twenty days. His feet were sore from the journey and bleeding and bruised. His hair was long and his beard, too, needed trimming.

'Those black men are not our brothers,' someone shouted, pointing at the *jihadiya*. 'They look more like slaves to me.'

'What kind of an army are you that need women and small children at your side?'

Nejumi began to falter. 'You know of our victories.' He paused, his voice drowned out by the clamour. Then he resorted to shouting at the top of his voice. 'When we took to the battlefield at Shaykan there were twenty thousand angels by our side. The prophet himself was there upon a white horse with wings.' At this they began to laugh out loud, and he knew he was losing the fight.

'You look like a band of gypsies, not a conquering army.'

'Where are your cannon and fine horses?'

'Look at those mules, there's no muscle on them. They're just skin and bone.'

'Like the rest of the bandits.'

'We need food,' shouted Nejumi hoarsely. 'Provisions, stores for the journey north.' The crowd was beginning to disperse now. He stood there, shaking, speechless; eventually he accepted Halim's hand to step down from the stand. 'I'd rather face a charge of the fiercest cavalry than go through that again,' he muttered. 'But they are right, I do look like a mad man and a fool.' Together they led the men away, back towards the open spaces.

◆

It was the same wherever they went. Instead of greeting them with open arms, as conquering heroes, the people boarded up their doors and peered from small clay windows with dark, suspicious eyes. They spat from rooftops at the ragged column, and they called out jeeringly, 'Is this the great conquering army of the Mahdi?' Someone threw a crust of dry bread and a woman trailing along behind ran forward to pick it up to feed her children. It was harder than a stone.

'Look at these gypsies. Would God send out an army as wretched as this against the might of the khedive?' the onlookers asked. 'Might as well send an army of mice.' Nejumi rode on, through the hail of rotten fruit and date-stones and goat droppings, head bowed, cursing the day he had drawn this battle.

They slept that night in the desert, and by dawn they had reached Arqin. But the steamers were there and the cannon blasted away mercilessly, breaking them apart. They were forced to fight, for they needed water and could not push on further. From then on the gunboats moved with them, patrolling the river and dropping fresh troops on the beach to attack in a series of light skirmishes. They fought for three days before turning and heading into the desert once again.

They were down to less than half of their original strength. A despatch had arrived promising fresh troops from the south. When they turned up, of course, they were boys too young to know anything of war and men too old to be of use.

'Look,' noted Halim, as they watched the new arrivals file by, 'they even brought their grandfathers to take care of them.'

Of thirty-five artillery men, they had only three gunners left. This was of little consequence, however, since the mules to drag the guns had also died, leaving them, effectively, with only one gun, which the men dragged behind them. They had enough ammunition for one good day's fighting and that was more or less it; the rest they abandoned, since without guns and gunners it was dead weight. The riflemen of the *jihadiya* were deserting in droves. 'The first sight of their former masters and they are gone,' remarked Nejumi one evening. 'Unlike you, Medani, old man?'

The old cook gave a dry cough that might just have passed for a laugh. The ligaments in his throat stuck out like dry rope. His skin

190

was like a worn water-bag. He had been blinded when a shell had exploded in the breech of one of the cannon some weeks ago, and a grubby cloth was tied across his eyes. He stumbled along, supporting himself on the last of the two wheeled wagons. 'Wait until my eyes heal,' he cackled. 'Then I'll show you how to deal with these monkeys.' And then his throat dried up and he turned to spit, managing to catch Halim on the leg. Halim simply wiped it off on his *jubba* without a word.

They sat in the sun, fiddling over their shelters. The whole camp was made of such flimsy affairs. A dog was barking in the distance. The camels were lying in the sand half-dead. A woman was soon to have a baby. Out here, now? It amazed Nejumi that even at such times, the cycle of life continued. He chastised the soldier, however, for bringing his wife along in such a condition. 'I could not stop her, my lord. She has family in Shallal,' explained the man.

◆

A letter arrived that day from the Egyptian side, from the *affranji* officer named Grenfell. Halim and Nejumi sat cooped up in the sand, under their tiny scrap of shade, reading the letter together. A puppy dog wandered up and began licking their bare toes.

> So I have come, and after me thousands upon thousands of English and Egyptian troops are about to arrive. I had in mind to wipe you out and obliterate your traces, but on my arrival I looked upon you and saw your weak and pitiful condition. I found you dying of hunger and thirst. I pity you, Wad al Nejumi, for the pretender to the khalifa has put you in this wretched position as the only way in which he can slay you. He put his nephew Yunus in your place to rid himself of you and your friends. There are no friends waiting at Binban for your arrival, only English and Egyptian armies. They await your coming, hour by hour, to drink your blood and send you to destruction. The ways are closed to you. Between you and Binban are hundreds of leagues of sand and rocks, dry and waterless. If you go forwards the victorious armies await you.

If you turn back the armies of Halfa are standing watch for you and if you stay where you are, hunger, thirst and pestilence threaten you. I call upon you to surrender, your life and the lives of your commanders shall be preserved from all evil.

Nejumi sighed and put down the letter in the sand. He reached out a hand to ruffle the mongrel dog's flea-bitten head. 'He doesn't mix his words, this Garanfil.'

Halim agreed. 'He certainly does not.' He was concentrating on holding up the spear that supported their shelter. The cotton fluttered and its shadow shook like an unseen spirit passing over the ground. Halim was beginning to see *jinns* everywhere. He muttered a prayer for protection.

'A man could die of sorrow reading a letter like that.'

'What do you suppose brought them here?' asked Halim.

'Well,' Nejumi speculated. 'The same as brought us, I suppose.'

'I hear that in their country a man can only take one wife, and they don't approve of slaves. So if he wants to find himself in the arms of another woman he has to leave his country and travel a long way. And they say that when it rains in their country, it is hard like small stones and white and colder than the bottom of a well in winter.'

Nejumi was watching a hawk turning elegantly through the hot air. He was hot and thirsty; he could not apply his mind to the concept of terrible cold. He stretched out his legs lazily and closed his eyes. Halim did the same; they both tried to sleep.

When the sun began to burn, Halim rubbed his eyes and sat up. Someone was skinning a dog nearby. He nudged Nejumi awake. 'You ought to write back to that Sirdar Grenfell and tell him to go home to his rain.'

'I have already decided that,' replied Nejumi, still half asleep. 'We have nothing to lose. If we win we shall gain many things: food, shelter and ammunition. But if he wins, then he gets nothing but this old *jubba* and a broken spear.'

That evening Nejumi called his scribe. He clapped the boy on the shoulder and turned to his friend. 'You know, Halim, my personal guard have deserted me, run away. Even my water bearer took the mule and escaped one night, may the jackals feast on his bones. The only one I have left is the writing boy.'

When he finished dictating, his face cracked into an angular smile and he licked his dry lips. 'When the world is said and done all we have left is words in the hands of boys like this.' He asked the young scribe to read back the letter, while he sat gazing down into the sand at his feet, his arms gently wrapped around his knees and the flames of the fire flickering in the dark hollows of his eyes.

The boy read: 'We say to you that we were sent from our lord only to summon the people and the Muslims. What you have mentioned about the abundance of your soldiers and the nearness of your approach does not awe us, nor cause us to fear, nor should it unless this were the place of the two worlds of men and *jinn*.' Out of the darkness faces were drawing, assembling around this innocent boy whose small, uneven voice rose up from the sand and spoke of their hearts and longings to the world beyond. Beyond the hills and the river, beyond the gunboats and the desert, there were men just like them, waiting to hear, waiting to know, not wishing to go to their deaths in a state of doubt. Beyond the footprints and the stars, there was righteousness and justice and good. They stood silently in the darkness, cupped like a pair of hands around the frail voice which was theirs. 'We fear none, but God on high. No quantity of powder and shot will avail you without His help. That is why your generals Hicks and Gordon and their armies perished, despite their numbers. It was inevitable, the will of God.'

When the boy had finished reading, Nejumi got to his feet. He looked around the faces reflected in the blue light of the stars. 'People,' he began, 'they wish to turn us back with accusations of cowardice. They try to fight the light of faith with their ignorance.' He waved a hand out towards the plain beyond them, which stretched flat and unbroken towards the moon. 'These are your lands. They are the lands of your fathers and the lands of your children. God is with us because we are right. What is God if not righteousness? Can anyone tell me that?' There was not a sound, not a single child stirred in his sleep, not a hand was raised nor a throat cleared; the people held their breath as though a flock of birds were passing overhead. 'These people want to take your land, and call it theirs. They claim the right to do this solely because they have bigger and better weapons, because in that land of theirs which we have never seen they have money and gold and men, thousands upon thousands of men who will fight for them. They have ships laden with guns, while we have mules with sharp bones.' This drew a snigger of laughter and Nejumi felt himself smiling too. He took a deep breath. 'They are waiting for us and we will go to them. We go in the knowledge that God is with us and will help us. Because without our faith we have nothing to face the unbelievers with. Know then that your hearts are good and go.'

He dismissed them and they dissolved gently into the inky night. Nejumi sat down on the ground and noticed that the boy was rubbing his eyes and yawning. He reached forward and slapped him playfully, but firmly, on the back. 'Your job is not finished yet.' And so the boy prepared his ink-well and selected a quill carefully, holding it up to the light. Then, crossing his legs, he unrolled a sheet of paper and nodded: he was ready. Nejumi dictated a letter to the khalifa in Omdurman. He sat close to the boy, with his lips almost touching the boy's ear. On the hard ground beside them Halim slept restlessly, tossing and turning and moaning.

The boy yawned and scratched his ear. 'The last line?' he asked.

Nejumi repeated, 'As far as the Egyptians are concerned, reports that at heart they are followers of the true faith and believers in the mission of the Mahdi, are incorrect. Nowhere have I been received as anything but a pariah dog. Many of the sheikhs are capable of betraying us for a few handfuls of gold from the purses of the Turks.' Now he paused. 'Our purpose here is doubly hard and our chances are getting smaller with each passing day. I write this to you so that you may know that it is the faith in our hearts that gives us the courage to continue. Your loyal slave and companion, Abdel Rahman Wad al Nejumi.' The boy added the signature with a flourish despite his fatigue, which brought a smile to Nejumi's face. 'How old are you, boy? And don't bother to lie to me. It makes little difference now.'

The boy wiped off his quill carefully and restored it to the leather case. He stoppered the ink-well and bound it with a leather strap. Then he packed the quill case and the ink-well into the pouch which he used as a pillow when he slept and which never left his side when he was awake. 'My mother told me that I was born with the moon of Sha'aban in the hegira year of 1294.' He lifted the flap of his writing pouch to show the date inscribed there. 'I wrote the date for whoever finds it when I am killed.'

Nejumi nodded. 'You write well for your age.' He was tired now, and waved the boy away. 'Go and sleep, boy, it's a long day that awaits us.' He stretched himself out on the ground and pulled the thin cotton wrap over him as a sheet. 'You have a gun, boy?' he mumbled, half asleep.

'My father's rifle.'

'Well just remember when it stops working that the Turks are no longer killing their prisoners. Don't get yourself killed unless it's absolutely necessary.'

'I would rather die a martyr than surrender to the infidel.'

'Very good, boy,' yawned Nejumi. 'I salute your courage. But someone has to get out of here alive to let the world know our story.' He turned over on his side. 'Think about it.'

◆

The reinforcements sent from Omdurman were a disappointment. They were weak from lack of proper food and the long journey away from their homes had made them dishonest. Nejumi was surprised to find out that many of them had been in prison in Omdurman. 'Why is the honourable khalifa sending me murderers and rapists?' he asked Abdel Halim. 'Does he think so highly of my character?'

'It must be all that he has got left.'

In the first three days they lost two men through petty squabbles. 'If they carry on like this we won't need to fight the enemy. The men will kill one another right here,' snarled Nejumi when the news reached him.

After sixteen days they moved on from Balluja towards the town of Tushki. The river they avoided. The gunboats were still a threat and the Turks had taken to setting ambushes on the banks, piling dates to lure the hungry men and then firing upon them with machine-guns or capturing them while they were absorbed in the business of eating.

195

Their plight was becoming more and more desperate. There were tales of parents who abandoned their children along the road, unable to carry them any further. Having eaten their camels and most of their mules, some of them even ate their slaves. Men vanished from the camp in the night, leaving behind wives and babies.

They reached the plain at Tushki and the enemy were waiting. The horizon clouded over with dust as the cavalry charged. With heads light from lack of sustenance, they saw *darawish* dancing on the wind as the lances of the enemy came down and split them in half. Women ran screaming; children crawled beneath the hooves of charging horsemen. The *ansar* scattered to the wind like a handful of dust. Nejumi's horse was shot from under him and he was wounded in the shoulder. He managed to pull the men back and a small group of them reached the safety of a patch of high ground. They lay there gazing out at the scattered corpses of their friends and families. The breeze tugged at the clothing of the dead as though invisible children were trying to rouse them from slumber. The sound of weeping carried on the wind. Nejumi lay back and closed his eyes to the sun. Beside him lay Abdel Halim, gasping for breath. They had rifles and ammunition. 'If they come, then God be ready for their souls,' said one man; the next moment he lay on his back with half of his head blown off by a flying shell to reveal the oozing red stuff of his brain. The flies buzzed thick and black, the fierce flies of the desert.

Nejumi's fine beard was peppered with red dust and there was a terrible pain in his chest. 'Abdel Halim,' he gasped. 'It seems to me that since we are in no position to retreat we will have to wait until dark to make our final assault into Egypt.'

Abdel Halim smiled as best as he could manage. 'I think that in fact we are in Egypt and therefore, sire, we must have conquered her.'

'Then we are liberators,' laughed Nejumi. He jerked a thumb over his shoulder towards the enemy lines. 'Who is going to go and tell them?'

The second attack came in the early afternoon. Nejumi, on his knees firing his rifle at the advancing *jihadiya*, was shot in the chest. The bullet went straight through him and struck a black rock protruding from the sand. It ricocheted upwards with an awful wailing sound. Tears filled Halim's eyes. 'That was his spirit going to heaven,' he said.

They picked up the broken body and tied his wrists with harsh dry rope and strapped him over the back of a half-dead camel and whipped it hard, sending their fallen hero on his final journey home.

27. Omdurman, 1890

As he hurried through the darkened streets, Hawi was muttering to himself, his head filled with the wild talk to which he had listened that evening. Plots were being hatched and bonds of subterfuge formed. People were emerging from the shadows. The very same men who had pledged their allegiance to the khalifa were now set on beating their own path to the top. Some of them had real grievances; others pointed enviously at the way in which the khalifa favoured his own people over all others. Inside the khalifa's camp itself, all was not well. The messengers who had been sent west to the Ta'aisha in Darfur with promises of a safe conduct to the capital, had been murdered. The khalifa's own people were turning against him. 'His father was a crazy cattle herder who had visions. Is that any basis for an Islamic state?' the merchants said.

The clandestine meeting from which Hawi was now returning had been attended by more than fifteen notables. Many of those who sat upon the councils of state by day, smiling and agreeing with the khalifa, gathered at night around the *ashraf*, who had lost much of their standing following the Mahdi's death. Their flags had been taken from them and Muhammad Sharif, their impatient leader, appointed as one of the original khalifas by the Mahdi, was now living in poverty. If the rumours were true there could be an uprising any day now. Resources were overstretched owing to trouble in the east with the Ethiopians, and unrest in the western reaches.

The streets were overflowing with refugees. Forced to leave their homes or face starvation, they flocked from the regions to the capital in search of work and food. But there was not enough, so they lived in the streets, scavenging what they could. They went knocking from door to door, bowls in their hands.

Hawi cursed his stupidity at having been delayed so long after nightfall. It was something he had cautioned himself against on numerous occasions. He pulled the scarf around his face and moved at a steady trot, unable to run as fast as he once could. Turning a corner, he came upon a group of people assembled like a huddle of crows on the ground. He slowed his pace, trying to think of another route; but he was tired and any detour would involve a lot more walking. He advanced carefully, his slippers slapping lightly against the soles of his feet. He carried no weapons, not even a dagger in the pocket of his *jubba*. As he approached, the people noticed him. They stopped what they were doing. Hawi kept walking. Then, without a word, they all scattered, running and jumping, slipping into the shadows of the walls.

On the ground lay the mutilated and rotten corpse of a mule. It must have died several days ago. There was an awful stench. Hawi's stomach turned over, and he rushed on, trying not to vomit on his clothes. They would surely die from eating meat like that. He covered the remaining distance quickly and banged feverishly on the door for the servant to let him in.

◆

The following day Hawi went in search of the *qadi* to offer his services. The man did not dare refuse him, so from that day on Hawi went to the government offices near the central compound. He was given a room and a mat for the floor and a box covered with a sheepskin to sit on. Every day he heard tales of loss and pain, of misery and desperate sorrow. Every day he said to himself, 'I must try to help.' He gritted his teeth and closed his eyes, repeating these words to himself: I must try.

They had nothing. They slept in streets haunted by cannibals and wild dogs, with one ear open for the calls to warn that the mad ones were coming. '*Jayakum!*' they shrieked; they are coming for you. They picked up their children and fled. In the mornings they came to the government office, to sit in row after row in the sunshine and wait their turn. They saw the young *ansar*, men too young to remember Shaykan. These peacocks strutted around in their fine feathers, lords of a new era. The young were to be trusted in place of the old, for the young only knew what you told them, while the old remembered, and those who remember are capable of dissent.

One day a woman died in front of Hawi. She was a Zaghawa woman whose husband had been a soldier for the Turks, but he had joined the ranks of the faithful when the garrison at Bara fell, and after the war he had sent for her. She had not been able to find him, and had travelled for two years to get here. She had been raped by a band of brigands: thirty-one men, she had counted them. She had swum the river and her child had been taken by the stream. Now she had nothing in the world but her husband. Hawi indicated to the notary to take her name and the village where she came from and to ensure that she was given the pension of a soldier's widow. But it was of little consequence, for in the act of reaching for a cup of water to drink the woman fell to the floor, like a loose bundle of bones in a sack. The guards and Hawi and the notary looked at one another. Finally Hawi waved a hand to the guard by the door. 'See if . . .' The guard knelt beside her, but there was no sign of life. 'See how simply life slips of out the door, with less trouble than a bird,' Hawi thought.

◆

That morning, as was now his custom, Hawi made his way as usual to the khalifa's compound, the nerve-centre of the administration and a place now regarded by the people as a holy shrine. He had to fight his way forwards through the press of bodies at the gate. Wailing babies were held up towards him. 'Take my child,' the women would cry. 'Take my child so that he might live.' The guards pushed people back roughly and the long *courbaj* snaked out.

'Don't do that,' moaned Hawi, but the young soldiers sneered at the old man.

Once inside, Hawi crossed to an inner yard, in which a *rakuba* provided a little shade for those who had reached the front.

Shouts were heard as a man was dragged from the room. The notary, a pale, bald-headed Egyptian, was dealing with the matter. The man's son had been caught stealing and was to be punished by amputation of the hand. There was no room for appeal, the notary

200

explained, unmoved by the father's weeping for his son. The rules were very clear. Hawi sat down behind the table. The Egyptian, who had been inherited from the khalifa's administration, was a born cleric, operating in a calm, unhurried manner and with an air that always conveyed scorn. Hawi despised him, but he could not manage without him.

The first case was brought in, a man with a large square face which suggested simplicity of mind.

'What is your problem?' the notary snapped.

In his hands, the man held a sheaf of papers. He looked down at them as if hoping they would speak up for him.

'What have you got there?' Hawi asked.

The man glanced over his shoulder. 'These are the titles to my land,' he explained.

Hawi held out his hand. 'May I see them?'

The papers were greasy and brittle. They came to pieces as he unfolded them. The ink was faint. 'Where is your land?' Hawi asked.

'Gallabat.' The man, who stood with his shoulders bowed, peered up from under large eyebrows. 'I walked all the way from there to here. My mule died. They took my horses. They took my wife and children. They said the land was to be occupied by the army and the food in my stores was to feed the soldiers.'

'There is a war being fought in those regions,' the notary insisted on reminding them. 'Be glad that you have the honour of contributing to the struggle. This is a *jihad*.'

He was about to dismiss the man and his case, but Hawi raised his hand. 'Wait,' he said. He got to his feet and looked into the glassy eyes of the Egyptian. 'Can we not help him?'

The Egyptian said nothing. His face remained immobile. Hawi turned to the man. 'You say the soldiers took your land?' The man nodded once. His doleful eyes followed Hawi around the room until he stopped and turned to address him. 'Go home,' he said. 'The army will not stay long and you will soon have your land back.' He stepped closer. The big man's jaws were moving but no sounds were emerging; he twisted the small cap from his head between his hands. He looked pleadingly at Hawi but Hawi had nothing to give. 'Go home,' Hawi said finally. '*Allah karim*. We have no miracles here today.'

◆

Soon after this Hawi fell ill with fever. For ten days and nights he hung between life and death. His body was racked with pain and sweat poured from him. The servant soaked sheets in water and draped them over him to cool him, but he could hardly feel the change. The Khalifa Abdullahi sent a messenger to stay with Hawi and inform him if he died. They summoned everyone who might be of help; doctors and learned men rushed to his bedside because the order had come from the house of the khalifa. Every cure was tried. They held incense under his face and told him to inhale; they burnt pages of script from the holy book; they left a boy to recite day and night by his side.

'If the sickness doesn't kill me,' Hawi gasped, 'the cure will surely do the job. If it is God's will then I will go.' He fell back, seized by a new spasm of pain. On the morning of the eleventh day, he began coughing and spluttering. He rolled over and began to retch. There was a wriggling sensation in his throat and he reached in and pulled out a long, grey-coloured worm. The servant ran in circles, as though a *jinn* had taken hold of him, screaming and wailing so loudly that the neighbours arrived to pay their respects, thinking that the master of the house had died. They looked at the worm sitting in the pool of vomit on the ground and they nodded their heads. 'The whole town is cursed,' they pronounced. 'The water is poisoned, the riverbank is spread with rotting bodies lying like dead lizards in the sun. The town is full of mad people who eat their own children.'

◆

A visitor arrived one night, some months later – a dishevelled, haggard figure, who seemed unfamiliar at first. The servant showed him in with an air of such foreboding that Hawi wondered what was wrong. Then he recognised Sheikh Abbas. It took him a moment to recover from the shock of seeing Abbas in such a state.

The sheikh managed a weak smile. 'When you came to me all those years ago I mistook you for a beggar. But now,' he gestured to his clothes, 'look at me.' He explained that he had been arrested for arguing with a local notable. His lip trembled as he spoke.

'What, is it your family?' Hawi sat up and stretched out a hand.

Abbas shook his head. 'Worse. They said that all written works apart from the Mahdi's selection of wise sayings,' a shake of the head at the mention of this, 'were subversive materials. I forbade them to enter my library, so they burned it.'

'What?' Hawi was aghast.

'It's all gone,' murmured the old man. He raised his bloodshot eyes towards his friend. 'We live in an age when being able to read is a crime, punishable by death. My boy, we are all in terrible danger.' He unwrapped the rosary beads from his wrist and began turning them through his fingers. 'They say,' he said, 'that it is the blockade which is starving us to death.' He turned his face to Hawi. 'How can they stop people trading with us? These *affranji* must have some powerful gods.'

'They have money and guns,' murmured Hawi. 'These days that counts for the same thing.'

'I hear that more people are being arrested.'

Hawi glanced sideways. 'Arrested, why?'

Sheikh Abbas shrugged, never taking his eyes away from Hawi's. 'Too much loose talk. People get upset about something and one day they say too much and someone else goes running secretly away in the night. The next thing you know the man with the loose tongue is lying in prison.'

'Who?' Hawi asked quietly. 'Who is disappearing?'

'Everybody.' All kinds of people: telegraphists, clerks, teachers, sheikhs from the regions, bakers, cattle-herders, river pilots. Women too.' He lowered his voice. 'There are spies everywhere. He fears a conspiracy.' He leaned forwards. 'That is why I came to you. You are close to him. People are jealous. You must be careful, my boy, for the dogs are hungry.'

28. Omdurman,
July 1894

'I am surrounded by dog-children and lame women,' howled Khalifa Abdullahi, hurling a date-stone, which bounced off a copper jug in the corner of the room and ricocheted upwards to vanish between the dusty rafters of the high-ceilinged room. Children and servants scurried away down the stairs; pigeons took to the wing, flapping nervously up to sunlit rooftops.

Hawi stood in the middle of the Persian carpet (rescued from the palace at Khartoum) and said nothing, not quite sure for what purpose he had been summoned. The khalifa paid him little attention. His bad moods were becoming more frequent. The side of him which was inclined to act rashly was gaining the upper hand.

He was engaged in a long-winded dirge, lamenting the recent defeats in the east and the loss of his valuable towns. 'First that fool Digna loses Tukar. And then Halima,' he made a little wiggle of his hips at the mention of his nickname for Musaid Qaydum, the Habbani commander of the army in the east, 'goes and runs away.'

Hawi remained silent.

'Why,' Abdullahi roared, 'am I surrounded by idiots?'

And Hawi thought to himself, because those who could be trusted were honest, and this made them vulnerable. The strong ones, the brave ones like Nejumi, you deemed dangerous and now they are gone. This is the age of sycophants. The khalifa wiped his shaven head with a cloth and sat down in a large ebony armchair with lion's paws carved into the feet and arms. He indicated for Hawi to take a seat on the wooden divan opposite. 'What,' he asked after a moment, 'did you think of my ride the other day?' He slapped Hawi on the arm in an attempt at joviality. 'Impressive, don't you think?'

On the day the news arrived that the Italians had attacked and taken Kassala, he had mounted his horse with all his warbraids and shields and then, sword in hand, had ridden down to the river, followed by an entourage of bodyguards and slaves and servants brandishing rifles which they didn't know how to use, shouting and cheering and blowing horns and beating drums. He had ridden straight into the water, having first ensured that the townspeople had followed. Then, raising his sword high, he had declared, 'God is greater than the Italians!' and there had been a mighty cheer in reply.

Hawi now tried to think of something to say. 'It had the desired effect, in any case.'

The khalifa spat on the floor in disgust. 'Hawi, you irritate me when you make such small-talk. Am I a woman that you are courting? Tell me what you think or I'll have you castrated. Not that that will make any difference to you,' he sniffed, alluding to Hawi's refusal to take a wife from among the many slave-girls he had sent to him.

The rotund khalifa now paced the room restlessly, preparing to discuss what was on his mind. 'The Italians gather in the east and the British sit in Egypt.' He shook his head mournfully. 'What am I to do?' Pulling a large sword from a scabbard hanging on the wall, he poked clumsily at some unfamiliar flags lying in a heap on the floor. 'Belgians!' He lunged. 'They are four days' march from Hufrat al Nahas. These rags were sent by Arabi Dafallah. He says that the British and the Belgians are fighting over the marshlands of Equatoria.' The heavy jowls shook with mirth. 'Can you imagine? These infidels are fighting one another over our land.' He waved the blade in a circle. 'God speed them on their way to hell.'

Hawi considered the matter. 'You are expecting the English to come back.'

'Even the English cannot sit polishing their boots in Cairo forever.'

Weighing the sword in his hand, Abdullahi went to stand by the window. 'There seems to be no end to their desire to carve up land that does not belong to them.' He turned back to Hawi, with a puzzled look on his face. 'You know, I wrote to their queen telling her of our mission.' He looked crestfallen. 'I told her of the Mahdi and the visions and the betrayal of the true faith, of the corruption and oppression we have suffered in these lands.' He examined the blade of the sword carefully, and threw it aside. 'Hypocrites! They

205

are only interested in slavery, they say. I never heard of a Turk who didn't have twenty slaves to himself.'

Hawi cleared his throat cautiously. 'What,' he asked, 'will happen, if they do come back?'

'The English?' The khalifa raised an eyebrow in mild scepticism and dismissed the threat. 'I am more concerned about the Italians. I shall send a new line of reinforcement to the Atbara river to hold Halima's hand. God knows what the Italians think they are doing there.'

Suddenly he sat down heavily and wiped a hand across his face. 'I am tired of this fighting,' he sighed. 'Not one of my generals can take an order without argument. They quarrel with each other all the time, instead of facing the enemy. I listen for the voices,' he continued in a murmur. 'I wait for the visions to guide me, like they did in the early days.' He stood up and scratched his belly, staring at his feet the way a man might gaze into a dry well. 'I loved him like a brother. When we met, each of us was in his own way lost, unable to find a way forward alone. But together we were invincible. We walked in the month of Ramadan, through the rain, from Aba to Jebel Gedir. I was by his side. Everywhere we went, people took our hands and embraced us. They fell at our feet, begging us to take them with us. We had nothing: no food or clothing, no money and only a few old ostrich guns.' His voice tailed away. In the distance Hawi could hear the sound of a steamer rumbling across the river. 'He was not supposed to die, not so soon.' The khalifa's arms fell limply to his sides and he shook his head. 'Not so soon.'

As Hawi walked softly from the room, his hands were shaking. He descended the stairs and crossed from the shadow of the house into the sharp light that filled the courtyard. He heard the voices of women squabbling somewhere; a handful of chickens pecked at the hard ground. The guards opened the gate to let him through and he passed with a sigh of relief into the street where the people walked.

PART 5

Apostasy

29. Cairo,
1896

The candles flicker in their blue glasses and the room seems to shiver. It is the early hours of the 13th of March 1896. The band is reeling through a long nocturnal version of a number made popular by a man named Bilal Abdel Tawwab, otherwise known as the Wizard of Nubia. No one in the Club Anubìs recognises the song, except the waiters who slip between the tables, clicking their fingers surreptitiously to the charming and somewhat suggestive song.

The officers of Her Majesty's armed forces are in their cups. The musical background is part of the mysterious veil which has descended over them since their landing. It is invasion by euphoria: they are here in the name of God and righteousness.

At the centre of the room sits a large, vulgar party which dominates the proceedings. Belgian attachés leave hurriedly with their stoical ladies in tow, muttering darkly of plots in Equatoria, passing comment on the bestial nature of their cousins from across the Channel. On the far side of the room, the Coptic proprietor, hair slicked back in a smooth dome, sucks deeply on the bubbling *shisha* and directs his inscrutable gaze at the offending group.

At the centre of the collection of rowdy men is a prematurely grey major, flanked by eager young pups whom he has been entertaining with stories of bravado. Soon the leash will be loosed and they will go barking upstream like rabid bloodhounds.

In eleven years Major Hamilton Ellesworth has changed little in outward appearance. A little more flesh round the jowels, perhaps, somewhat deeper etching under the eyes, and a number of grey hairs. He has reached the grand old age of thirty-six but he is not quite ready to throw in the towel just yet. He too has a mission.

'Gordon's strategy was quite off track of course,' someone is braying. Ellesworth yawns, stiff with brandy. The voices grate against his ears.

'Quite,' another bell chimes. 'When Woolsely got there, they could have launched a full assault on Khartoum and knocked the desert heathens back on their heels.'

'You forget,' growls Ellesworth, rousing himself suddenly. All eyes turn and he wishes he hadn't opened his mouth. He blinks and licks his lips. 'Lines of communication . . . cut.' His eyes roll around the young faces. They look the way he ought to look. 'Besides,' he adds, 'no political support from Whitehall.'

The young Lancers nod to one another. 'Well, he was an odd bird all right,' comments one of them. The others seem to agree. One of them begins to giggle.

'Lone!' Ellesworth's fist crashes on to the table, making the glasses and the waiters jump. He squints at the candle flame. 'He was abandoned. Left alone. Completely and utterly alone.'

◆

Hamilton Ellesworth had volunteered for this posting, although he could not, if asked, explain exactly why. He had turned up one day eight months ago and begun hanging around the staff officers, pestering for a recommission. After all these years, there were few who remembered him. He was staying in cheap, unsavoury lodgings near the bazaar. When they asked him why he wanted to get back in at this late stage in life, he said, quite honestly, that he did not have anything better to do.

He had begun to dream of the river, although he did not attempt to explain this to the recruiting officer. They could not turn down a man with such experience. They adjusted his rank and pay according to his age and then proceeded to avoid him. Some said that he had spent too long living in the slums and had gone native. Others whispered that his wife had gone insane, and that he had subsequently abandoned her. His friends became the junior officers; younger men who were more eager and less discerning.

The morning after the drinking session at the club, Major Ellesworth was summoned to an urgent general staff meeting. The hall was crowded, for such a call had been anticipated for some time now. After the usual formalities it was duly announced that at 3 a.m. the previous night (around the time Ellesworth had been throwing up in an alleyway near the Husseiny Mosque), the *sirdar*, Major General Kitchener, had received the orders he was waiting for. A telegram had arrived from London authorising the advance into the Mahdist territory of Dongola as far as Akasha, and there was a strong possibility that they would eventually continue to Khartoum. There was cheering; but Ellesworth found himself coldly detached, unmoved.

So Gordon was to be avenged. A few years ago, he reflected, he might have swallowed it. Now he suspected ulterior motives.

His suspicions were confirmed when, as though reading his mind, the short, robust figure of Colonel Wingate stepped to the fore. He lifted up his chin. 'Gentlemen, we believe that the Mahdists have struck a terrible pact with King Menelik of Ethiopia. The intention is crystal clear – to rid the land of all Christians.' He let this sink in. 'The Italians are taking a lot of stick from the Dervishes. It is our intention to relieve some of that pressure by moving up the Nile into Dongola province.' He indicated on a map that was placed on a stand beside him. 'The Italians have been begging for our help for some time now and they have done quite a job in establishing their Eritrean posts. Now they have taken Kassala for us and I think we ought to give them a little something in return.' He glanced over towards Kitchener, who stood stone-faced, eyes like glazed china, listening to his intelligence officer taking command. Wingate stroked his moustaches and took a second to consider his position. He decided a tactical retreat was in order. 'Our reports tell us that the forces of the khalifa are spread out, with poor communication, and morale is low.'

At this point he gave the floor to Kitchener, who kept his message short and to the point. 'Never underestimate these fanatics,' he purred. 'Those of you who have seen action in the upper regions will know, but many of you are new and I can only reiterate what has been said before. Your average Dervish is slippery as a greased snake and twice as deadly. Men have lost their lives in going to the aid of a wounded comrade. They can hide under the smallest stone and they are lithe as monkeys.'

'E's all 'ot sand an' ginger when alive, An' 'e's generally shammin'

211

when 'e's dead,' came a voice from the back, to be met by a ripple of light laughter.

Kitchener paused for a moment before replying, 'A connoisseur of letters. Well, Mr Kipling may be of some comfort to you but I wouldn't try quoting him to the natives.' From the corner of his eye he discerned something very like a smirk on Wingate's lips. A trick of the light, perhaps?

Ellesworth saw through all this. The Italians were losing the battle. They had lost Adowa to the Ethiopians, and unless the pressure was taken off them, they would lose everything. Nothing to do with Gordon; this was about land. He had stepped closer to the window to allow the breeze from the river to refresh him. Then, as if from a great distance, he heard a voice calling his name. He turned from the window to find that the entire room was staring at him. 'Major Ellesworth?' Wingate said. 'Perhaps you would like to add something to what has been said?'

'What?'

Wingate smiled encouragingly. 'Considering that you are one of the fortunate few who have ventured into the Mahdist territory and returned in one piece.'

Ellesworth's mind was a blank. He detected a note of sarcasm in the last phrase, and his thoughts became caught on this nail and tangled themselves up. Were they laughing at him?

'Major . . .?'

People were beginning to nudge one another and lean over to whisper. He shook his head to clear it. 'I . . .' he began. He tried to smile, but the result was, he knew, ghastly. 'It's . . .' he murmured, trying to shake the words free from the knot inside his head. 'Nothing.'

They turned away and he breathed a sigh of relief. As the voice of some other officer droned on with details of logistics and so forth, he felt Kitchener's eyes upon him.

◆

That night found him back in his usual corner at the Club Anubìs. The place was almost empty and had a sleepy, abandoned feel to it.

He was working his way steadily through a bottle of brandy and had reached that euphoric point in the proceedings when he imagined that he could singlehandedly lead the entire force upstream and retake Khartoum without more than a handful of casualties on the Egyptian side. He was shaken from this pleasant reverie by the arrival of two lieutenants at his table. By their familiar greetings and jocular irreverence he decided that he must have met them before. They sat down without being asked and immediately began calling out in crude tones to the waiter who was dozing on a stool by the bar. Ellesworth was not in the mood for entertainment. He noticed that the atmosphere in the club shifted with the arrival of the two loud foreigners. The band, which had been taking a nap, were now beginning to stir in their seats and the owner, in an ugly mood, kicked them and told them to do what they were being paid for.

The two soldiers settled down somewhat when the brandy arrived, though they offended the waiter by making a private joke about him. Ellesworth saw the proprietor watching them from the corner. He leaned forwards. 'Listen, chaps,' he began, only realising how drunk he was the moment he opened his mouth to speak. 'I have seen people knifed on their way home from this place because they upset someone or other.'

'First bloody monkey that tries it on with me has got it coming,' retorted one of the men, clumsily pulling a large revolver from his pocket. The second one hee-hawed in agreement. Ellesworth looked at them both as though they were from another planet. They must have thought his expression was intended to remind them of his rank, because with a good deal of shuffling and straightening of tunics they sat up attentively.

'I thought we were the occupying army here,' whined the second one, peevishly.

'It's a tricky situation. We are and then again we aren't. This isn't really part of the British empire.' Ellesworth, who was not in the mood for talking, waved the matter aside with his hand.

'But we more or less own it,' the other man said, looking to his friend for confirmation. 'Far as I understand it, that is.'

Ellesworth took another sip of brandy. 'Something like that,' he said. It was easiest to agree.

The other one spoke now, thrusting his face forwards, red and angry from the sun. 'It's us that's going down there to get this bloody merchant of death, this caliwalfa.'

Ellesworth was having difficulty focusing his thoughts. 'Well, they are supposed to be coughing up the costs, either now or later. And their men and officers will be fighting alongside regular British Army units.'

The two men laughed at this, turning to one another and winking. 'Oh yes,' said the first, 'and a bloody great help they'll be.'

Ellesworth's voice grew harsh. 'It's a long way from here to there, gentlemen, and when the time comes we are going to need every man we can summon.' He took a deep breath, feeling the room begin to spin.

There was a pause. Then the second soldier leaned forward. 'I say, sir,' he gurgled. 'You've been there. What's it really like?'

After a moment's contemplation, Ellesworth replied, 'The sunsets are worth dying for. They are like fine music. The light fades the way a man's face drains of colour when he lies bleeding to death in the sand.' It was only when he had finished speaking that he realised they were laughing at him – looking aside, gritting their teeth, covering their grins like schoolboys. Whatever happened next was a blur. Ellesworth tipped over the flimsy table in getting to his feet. He managed to draw his revolver and let off a couple of shots before the waiters and the band descended on him. For a brief second all the lights went out and then he landed on his back in the trickle of dirty water that ran down the alley outside. He got to his feet and dusted himself down. Some time later, as he wandered back to his lodgings, he recalled with vivid clarity the details of his return downstream eleven years ago.

30. The Nile, September 1884
(Eleven Years Earlier)

The night is black. The river beats like a flock of velvet wings and one has the impression of being perched unsteadily on the edge of the abyss. Iron creaks and timber groans; the engine has been struck dumb in sheer fright. Voices break the spell only tentatively, enquiring as to the extent of the damage. The bow of the ship overhangs the rocky lip of the cataracts. Ellesworth is there in the faint damp hiss of the storm lanterns; a blurred figure in the background, watching.

The captain has his own worries. His eyes and ears are only for the river that swirls around them: his wife, his mistress, his master. He feels it is turning against him and wonders what he has done to betray its trust. He calls forward to where the lookout is craning his neck over the reinforced bow. The boy turns and shakes his head. They are aground. Nothing to do.

'We must e'wait until morning e'Sir,' says the *shallali* captain apologetically, feeling every miserable bone of his humiliation sticking in his throat. He is the last of a long line of pilots who have been navigating these waters since Cleopatra's time, or so he says. The rock upon which they are now poised has tonight of all nights decided to move. He curses his luck.

A voice, plaintive and faint, comes drifting from the bank, 'Colon-elly Estew-art? Estew-art basha?'

The stiff figure of Lieutenant-Colonel Stewart moves to the port rail and peers towards where a lantern is being swung. He locates it and lifts his eyeglass. A group of shadowy figures, soft cotton billowing blue in the starlight, huddle round an oil-lamp like moths. 'Yes?' His voice reverberates as though the darkness were a deep well.

A conversation ensues between the pilot and the men on the shore. The tone sounds to Ellesworth almost casual.

'Are you stuck?'

'A rock has caught us.'

'The waters are low this year.'

'Yes, by God, they are.'

'What are you going to do?'

'What can we do? We have to wait until morning.'

'Okay, well why don't you send the others ashore?'

'No, they have to stay with the boat, it's not safe.'

'What is not safe? We are your friends, how do you think we knew you were coming?'

'Who knows?'

'I'm telling you, send them ashore. We have food and fires; rooms for them to rest. You are our guests here and we insist.'

'Thank you, brother.'

'Just ask them, tell them what I say and then ask them. Tell them that we insist that they are our guests. The journey is long and one needs to rest. Don't you have women on board? You can't ask women to stay the night on a boat which may sink at any moment.'

'Sink? Who said anything about it sinking? This is my boat.'

'Well, it doesn't look very good from here. Anyway, better to wait until it's light.'

Stewart paces up and down. 'Keep your rifles trained on that group,' he mutters to the few soldiers who line the bilges on the port side.

'A trap, sir?' Ellesworth asks.

Stewart is frowning. He is in a difficult situation. The boat needs to lift off the bottom. The more weight they can remove, the better the chances. Less than a day's journey downstream lies the camp of Kitchener and his men, and not far behind them is the rest of Wolseley's Relief Expedition. No Dervish would dare to try anything with such a large force so near at hand, surely.

'We have no choice,' he decides, straightening his back. 'I'm afraid we are going to have to trust the thieving black bastards this time.'

Herbin, the French consul, is standing to one side. He rests his hand nonchalantly on the railings and one could imagine him striking a similar pose in a Paris ballroom with a silk suit and a glass of champagne, stroking his whiskers like a cat. He is no fool. He has lived with danger for months. This, however, is getting close to the

216

bone; less than one hundred miles to go. The pilots have proved themselves to be superb at their job. Up to now, they have managed to glide smoothly through the rocks of the cataracts without problem or delay. There is only one of these obstacles left and this he understands is easy in comparison with Sabaloga and the rest of those which have been put safely behind them. He calls the young captain over. He knows that Stewart, though an admirable and competent officer, does not like him, which he puts down to some strange British military code that he will never grasp. The man obviously feels guilty for having abandoned his respected commander, the possibly noble but most certainly very foolish General Gordon. They parted from him at Khartoum, where any man possessing an average number of faculties would have realised that it was pure madness to remain, surrounded as they were by a million blood-thirsty savages who regarded all white men as satanic infidels and saw it as their duty to take off their heads with a blunt knife and feed them limb by limb to the jackals. All this he has explained to Ellesworth over the course of the evenings they have spent together in the somewhat makeshift and cramped salon which has been provided for their comfort.

'Captain, what is your assessment of the situation?'

'Well, sir,' and Ellesworth speaks excellent French – another reason for Herbin to like him, 'Colonel Stewart feels we have to trust them.'

Herbin smiles at the younger man. 'And you, captain, what do you think?'

Ellesworth does not know what to think. He does not wish to set foot on land again for fear of getting lost once more. He shrugs his shoulders. 'We can get horses, camels and guides to take us the rest of the way to Merowe. We cannot continue this way. The boat may be irreparably damaged.'

With a beaming smile, and slapping his hands against his sides like a penguin, Herbin says '*Alors*, we have no choice, as you say.' He sees quite clearly that military men are only capable of functioning as links in the chain of command. This is their training. They are not trained to think as such. And this despite the qualities which Ellesworth has displayed so far. 'Captain, I shall gather our Greek friends together and we shall pool our resources.' He sets off with a wave, saying over his shoulder, 'I have never known an Arab who would not sell his grandmother for the right price.' Then he vanishes inside the salon, where the merchants are still busy gambling their fortunes away.

◆

When the small boat drew up alongside it contained only three men, two on the oars and an elderly grey-haired man in the bow holding a small lantern. They helped him aboard. He stood there proud and smiling, intent on making a good impression. Ellesworth noted that he was dressed not in the green patched *jubba* of the Dervishes but in a spotless white *jubba* with a silk shawl around his shoulders and a fine scarf wrapped on his head. He was quite dressed up for the occasion – a little too much, perhaps, but in a shambling, endearing fashion. He began to speak, despite their requests for him to wait for a translator.

'Fetch the Egyptian,' snapped Stewart over his shoulder for the third time.

When the Egyptian officer finally arrived, he smelt of brandy and saluted everyone present in an insolent fashion before turning to the old man, who having finished his long, incomprehensible speech, now stood with his head bowed in silence. He looked up in surprise at the officer.

'Well, old man, what have you got to say?'

The other man began to smile, but then changed his mind and instead folded it up and put it away, having seen the glint in the officer's eyes. 'We come in peace,' he muttered absently, looking around the deck. He touched his hand to his heart and his head. 'We have no fight with the Egyptians, who are our brothers. Nor with the Turks, nor the sultan nor the khedive, nor the *Inglisi*, or, the *Fransawi*.' The old man tailed off as he noted the Egyptian's impatience. Then he came abruptly to the point. 'You cannot stay on this boat; it will sink into the river before morning.'

The Egyptian turned and translated carefully for the others.

'Ask him if they have enough horses and camels for us.'

'How many are you?' asked the old man, looking them up and down like a tailor measuring up a customer. A debate ensued as to whether or not this was confidential information.

'They have to know if they are to help us.'

'Colonel, we have no choice,' Herbin intervened finally. 'If this man is genuine then we should not risk offending him.'

'Sir,' replied Stewart in his sternest manner. 'You are a civilian and this is a military vessel. I would remind you that I remain in command and I will judge whether we are divulging information which could prove useful to the enemy.'

'Surely,' piped up Frank Power, correspondent for *The Times*, 'they will not harm us with the Flying Column less than a hundred miles away.' He had a habit of stating the obvious, but was apparently well respected in Fleet Street. 'Everyone knows the game will soon be up. At worst they may hold us captive, and it won't be long before Wolseley's cavalry arrive to release us.' Perhaps he was taken with the idea of being held captive – visions of exclusive reports flashing before his eyes. To the others, however, the prospect did not have the same appeal.

Colonel Stewart turned to the Egyptian dragoman. 'Tell the sheikh that I will come ashore with a small party to negotiate the details and that he will be rewarded for any help he gives us.' It was clear from the old man's eyes that this offhand manner was not to his liking. He nodded in a surly fashion and the Egyptian returned with his reply: 'All of you are our honoured guests and we will give you food and shelter until morning when you can continue your journey through our land. Let it not be said that the people of Salamat do not show hospitality to their guests.'

'We shall see,' nodded a sceptical Stewart. The preparations were made. 'I shall take twenty men and any of you who care to come along. My advice, however, is that at this point it is safer to remain aboard the *Abbas* until we have seen how the land lies.' His eyes returned to the darkened shoreline, where a single lantern still flickered among the shadows. The rocks and the sky seemed carved out of the same stone and the stars gazed upon them like a thousand pairs of eyes, distant and impartial.

Frank Power dropped his cigarette to the deck and ground it in with his heel. 'Don't think you'll get away with leaving me aboard a sinking ship.' He wore a tense, reptilian grin which had never endeared him to anyone. Stewart sighed.

Herbin stepped forward. 'I too must come along I fear, *mon colonel*.'

'Nothing to fear, Monsieur Herbin,' quipped Power. 'A spot of exercise before we meet up with the Flying Column will do us good. We are in the hands of the queen's finest.' It seemed that on this point at least all of the other passengers were in agreement with him. They all elected to go along. Only Ellesworth was left on board, with a handful of men and the crew.

Watching from the small bridge, Ellesworth heard the voices dissolve into the inky blue night. There was a wave of a lantern and then they were gone. The breeze blew gently through the hairs on the back of his neck. A bat flew squeaking overhead.

The night crawled slowly; the wind hummed through the rocks. Something shiny and black moved through the water, catching the corner of his eye. 'Crocodile?' he thought. The sound of laughter echoed from below. Someone had told him that many of the river crews could not even swim. If they wanted you, the river *jinns* would get you, no matter how good a swimmer you were.

It was three o'clock in the morning when the boat began to sway. He was half asleep, leaning against the timber shoring on the front deck. He waited for another sign, a confirmation. The stern lurched again. The weight was shifting. Start the engines, shouted a voice in his head. Something was bumping against the hull. He heard it again. The stern shifted again as the stream caught them; they were yawning slowly around in the water with a tearing sound from down below. Was that water rushing into the hold? Suddenly there was commotion at the helm. The two pilots were arguing with one another, struggling to hold the wheel. He got to his feet. 'Get the steam up,' he ordered. He looked down as another movement caught his eye. 'Lights!' he called. 'We need lights!' Figures were moving along the deck towards him. He turned and stumbled; knelt down and felt something wet and sticky. He drew his pistol just as a scream came from somewhere in the stern. How had they come aboard? He fired into the air and made for the short ladder to the bridge. The two pilots had vanished, leaving the wheel rocking this way and that. The boat swung and rolled, listing badly to starboard. They were being dragged stern first down the river by the current, picking up speed as they went. He heard a shot from somewhere and turned to see a boy, no more than twelve, with a dagger in his hand, coming towards him. He raised his pistol and fired. The boy clutched his head and screamed. The wheel was now hammering away, like the devil drumming with bones on a tree trunk. Ellesworth dropped down the ladder to find the deck awash with foaming muddy water that came up to his knees. There was a terrible crash as they slammed back into the rocks. A wave of water knocked him on to his back. Then, like a hand rising up beneath him, it lifted him and gently blew him over the side, light as a feather on the breeze. He stretched out a hand instinctively and his fingers gripped a timber, a piece of the armour come loose. He clung on, sobbing, begging for life, and floated away downstream – eyes wide, ears filled with the rushing, roaring sound of the world gone insane.

◆

On his return to England he never mentioned his experiences, never in passing, never to his wife. He was introduced at parties as the Survivor of Khartoum. The newspapers clamoured for his story, but he turned them all down. He became morose and introverted, a fact that gradually poisoned the rest of his life and those around him. He recalled as if from a great distance those days when nothing meant more to him than his love for Amelia Tamarind Walden. Of the nights he had spent wandering lost with Spratling, not one had gone by when he had not thought of her and whether she would be waiting for him on his return. There was no one in the world he would rather have shared his story with, but how could he expect her to understand what it was like? She fretted about him when he turned mournful and solemn, but the more she tried to express her sympathy, the more he realised the impossibility of the task. Her attempts to soothe soon began to smother him.

She had waited for him, even when he was reported lost. They were married within a year of his return. Her father was dying and it was her wish that he should see her settled before he departed from this world, despite the fact that she must have suspected some change in her beloved on his return.

They moved into the big house. With Amelia's inheritance they had little need for money and he fell into idle habits. He resigned his commission and stayed at home, working his way through his late father-in-law's library, rarely emerging, even to eat. Amelia sat in the rose garden in the rain, weeping secretly.

When their first child died during birth he declared that he was cursed. But she insisted they try again, though by now their marital relationship had deteriorated to such a degree that the chances of another conception were unlikely. As luck would have it, however, nature eventually took its course and she became pregnant. By this time her mind had begun to turn inwards as she blamed and punished herself for not being able to save her husband from his demons. She would find him asleep in the library, sprawled upon the fine leather-topped desk, a bottle of brandy knocked over on its side. She turned to prayer, but it brought her no comfort. Her distress of mind slowly ate away, unnoticed by him until it was too late.

31. Omdurman, 1897

It happened that one day Hawi ran into Sheikh Baladi, with whom he had not had any contact since the days of the Council of Vision, which had long since been disbanded. The sheikh seemed pleased to see him. 'What a coincidence,' he remarked. He asked Hawi if he remembered an evening nearly ten years ago now when the council had been presented with a strange case, a girl? Hawi did vaguely remember. Well, what a coincidence, laughed the sheikh, for the same girl had just that morning come before his court. 'Perhaps you would like to come one day and observe proceedings?' Although he was not keen on the idea, Hawi decided that it would be ungracious not to turn up for a short glimpse of the sheikh, who was now a *qadi*, at work. And so Hawi found himself sitting inside the stuffy hall of the courtroom. A stiff-necked *ansar* stood before them, his nose stretched towards the dusty rafters.

'What did she do, exactly?' repeated the *qadi*.

The guard shifted his weight from the one foot to the other. His eyes were fixed straight ahead of him and they bulged like those of small fish in dark waters. By the looks of him he was scared of the judge. Hawi sat against the wall on a small bench. On the far side of the room sat the woman, her head bowed. He remembered her now that he saw her. The guard began again. The girl had tried to stab both himself and another soldier. The other man was cut, but it was not serious. He had gone home to his wife in Darfur to recover. The soldier's eyes now flickered back and forth between an unmarked spot high on the wall behind the judge and somewhere above Hawi's right shoulder. He seemed nervous, and looked as though he were about to faint.

Sheikh Baladi was tiring of the delay. He stirred, rearranged his shawl and his *imma*. The grey wisps of his beard shook around his jowls. 'Finish the story, boy,' he growled, 'before we rot to death.'

223

Nodding obediently, the guard swallowed and began to speak. 'There were complaints from the neighbours about loud noise and fighting. Her husband was sick, in great pain, nearly dead when we arrived.'

At this point things took a dramatic turn as the girl leapt to her feet. 'It's not true,' she yelled. 'I was his slave, not his wife.'

'Keep quiet, girl, until we ask you,' growled Baladi. 'Then, as though it had suddenly occurred to him that this was in fact an opportune moment, he addressed her. 'Why did you try to hurt these men of the guard?'

The girl bowed her head again and spoke to her feet. 'They put their hands on me.' Hawi noticed that the guard was shifting his weight again.

'God protect us from the devil,' thundered the judge. 'Perhaps I should give you two hundred stripes of the *courbaj* to teach you how to treat women?'

The soldier stood sullen and silent, his eyes lowered. Baladi leaned down towards Hawi. 'What do you think?' he asked. 'I told you it would be amusing, eh?'

Hawi did not know what to think. 'We need to know more,' he whispered finally.

The *qadi* agreed. 'It is late,' he said to the soldiers. 'Take her back to the prison and keep her there until tomorrow. Come back here at the same time.' He waved a hand to send them away.

'Bring in the other witnesses,' he called out. He leaned down towards Hawi. 'We hear what they have to say and then we go and eat lunch in my house.'

A cluster of men and women with the look of simple people came shuffling into the room. 'Come along, come along. What do you all have to say?'

A small woman with no teeth stepped forward. 'She killed her child.'

A larger woman came to stand by her shoulder. 'What she speaks is the truth,' she hissed, swatting a fly from her face with a heavy flick of the wrist. There were nods and murmurs from those gathered behind them.

Baladi waved his hands in the air for silence. 'One at a time, please! Someone explain what this is about.'

The two women retreated and the crowd parted suddenly, leaving a gaunt, hollow-faced man alone in the centre of the room. He licked his lips and looked around for reassurance. 'It happened many years ago apparently. She became with child by a soldier. He promised to marry her and take her across the sea to his home. But his mind was confused by the sun and the battle, and so when he regained his senses he knew that it would never be allowed.' The man wheezed and coughed and spat copious amounts of phlegm on to the floor, but he spoke with the confidence of one who had been telling the same story all his life. 'They put her into a hospital when she came to this part of the world. She had a sickness which many suspected was the work of *jinns* living in her head. She watched her soldier sail away towards the cold north, alone, and she could not understand how one person could betray another in such a way, though she was no fool and fully understood the ways of men. She had trusted this soldier.' The sound of quiet weeping came from the back of the hot, crowded room.

Hawi held up a hand, and the old man paused. 'Old man,' Hawi asked, 'how do you know all of this?'

'I listen very carefully,' said the man slowly. He gestured with one hand for permission to continue. 'When the child was born, and it caused her great pain for it was her first, she saw immediately that it was not her child, but belonged to the people of the soldier who had put it there. She knew that it would always remind her of his betrayal and so she took it to the river and drowned it there, tying its arms and legs to a stone before dropping it in.' The women behind him were now wailing and shaking their heads from side to side at the horror of this. The man continued. 'But she was seen by a fisherman and he reported her to the *ansar* and they took her to the judge, in a court just like this one. They gave her to the one named Ibrahim, the foreigner who owns her now, thinking that it would please her; obviously it didn't.'

The witnesses were dismissed and shepherded from the room. Sheikh Baladi got to his feet and indicated the door. Hawi followed him. Baladi slipped his arm around Hawi's shoulders. In his other hand his fingers restlessly turned the beads of his *sibha*. 'Perhaps you might acquire a taste for this work. I could see your interest.' They marched on through the heat of midday. The *qadi*'s house was close to the khalifa's compound.

As they walked on through the throngs of people that crowded the main square near the Mahdi's tomb, touching the walls, kneeling down in prayer, Baladi asked, 'Why do they do this kind of thing?' He wrinkled his nose in distaste.

Hawi was surprised by the question. 'They take their children to see why their fathers and grandfathers and uncles died.' He paused. 'They don't want their children to forget.'

'All things will be forgotten, even them.' Baladi stopped racking up the rosary beads and turned to face Hawi. 'Is that how you see religious devotion?' Above the rattle of mule-traders and water vendors and the bustle of pilgrims Hawi struggled to hear what the judge was saying. '. . . it takes no time at all to win a battle, but it can take generations before the consequences of that battle are understood. Man is a stupid beast.' He turned a corner. 'You never see a bird behaving like that.' They reached the house and went inside.

Hawi suddenly grasped the other man's arm, so roughly that the sheikh gave a yelp of alarm. 'I have a question for you.' The sheikh stared at him. Hawi took a deep breath. 'That girl, if I vouch for her will you release her into my care?'

'You are a man of learning,' said Baladi, holding Hawi's gaze. 'And you are close to the khalifa's ear. I could not deny you such a thing.' He straightened up and began to unwind and re-tie his scarf. 'What kind of assurance did you have in mind?'

'I will vouch for her,' said Hawi.

Sheikh Baladi raised his eyebrows. 'Well,' he said, smiling, 'you seem to have given this some thought. This certainly explains your interest in the case.' He made as if to walk on, but once again Hawi stopped him.

'I will marry her,' he blurted out.

The sheikh looked confused. 'Marry her?' He shook his head. 'A woman like that?'

'To my servant, of course.'

'To your servant?'

Hawi nodded. 'It would be good for him . . . and for her.'

Sheikh Baladi shrugged his agreement and clapped his hands for lunch.

226

32. The Nubian Desert, 1897

Like fluid mercury, the line spills itself across the plain. To them the land is dead, made of rock and sand, stones turned hard and black in the furnace of the sun. All day they ride, like modern-day crusaders inside the clanking armour of flat wagons that deposit them in the middle of silent nowhere, surrounded by the wind; a place from which they will crawl like ants towards ... somewhere else. It is the middle of summer and the rocks and stones are too hot even to touch. The dust burns when it comes in contact with the skin. The men are going down with every kind of rash and pestilence ever encountered by the surgeons: fevers and cramps, attacks of blindness, sunstroke, an outbreak of vicious boils which swell up in the armpits before festering and finally bursting, releasing bloody streaks of pus. Their hands and feet are swollen and worn raw. Every other day someone reaches under a rock without turning it over first and finds a scorpion. There are sand flies and poison thorns which curl through the sole of a boot and into the foot. In the large camps there is dysentery and livid forms of venereal disease transported from the brothels of Cairo.

All of this and then the work. The task which lies ahead of them is to build a railway – to transform the floor of this desiccated ocean into a metropolitan tramway. To drive a million tiny iron stakes through the dark heart of the strange creatures whom God in his wisdom has chosen to abandon here amongst the calcified fishbones and crumbled towers. They wander in from time to time, materialising out of the heathaze, stepping lightly from a fold in the sand: whole families, snotty-nosed children and sleeping babies, patient men squatting together on their heels watching from a distance. They watch and they listen, fascinated that anyone should go to so much trouble to cross a desert.

The soldiers sing strange songs to remind themselves of home. And although they curse those stern-faced gentlemen who led them into this madness, they all share in the sense of proud achievement. The *sirdar* Kitchener strolls around, knocking idle rivets into place and slapping the men heartily on the shoulders.

All day and night the machinery rolls forward through the desert. The trucks glide along the rails carrying crates of ammunition; charges and detonators; mines and rifles; field guns and gatling guns; bayonets and booby-traps. They have flat-bottomed gunboats in sections. They have camel men and infantry. They have bully beef and new boots. They file down the tips of their bullets for maximum effect, so that they will flatten and explode into viscous fragments, harder to extract and more painful. The desert railway is the artery that feeds. And slowly, relentlessly, the thin silver trail crawls forward, like vertebrae along the spine of some unnamed arthropod.

◆

It is three in the morning. The moon burns through the black night like cold metal. The burly *fellah* kicks the sleeping bundles awake. He seems to enjoy being out of his bed before the rest of them, and then reminding them of this fact, night after night. Kadaro rolls to his knees and rubs his eyes. His body is stiff as a tree; every muscle is in hard knots. The prisoners shuffle, cough, hack and spit and turn their backs to glare at the moon as they piss. The men are a surly bunch: criminals, deserters, the lowest kind of men, turncoats and cowards, killers of women and torturers of children. They will turn on their masters the first chance they get.

They will work now until dawn, shovelling the small stones and gravel until the supply train from Halfa arrives. From this they will unload great iron girders that shine in the sun. They do it early, because later in the day the metal is too hot to touch without burning the hands. They clamber up and down like small animals at the command of the *Inglisi* officers and the *fellaheen* who bark at them like dogs. The railway crawls southwards at the rate of one or two miles a day. They are following a line drawn upon paper, which must be straight as the barrel of a cannon. The straightness of this line will not be sacrificed for anything. They cut down through banks and fill in washed-out *wadi*s. Through the dust and the wind they struggle blindly. Kadaro watches the engineers poring over their diagrams, scribbling notes and taking readings. They are evening out the desert, taking away the corners and the round edges which God put there the way one ploughs a field. Kadaro has noticed that some of the Europeans have the same weary look about them as his own people, as though they cannot see the purpose of this enterprise; only Kadaro can see. They roll out of the camp towards the south, clinging to the rim of the flat bed-wagon, feeling the wind on their faces. This is the moment he enjoys most of all: lying down feeling himself being swept along by this machinery. He laughs and claps his friends on the shoulder.

'Think,' he howls, 'that they go to all this trouble to bring this machine here so that we may float across the desert like *jinns*.'

They laugh, because the rest of the day they will be sweating blood through the pores of their skin. He has seen a man lose a hand because he was too slow to miss a moving girder. You have to be quick with this silver sorcery because it can easily turn on you. Kadaro does not want to be eaten by this machinery; he wants to tame it.

The first time he saw Major Ellesworth, Kadaro was standing near a pile of fallen girders beneath which an unfortunate fellow prisoner was trapped. A stave had given way and the old man had no chance. He was spluttering blood and someone ran to fetch water from the square steel box-wagons that came down from Halfa every day at noon.

The major had arrived astride the prow of the locomotive, clinging athletically to a convenient railing, and was coated in yellow dust. He stepped down and strolled over towards the scene of the accident surrounded by an entourage of Egyptian officers and subalterns, Sikh drivers in turbans and pale-looking station officers. He took his time, surveying the village of dust-blown canvas that housed twenty-five hundred men and which would be home to him for the rest of the summer. Kadaro stood beside the gang of men who were frantically pulling at the ironware. It was no use, Kadaro was thinking; the man is as good as dead. He was unable to take his eyes off the figure now approaching them.

The major began shouting orders. Time was being wasted. Hurry along. From the running-board of the engine, the Italian engineers surveyed the scene. They were laughing to one another, making comments in their own language. After an hour, the man's cries stopped. They carried on lifting the hot girders out of the way. The major had turned away by this time, however. He went to sit in the shade. Then the whistle blew and they were ordered back on to the wagons. It was time to move forward. Kadaro received a thump on his back and found himself propelled back into the shuffling crowd of linemen.

The following days went by in a similar manner. Each time Kadaro saw the major he became more convinced that it was who he thought. They led out the line of silver metal towards the unbending horizon. They hammered in the spikes to each alternate sleeper. Then they stood aside as the lumbering engine groaned and moaned and dragged itself inch by inch over the new track. Kadaro watched the engineers, their hearts in their mouths, leaning from the cab. For them it was like a delicate surgical operation; they moved that big engine as though running over a row of eggs. The next morning they would begin again, shovelling gravel into the ballast gaps and stitching up the spikes that nailed the iron ladder to the ground; the ladder up which the soldiers were to climb.

Often there was talk among the prisoners of escape, of sabotage, but they were too weary to do anything. They sat around a small fire in the evenings, watching from a distance as the English officers drank their whisky and their ale, and smoked their cigarettes.

'They have a good life, these people,' Kadaro thought to himself. 'They don't need anything.' He had seen the stores at Halfa. The mountains of bale wire and fishplates and spare boilers and machine tools and trolleys and a thousand other things whose purpose he could not even guess. The armies of the khalifa could never withstand this force. And he understood then that the battle was not between men of different colours or faiths, but between two different ages. The world beyond, a world he did not know, existed in a different age – an age that was so much faster than that which he knew, and so much wiser. This was a war between yesterday and tomorrow.

One night when the moon was only a thin silver scar etched on the inky sky he crept from the place where they slept and crawled on his belly with an iron spike in his hand. He reached the officers' tents where the glow of lanterns illuminated the shadows within. He lay there in the sand listening to the strange conversation, the words he could not understand. His hand clenched and unclenched around the weapon, and the more he thought, the more confused he became. He loved the shiny machine rails, but they would only ever be used to rule. He crept closer to the tent where the major was.

To his surprise he found the major standing with his back to him, pissing in the sand while singing a tuneless song. Kadaro crouched, ready to attack. He reminded himself of the time he spent in prison, of the girl, of that morning long ago on the bank of the river among the creaking canes. He lay there feeling the sand against his belly and the moment passed. Finally, painfully, his fingers unclenched and the spike fell from his hand into the cool sand. He turned and began to run. He cleared the camp without difficulty for there were few guards: where would anyone run? Out there was the desert and no one could survive in it for long. But Kadaro could and he knew it and so he kept on running.

◆

A week later he was caught, ten miles from the river, by a cavalry patrol sweeping for raiding parties. He lay with his ear to the cool stones of a well listening to them approaching; thirty men, mounted on camels. They chased him across a plateau of muscovite which glittered in the sunlight. When they roped him in he told them where he had come from, making up a story about a wife who was sick. They laughed. He was going back. The railway was too important, they said, otherwise they would have shot him as a spy.

The fires were burning smokily as Kadaro was led between the canvas walls of the camp. The voices of the soldiers came from the corners where they gathered to drink. Out of the shadows stepped a familiar figure: the major, his tunic unbuttoned to the waist. He stood there for a moment, swaying only slightly in the clear night breeze. He held up a hand. 'Just a moment, soldier.' The two men who were accompanying Kadaro saluted and halted. Ellesworth stepped forwards. In the flickering light that filtered between the dark walls he peered into the young man's face. He turned to the guards. 'Where are you taking this man?' he demanded. The guards explained the story. Ellesworth stepped backwards a pace and raised a finger. 'What happened to his leg?'

'The patrol had to immobilise him, sir. Rifle butt to the knee, I believe.'

Kadaro said nothing. Ellesworth dismissed the two guards. 'Don't worry about it, gentlemen, I will take full responsibility. This man is not going to try it again, I can assure you.'

They left, reluctantly, and Ellesworth turned to Kadaro. 'You ran away, that shows courage . . . and intelligence.' He nodded and tapped the side of his forehead to emphasise his meaning. 'This line needs people like that. This is only the beginning. We need people we can trust. I can trust you, can't I?'

Kadaro took a moment to weigh things up. He said nothing, not wanting to break the flow of what appeared to be good luck coming his way. 'You probably won't understand this, but you remind me of someone I once knew, a long time ago.' He stepped closer and swayed in towards Kadaro, breathing whisky fumes. Kadaro did not flinch. 'I know you. I know your people. That,' purred Ellesworth, 'is how I know I can trust you.'

He threw his arm around Kadaro's shoulders, supporting him and pulling him to his side. 'One day this land is going to be crossed by thousands of miles of track, upon which the finest locomotives will fly up and down from Cairo to the Cape of Good Hope.' He stabbed a finger into Kadaro's chest and stepped away. 'Engineers; station masters; brake men; conductors; all humming away happily.' He beamed and winked. 'No one wants to start a revolt when they are well paid and respected.' He broke off into laughter which stuttered into a cough, and waved a hand in the air as he tried to get the words out. 'You can stay in the stone age,' he stabbed, 'or you can be in at the start.'

33. The Battle of Omdurman, 2 September 1898

The Hour had come. That night the rain fell as it had never fallen before. Hawi sat beneath the shelter of the roof, through which the drops fell idly, disturbing his thoughts. The water now danced and splashed in ever-widening pools where an hour ago there had been hard dry earth. He could hear children's cries of joy and delight from the streets and surrounding houses. The silver puddles stretched and swelled. The water ran in long streams down the walls, eating away at the plastered mud and wattle. The deluge carried on through the night. He lay awake on his bed, listening. He felt as helpless as a baby.

All night through the rain he heard the distant voices of men, in anticipation, in discussion and in prayer. All that could be said had been said before. The fate which was drawing closer towards them with every hour had been coming for a very long time. Despite the assurances of the khalifa and his advisors, there was little hope in the hearts of the people. They had struggled for so long, and here was another war come to meet them.

Everyone had been mobilised for this battle. For weeks he had drilled in the sun with a wooden stick on his shoulder for a rifle, the real ones being locked in the armoury for the sake of security. It was all absurd, Hawi realised. In anticipation, a great parade had been arranged: all the great ivory *ombeya*s blew and the drums beat. Then, in the midst of all this, while men marched back and forth whooping, waving their spears, and the cavalry made endless charges up and down, Ali wad Hilu fell off his horse. In front of the Mahdi's tomb he fell right out of the saddle, landing on his back in the dust. The parade scattered in disbelief. People began beating their heads and tearing at their hair in despair. As if in mourning, the khalifa vanished inside the Mahdi's tomb and remained there for eight days of endless prayer.

Everything seemed to be falling apart. If the world was at an end, it

233

was not going to take place in the manner predicted by the Mahdi. The final battle would be much closer to home than anyone had ever imagined.

Hawi listened to the conversation as he huddled in his shelter. The men said that it was no longer the khedive who ruled Egypt, but the queen of the *Inglisi*, and that her men knew no mercy. They were here for revenge. They had bullets which exploded inside a man's body and spat the bones out of his back like so many watermelon seeds.

Hawi finally fell asleep, too exhausted to take issue with this talk. It was some hours later that he was woken by the arrival of his servant. The clouds still rumbled in the distance and the servant was soaked through and shivering with exhaustion. Hawi pulled him in under the shelter of the *rekuba* to discover that his clothing was covered with a sticky dark mess. 'Blood?' he asked, his head still spinning. 'Has the killing begun already?'

Hayatu gave a shake of his head. 'Not the blood of men,' he answered wearily. 'We have killed every mule, every camel, every horse and dog which could be used by the enemy.'

'Has he finally gone mad, that you, his army should be out there slaughtering donkeys on a night like this?' Hawi dribbled as he fell back into a deep sleep. He imagined he smelt dead fish and could feel the river rising, that the whole world was in flood.

◆

Sixty thousand men all told, ranging from young boys who could barely hold a sword above their heads with both hands to old men like Hawi who could hardly walk. Sixty thousand men walking into the sun: under the light-green flag of Ali wad Hilu marched fifty-five hundred souls, north towards the black rocks of the Kerreri Hills round which they would circle towards the plains. Behind them came the dark-green banner with twelve hundred horsemen and a total of twenty-eight thousand *jihadiya* riflemen and *ansar* who had spent the night crouched beneath the belly of the sleeping mountain.

◆

234

The swollen river was cluttered with iron-clad boats. The rumble of pistons and steam made the mud-worms shudder. The razor steel rings and the brass casings hummed. For two years they had been carving their way upstream. They nailed the sky to the burning desert and dragged its thunder from Halfa to Atbara. The locomotives rolled restlessly back and forth with their endless rattling chains of wagons, artillery and men. The wheels of modern industry, their name plates gleaming with sounds that would soon become familiar: Lancashire, Manchester, Sheffield, Leeds; faster and faster they spun.

◆

They are coming. *Allah i khalina min al shaitan.* This time nothing will stop them. The future is making its way upstream and the river is shaking in its bed.

◆

Night, and the one bad eye of the searchlight peers out. The boats patrol up and down, searching for anything or anyone that dares to move.

On the west side of Jebel Surkab, the Khalifa Abdullahi and his brother Yaqub sit with their twenty-thousand brothers from the Baggara, watching the beam of light rake the ocean of ink which covers the plain. 'What evil is it that the dogs bring to us now?' the khalifa asks.

◆

Dawn broke like the promise of a virtuous whore to find Hawi caught up in the atmosphere of haste and fear that pervaded the camp. The bare feet of thousands of men slapped against the sharp stones as they began to run. And even in that moment, just before turning the corner to face the enemy, there was still hope there, in the hearts of men who would not live to see another sunset. In Hawi's heart, too, there was the hope that they could do it once again. This time they would send the English dogs home, not because they were better or braver, nor because the Mahdi had proclaimed it, but simply because they needed this time. If they were ever going to learn how to listen to one another, how to be fair, how to rule a land as vast as this, then they needed time.

◆

The sky was dotted with clouds that bloomed like buds of cotton on a tree. The roar of men's voices filled his ears. He could smell their sweat, their stale bodies, their breath, their beating hearts, the blood that ran in their veins.

It was better when you were moving. When you are running you are occupied. All around him was dust kicked up by the horses as they galloped back and forth, shaking their hindquarters impatiently. When the enemy came within a certain distance, still a line of bush and thorns on the horizon, the shells began to land among them. He heard nothing above the roar, and though he was terrified, he would turn to look at the man next to him and he would see that this man was different from the one who had been there a moment ago. All along the line he saw the faces of brave stupid men running headlong towards the guns and he knew that he was proud to be here, to be a man among them. With each heartbeat it seemed that he lived and died another life. He was young, he was old; he was brave as a lion and then as frightened as a mouse; he was invincible, and he was dead; he was proud to be among these men, and he was ashamed of the spear that he carried in his hands. He heard their chanting like the music of God in his ears and then the rifles erupted and they were running in different directions and there was confusion broken only by brief moments of clarity. The smoke of the rifles cleared and suddenly he was alone. Before him lay a man; a young man with the white flag of Osman Azraq beside him. Leaning down, Hawi lifted it carefully, and then holding it high he began to run in that awkward, clumsy fashion of his on towards the sparks and the flames, into the smoke, towards the end of the world.

◆

The plains were scattered with the bodies of the faithful: old men, young boys, children armed with carved wooden swords. The soldiers advanced cautiously, bayonets fixed, prodding the last vestiges of life from the blood-soaked rags. Behind the soldiers came the looters – an unpleasant crowd of scavengers who had attached themselves to the column at various points along the road from Cairo. There were good pickings here. The groans of the dying lingered on through the night.

◆

They said that out where the wings of hawks drew black circles, there were thousands of bodies that lay like leaves shaken from a tree, spread across the Kerreri plains. Hawi was woken by the crowd which had made its way out in the morning sun to try and find their fallen relatives. A day had gone by and the corpses were swollen with the heat. The stench was awful. Here and there relatives wept over the discovery of a son or a husband or a father. For years afterwards some widows went wandering in their black shawls like crows, picking up the bones of men and collecting them as some kind of memorial to the ones they had never found.

Hawi dragged himself out from under a pile of bodies. He made his way slowly back to the town, or what remained of it. All along the road lay the dead and dying. People were digging holes in the ground to bury them. The soldiers rushed by in a great hurry, dragging carriages and shiny cannon.

The town was still in a state of panic and pandemonium. Whole streets had simply vanished. Dull heaps of churned-up mud grew like anthills from the ground, circling deep holes that had appeared in the earth. There were dead bodies, divided into parts by some macabre hand. Disgorged entrails lay turning grey in the dust. Dogs loped around, feeding in a frenzy. A woman kneeled in the street, silent, her body racked by sobs which remained unheard.

People walked through the streets in a dazed kind of way, talking to no one in particular, feeding on the stream of words that passed through them like a common voice.

'There are no longer any differences between us,' Hawi reflected. 'We are all lost.'

They congregated among the ruins out of a common desire to confirm and comprehend. People said that the clouds of red dust came from the fortifications which had been built along the riverbank stretching north towards Shambat. The guns that were intended to fire on passing boats had vanished in a cloud of dust and straw. At one stage there was cheering as the roar of guns from the iron-clad boats prowling the river faded into silence. When they started up again, people said that the final Hour had surely come since the unbelievers had been raised from the dead. A hole had appeared in the Mahdi's tomb and the single white tooth aimed at the sky was shattered like an egg.

Someone took his arm and told him urgently to come. They rushed together through the streets to the place where his house had stood, now no more than a heap of mud. The sky grew black. He searched and finally found Noon, lying on her back, surrounded by a flock of neighbours. Her eyes were open though she was not dead. He knelt beside her and lifted her carefully into his arms for the first time, for they had never lived as anything but companions.

'It is I,' he said.

She dug her fingers into his arm. 'The world has gone black,' she said with a kind of wonder.

The tears which rolled down his face did not hurt. He no longer heard the screams of the dying and the insane. He crouched on the ground, his arm around the shivering girl. If this was not the inferno of *Jehenum*, if this was not hell, he asked himself as the air was sucked from his lungs and replaced with burning dust, where else could it be?

34. The Palace, Khartoum,
September 1898

The smoke cleared and the night passed. The clouds were swallowed in the dull pools of rain, and the *sirdar* entered the fallen city dragging the khalifa's flag behind him through the muddy ground. People looked on with eyes glazed with fear at the Highlanders in their kilts playing instruments that looked like dead goats.

They tore down the remaining walls of the Mahdi's tomb, ripping the embroidered cloths, the holy inscriptions and the silk, all down. They dug up the grave and held the bones up towards the sky. 'See here,' the soldiers shouted, 'he is as dead as any man. His remains are here. He has not gone to sit beside the Prophet and God, he lies rotting here.' They threw the bones into the river, except for the skull, which the *Sirdar* Kitchener kept as a souvenir in a jar of kerosene.

◆

Ellesworth consoled himself with the thought that now he would be at peace with himself, at last. He lay resting on the infirmary ship. Fellow officers wandered by, nodding in salute. From the cot where he lay he could just see, over the armoured railing, the gentle sway of a palm tree. He remembered little of the battle itself.

The enemy were approaching like a tide rising from the bed of a deep unfathomable sea. The air was still damp from the rain and rusty bronze pools of water were left stranded on the flat plain. The men began to fidget, yelling curses at the approaching dervishes. 'Never mind that! You must wait until they are within range. Wait for it!' But he could not bring himself to pace along the front of the line as Macdonald had earlier, making the men wait for the order before opening fire. Instead he stood on the side where it was somewhat safer and contented himself with shouting. In the distance he saw shells from the right wing fall in among the dancing hordes of white cotton and glittering metal. The shells fell like pebbles into a pond, sending out little circular ripples of dead and wounded men. His head was in a state of disbelief: he was not here, this was not happening. Above the noise and smoke and the crash of Colonel Maxwell's artillery from up on Jebel Surkab behind him and the howling of the dervishes it was impossible to hear a thing. They were almost upon them and he gave the order; too soon. There was chaos. Firing in all directions, the smoke from the damn Martini-Henri rifles making it impossible to see what was going on. The sound of the Maxim guns popped away in the back of the head, mowing down the advancing dervishes; but they still came on. The shout came along the line that they were low on ammunition and for a moment Ellesworth's heart was in his mouth as the enemy kept coming: fifty, forty, thirty yards. Then, like a miracle, the Lincolnshire Fusiliers appeared on the right flank, moving with machine precision; turning, loading and firing with devastating effect. This would be called a resounding victory when it was over, but at the time it was more like holding on by the skin of your teeth.

A gang of five hundred cavalry men came charging towards them. It was pure suicide. The horses kept coming. The order was given and the barrels swivelled. The machine-guns barked and stammered and in a blink of the eye the line of horsemen was cut in half. On and on they came and with each step their numbers were depleted. The last horseman – wounded, blinded by blood pouring from a wound in his head – charged and then faltered. The guns fell silent as this spectacle unfolded. The rider turned in a circle, surprised perhaps by the lull. He cocked his head to one side, listening. Then locating his enemy he gave a shout and kicked in his heels. A burst of fire tore him down; horse and man crumpled to the ground.

Ellesworth's body was shaking. He could not think. He could not speak. He shouted whatever came into his head. At some stage he recalled turning to look southwards towards the town which they had come to conquer. He saw a simple collection of mud walls and the cracked and crumpled shell of a tomb. It all seemed so hopelessly inadequate to justify such time and effort; too small a price to pay for all of these lives which now lay strewn across the plain.

The army was wheeling and checking its machinery. He looked at his watch. Not yet midday. The battle had taken only four hours or so. Four hours – and eleven thousand enemy dead at the cost of forty-eight Englishmen. A strange mixture of awe and revulsion went through him like a shudder: a man could not feel honour at having wreaked such havoc. The age of war was a quaint memory; this was the age of meticulous slaughter.

◆

Three days went by and the bands piped down. The drummers were eating bully beef and biscuits. The Union Jack was fluttering beside the khedive's gold crescent and star among the ruins of the palace, now inhabited by wild goats and pale-green lizards and overgrown with red tamarind whorls. The officers had finished singing and were lining up to allow a correspondent who was turning the crank of a moving-picture camera to take one final reel of them gathered at the site where Gordon had lost his life almost fourteen years ago. The officers stood, hymn books in hand, and they performed a rendition of 'Abide with me'. Despite the gravity of the ceremony, the *sirdar* was in high spirits. He wandered round, clapping men on the back. Ellesworth had never seen Kitchener like this before.

'Excellent work. Well done, all of you. Now the old boy can sleep soundly in his grave.' The *sirdar* stroked his moustache and someone next to Ellesworth murmured under his breath, 'If anyone can work out where they put the poor bastard.'

On the periphery of the crowd Ellesworth caught sight of a face which struck him as being oddly familiar. An old man was standing beside the trunk of a thick palm tree. He was thin and grey and shuffled from one foot to the other like an idiot. The skin hung in wrinkled folds from his face. He licked his lips from time to time and appeared to have no teeth left. Ellesworth summoned his adjutant and asked him to bring the man over. 'Ask him who he is,' he instructed the Egyptian.

The corporal turned to the man and spoke. He laughed and explained to Ellesworth. 'He is crazy man.' He gestured to the overgrown ruins behind them. 'He say this his kitchen and he want it back.'

The old man stood swaying from side to side as if in a trance. Ellesworth could not think why he had appeared familiar. 'Ask him . . . if he knows where the remains of General Gordon are located.'

The corporal gave the major a long look and then turned to put the question. The man paused, tilted his head to one side; then, clicking his lips and shaking his head, he grinned like a lunatic. 'Nejumi, Nejumi will return,' he repeated over and over.

The corporal looked at Ellesworth as if to say, 'I told you so.'

Ellesworth could think of nothing more to say so he dismissed the man, who slid back towards the bole of his tree and remained there, licking his lips and watching the proceedings, shaking his head from time to time, smiling and clicking his tongue.

Epilogue
The Far North

Once again he came travelling and once again he was a stranger in his own land. He passed through villages and towns, places deserted and no longer habitable by anything but stray goats and dogs. He met crowds of people who reminded him of the pilgrims from many years ago. He noticed that people in such despair had already forgotten the lessons of the past. They were resigned to their helplessness. He felt his age leaning its weight on him. It struck him that all had been for nothing.

Later on, he was unable to recall where or when it started, but at some stage he had decided to act. 'Out of chaos, man has always found hope,' he repeated to himself. 'Someone must take the first step.' As the road grew under his feet so it became clear to him that there was no one else left: it was he who must speak.

He found himself in the ruins of a village whose sons had been cast beneath the iron wheels of the war. There was no one in the marketplace but for a few old men sitting in the shade and some children. Handing the halter of the mule to the blind girl, Noon, who now travelled with him wherever he went, he stepped on to the top of a mound of dirt and bones and began to speak. Some children began to laugh and pull faces, others started to throw stones. He continued to speak despite this, for with each blow that landed his conviction grew stronger and his doubts receded. What did he speak about? Many asked this question afterwards and few could remember with any clarity. He spoke to them of religion and of the world. Of the way in which religion could be used by men who sought only power and that this was the worst betrayal of all, and that what had happened once could easily happen again. He told them that the only defence anyone has against such a betrayal of their faith is to understand their faith, to arm themselves with knowledge. He noticed

243

that children began to pay more attention. First the older ones and then the younger ones, keen to imitate. By the end of seven days he had a regular crowd which assembled every morning at his feet, none of them being older than thirteen. The parents looked on suspiciously when he moved his lessons to a more comfortable spot beneath a large neem tree where the breeze from the river came and lifted their spirits. He told them to look amongst themselves to see how different they all were; how their names contained the names of their father's father, and his father before him, and so on back into time, and that each of those names contained a story and very often a journey was connected to that story. That there was a place where all of their stories met and crossed and that this was a place that had to be shared.

At night he and Noon lay silent and alone out in the scrub, living on the scraps people might have thrown them out of pity. At times his head ached from thoughts of despair.

He remembered one day that this was the beginning of a new century according to the calendar of the Christians who now sat in the capital. We shall be dragged into their time now, he thought, and God help us.

When his thoughts became tangled he let himself return to his earliest arguments: his re-interpretation of the words of the Prophet. He sat each night stirring his ink so that he might begin again the next morning with his notes. He had collected, in the space of a short time, a huge, loosely tied bundle of yellowed scrolls. His thoughts rushed forth in a great wave, and he would only stop writing when his wrist began to ache or his vision began to blur so that he could no longer even see the page. In this period his health suffered. He was travelling so much that his legs were worn to the bone. He slept little and the effect of a sporadic and spartan diet was beginning to tell. Many days he and Noon went without food. If truth be told he preferred to settle for unripe dates than sit beside a begging bowl in a village. He had hoped to find a family to take Noon in and care for her, but people had enough trouble of their own. Also, people who were not normally suspicious of travellers would begin to wonder when they saw the influence he had on the children. More than once he was run out of town by furious women or old men shaking sticks. They thought he wanted to steal the only thing they had left.

◆

They reached a dusty place which was nothing more than two trails intersected by the iron road of the English. Hawi's eyesight was now so bad that he realised where he was only when the mule came to a halt by the well. They slept in the ruins of a small mosque. The town was a place of much bitterness, he was told; it had been badly hit by the battles in those regions.

Hawi climbed upon the fallen stones of the mosque and began to speak. The people, as usual, were slow to come to him. He stood upon a pile of rubble, holding his hands up before him as though he were reading from his palms.

'Blessed are the strangers!' he recited. 'Islam started as a stranger and it shall return as such. We have seen something that could be described as the Final Hour. It is written that when the woman gives birth to her mistress, when you see barefoot and naked shepherds living the life of extravagance, then the Signs are with us and the Hour has come.' He appealed to them. 'Is this not what we witnessed in the later years of the Khalifa Abdullahi's rule? Did those around him not begin to grow fat and rich, and who were they if not simple herders of cattle and goats? I was there, I saw.'

There was some indignation at this. Someone at the back shouted something obscene. It seemed that many had been loyal to the khalifa in these parts. A small crowd was assembling itself on the far side of the open square. The marketplace was crowded today and the clear air was filled with an optimism which encouraged Hawi. He raised up his hands for patience.

'History repeats itself, but never in the same manner. Place is not spherical and nor is time. Both are helical structures, like the fruits on the tamarind tree.' He turned his hand in spirals in the air. The children were enchanted by his conjuring. 'The end of the cycle resembles the beginning . . . but is distinctly different.'

The ugly element in the crowd had now pushed its way, not without difficulty, to the front.

'You are not a believer,' someone shouted.

'We gave our sons and fathers for the faith. What have you given?' came another.

Hawi smiled and nodded. 'Brothers, I implore you,' he held up the palms of his hands. 'We must remember who we are. We have been through so much suffering and pain together. That which went before was wrong. We must have the strength to learn and to change.' The crowd was beginning to drown him out. He had to raise his voice until his lungs hurt. '"Every day He has a fresh concern." People say that only that which is imperfect evolves and develops. This is not so. Perfect men aspire towards something more. Perfection is a fluid state of renewal and progression, not stagnation.'

The crowd were pressing forward from every angle. Hawi felt their arms reach for him. He pushed back and held up his hands. His words were coming in gasps. 'The tiny shoots of fresh grass at the bottom of the mountain are more perfect than the mountain itself.'

The fury of the people was suddenly naked and clear. He withdrew as though a dog had bared its teeth at him. 'What . . .?' he asked, bewildered by age, by the world, by lack of food and shelter, by ignorance and accident. 'What?' he asked.

The hands reached out, touching his clothes, pulling him, drawing him down into the crowd. He heard the roar of their voices. He saw their faces transformed as though by evil or sorcery. Where there had been light a moment ago there was now a darkness. A black shadow covered the sky. A tiny spot on that flat ochre plain of powdered rock and bone. A woman's face swam towards him and he saw her transformed as she spat upon him. They are only people, he told himself, simple ignorant people; they know no better.

He tried to call out for Noon. He felt himself lifted from the ground and herded towards the iron tracks and the houses built by the railway company for their workers – a small collection of conical shapes, like clay heads resting on the flat ground. The crowd drew to a halt and called for the station master. They needed someone to judge their case. The station master was, for the moment, the closest thing to any form of authority here.

After a time a man could be seen, peering from the shadowy recesses of the hut. He seemed reluctant, but eventually, grumbling and cursing, he stepped out into the afternoon light, which was jaundiced and discoloured, like worn canvas. He pulled a cap down on to his head and wore a tattered khaki uniform that hung loosely from his shoulders. His face had changed; he was older and a certain stiffness had come over features that were once pliant with youth. Kadaro did not even glance at the blind girl who lay at the foot of the crowd. He rubbed his eyes, annoyed at having been woken from his sleep.

'What is going on here? he demanded, realising that the crowd were angry. He looked at the pathetic figure of a man whom they held captive – barefoot, his shaven head covered in scabs, his clothes soiled and torn. Kadaro pointed a hand. 'I know his kind. We don't want tricksters and thieves in our town. Only the harshest punishment is good enough for them.' He sniffed and straightened his tunic. Something more was called for, he thought to himself. He pulled a switch from the hand of a man who stood beside him and waved it in the air. He cleared his throat. The words poured out; words which were drummed into the head of a little boy many years ago; words he had forgotten.

'Beware the false prophets,' he quoted. There was a rumble of approval. Kadaro, his chest heaving with confusion and anger, continued, feeling the crowd before him, warm and large. '"How do we know them?" they asked. "You shall know them by their deeds!"' The crowd rose as one; a seething wave of indignity. They had paid too much to be told that they were wrong.

Hawi watched all this as though he were floating overhead. He realised sadly that people do not want to accept the beauty of the manifold world which God in all his wisdom created. They want everything to be the same. On the one hand they¯praise God for his magnanimity, while on the other they cling to the idea that there is a common man, a perfect picture towards which everyone should strive. They will not accept that each and every one of them is created uniquely, that each has his own talents and gifts. In their hearts they know that this is the wonder of life, but they do not wish to know it. And so they turn against anything which reminds them of this truth – against strangeness, the outsider; against him.

All of these thoughts went through his head as they fetched the rope. They made him stand in the sun while everyone, now silent, looked on. At a short distance away a flock of children watched, terrified and so fascinated that they were unable to avert their eyes. They will remember, he thought as his hands were bound behind his back. The sun hurt his eyes, made them ache, made his head hurt.

At one stage he fell to the ground among the scuffling feet and the dust. His mouth filled with straw and the acrid dryness of mule shit. He tried to rise, coughing and choking, and felt the weight of them on his back. They mounted him on the same white mule upon which he had arrived. He did not feel shame. 'This is how it should be,' he heard himself say. You live long and you see much. This time must come for all of us. This was the moment for which he had been preparing himself almost all of his waking life.

But suddenly he realised with a jolt that at the very centre of him there was a hollow, that he had somewhere along the way lost something essential. It struck him suddenly like a knife thrust through the vital organs of his body: he had lost his faith. He reeled around now in desperation, his panic complete. All of it was worthless, all of the hours and years, all the nights he had lain awake and struggled to come close to the source – wasted. What then had his life been for? In the name of the Lord so much pain and suffering he had witnessed in silence: God is Greater, he who knows and sees, he has a reason. But what reason could exist now? Why had Muhammad Ahmad al-Mahdi never reached Kufa or Baghdad? Because there was a reason. Never ridden in triumph through Medina? Because there was a reason. And the reason? God is good. He is the Compassionate and the Merciful.

He raised his face from the rear of the mule and saw the crowd of onlookers. His head was spinning in the way of a bearded *darwish*, hair filled with birds' nests and dust. He heard their wailing rise and fall on the wind; the jibes and the chants reached him the way the *khamsin* blows in from the desert. It was they, after all, the simple people, who could not learn to love their fellow man; who could not listen, whose only protection was hatred and distrust.

'Apostate!' they roared, and he did not argue, for in that moment he knew it was true. He raised his eyes towards the sky, searching, begging. Then he closed them and a single tear crept down his wrinkled face. When he opened his eyes again it was to see a white

248

bird curling across the sky. An owl or a dove? Then, as oddly and as easily as it had come, his doubt vanished. He began to smile and he opened his mouth to recite the opening prayer: *La illaha il Allah.*

Kadaro brought the switch down on the mule's hindquarters and it started off for home, leaving Hawi the apostate hanging in the soft afternoon breeze.

The crowd dissolved slowly, vanishing back the way they had come, talking in subdued voices to one another, leaving the blind girl on her knees in the dust beside the body that swung gently from the telegraph pole by the railway line. Between sobs she gasped out a few words at the disappearing backs of the people.

'He was right,' she cried. 'He spoke the truth.'

The station master dismissed the matter with a curse and turned to go back inside his shady hut. He was tired and needed his rest.

Glossary

Afareet (plural of *afreet*)   A powerful form of *jinn*, a hostile spirit commonly believed to inhabit or take the form of smoke.

Affranji   A person of the Franj, or Franks; a Western European.

Alim   (plural: *ulama*)   Religious scholar.

Amir   Prince; also used to denote a commander in the military sense.

Angareeb   Traditional wooden bed, strung with palm fibre ropes.

Ansar   The devoted followers of the Mahdi; the name given originally to the supporters of the Prophet at Medina.

Ashraf   Term denoting descendency from the Prophet – a claim made by the Mahdi himself. The Mahdi's relatives/clan became known as the *ashraf* and were led by Muhammad Sharif, one of the four khalifas.

Assida   Staple type of porridge made from sorghum flour.

Bamia   Stew made with okra.

Bash-Buzuq (*Bashi-Bozuk*)   Turkish term meaning 'unattached'; signifies the irregular cavalry units of the Ottoman Empire, greatly feared for their savagery.

Bimbashi   Military rank – equivalent to sergeant.

Courbaj   Long whip, often made of hippopotamus hide.

Danagla   From 'Dongola', denoting the people from that region.

Darwish (plural: *darawish*)   Dervish – a Sufi devotee.

Fago   Radish-like root which grows wild and can be eaten.

250

Fellah Peasant.

Gorassa Staple pancake-like food made from wheat flour.

Haboob Dust storm.

Hegira Migration; the migration of the Prophet from Mecca to Medina which marks the beginning of the Muslim era.

Hijab Amulet or lucky charm, made of leather.

Imma Type of headgear resembling a turban; long strip of cloth wrapped around the head.

Jehenum Hell, hell fire.

Jellaba Term referring to Arab traders in Southern Sudan.

Jihadiya Slaves confiscated from traders and enlisted for military service by Egyptians.

Jinn Airy or fiery spirit, capable of changing form. Created from smoke and flame (as opposed to clay and light from which men and angels were created).

Jubba Long, loose cotton shirt.

Kamanga Colloquial term for local form of hashish.

Maʿalish 'Never mind.'

Mashrabiyya Carved wooden screen, commonly used in the Middle East to cover windows.

Merissa Fermented drink made from sorghum maize.

Ombeya Large trumpet horn made from elephant tusk.

Qadi Judge.

Rakuba Simple, verandah-like shelter covered with reeds or palm fronds attached to the side of a house.

Sanjak Turkish military rank – officer equivalent to captain.

Shallali Person from the region of Shallal in Nubia.

Sharia   Islamic law.

Shayn   Ugly.

Shimal   North.

Shisha   Water pipe.

Sibha   Prayer beads.

Sirdar   Turkish military rank, equivalent to governor.

Sirwal   Long, loose-fitting cotton trousers.

Sura   The name given to the chapters of the Koran.

Tarboosh   Fez, Turkish headgear.

Tariqa   Way or school within the Sufi religious tradition.

Ulama   See *alim*.

Wadi   Valley.

Wakil   Deputy; administrative official.